Southern Comfort

Books by Fern Michaels

Santa Cruise
No Way Out
The Brightest Star
Fearless
Spirit of the Season
Deep Harbor
Fate & Fortune
Sweet Vengeance
Holly and Ivy
Fancy Dancer
No Safe Secret
Wishes for Christmas
About Face
Perfect Match
A Family Affair
Forget Me Not
The Blossom Sisters
Balancing Act
Tuesday's Child
Betrayal
Southern Comfort
To Taste the Wine
Sins of the Flesh
Sins of Omission
Return to Sender
Mr. and Miss Anonymous
Up Close and Personal
Fool Me Once
Picture Perfect
The Future Scrolls
Kentucky Sunrise
Kentucky Heat
Kentucky Rich
Plain Jane

Charming Lily
What You Wish For
The Guest List
Listen to Your Heart
Celebration
Yesterday
Finders Keepers
Annie's Rainbow
Sara's Song
Vegas Sunrise
Vegas Heat
Vegas Rich
Whitefire
Wish List
Dear Emily
Christmas at Timberwoods

The Lost and Found Novels:

Hidden

The Sisterhood Novels:

19 Yellow Moon Road
Bitter Pill
Truth and Justice
Cut and Run
Safe and Sound
Need to Know
Crash and Burn
Point Blank
In Plain Sight
Eyes Only
Kiss and Tell
Blindsided

Books by Fern Michaels (*Cont.*)

Gotcha!
Home Free
Déjà Vu
Cross Roads
Game Over
Deadly Deals
Vanishing Act
Razor Sharp
Under the Radar
Final Justice
Collateral Damage
Fast Track
Hokus Pokus
Hide and Seek
Free Fall
Lethal Justice
Sweet Revenge
The Jury
Vendetta
Payback
Weekend Warriors

The Men of the Sisterhood
Novels:

Hot Shot
Truth or Dare
High Stakes
Fast and Loose
Double Down

The Godmothers Series:

Far and Away
Classified

Breaking News
Deadline
Late Edition
Exclusive
The Scoop

E-Book Exclusives:

Desperate Measures
Seasons of Her Life
To Have and To Hold
Serendipity
Captive Innocence
Captive Embraces
Captive Passions
Captive Secrets
Captive Splendors
Cinders to Satin
For All Their Lives
Texas Heat
Texas Rich
Texas Fury
Texas Sunrise

Anthologies:

Home Sweet Home
A Snowy Little Christmas
Coming Home for
Christmas
A Season to Celebrate
Mistletoe Magic
Winter Wishes
The Most Wonderful Time
When the Snow Falls

Books by Fern Michaels (*Cont.*)

Secret Santa

A Winter Wonderland

I'll Be Home for Christmas

Making Spirits Bright

Holiday Magic

Snow Angels

Silver Bells

Comfort and Joy

Sugar and Spice

Let it Snow

A Gift of Joy

Five Golden Rings

Deck the Halls

Jingle All the Way

FERN MICHAELS

Southern Comfort

KENSINGTON
PUBLISHING CORP.

www.kensingtonbooks.com

Prologue

Atlanta, Georgia
March 2002

Detective Patrick Kelly, Tick to his friends, signed out of his precinct and headed to his car, an eight-year-old Saturn with 120,000 miles on it. It purred like a baby when he turned the key. Then it sputtered and died. He'd given it too much gas and flooded the engine. He knew the drill—wait five minutes, try again, and if he was lucky, Lulu would get him home.

Sally, his wife, had named his car Lulu but never told him why. She'd just giggle and say it was a lulu of a car. Sally drove a ten-year-old Honda Civic. The only good thing about owning two old cars was not having to make car payments. Everything was about cutting corners, saving for college for the kids, and doing without.

Tick sighed, leaned back against the headrest, but didn't close his eyes because, if he did, he'd go to sleep. He'd worked a double shift because Joe Rollins had a ruptured appendix, and he'd filled in for him. He couldn't wait to get home to Sally and the kids, take a shower, maybe eat something Sally kept warm for him, and go to sleep with her spooning into his back. When he felt his eyelids start to droop, he turned the key, and, miracle of miracles, Lulu turned over. He was on his way to his family, whom he loved more than anything on earth. He loved them more than he loved his job, and he dearly loved his job. There were days when he hated the job, but the love always won out. He truly believed he made a difference. Where his family was concerned, there was no doubt: He loved them twenty-four/seven, unconditionally.

When he worked the late shift, he always let his thoughts go to his wonderful little family as a way of unwinding on his way home. He'd met Sally in the seventh grade, when she transferred from out of state. He fell in love with her that day when she stood in front of the class, and said, "My name is Sally Pritchard and I'm new today." He'd seen the sparkle of tears in her eyes and knew instinctively that she was afraid. Afraid the kids wouldn't like her, afraid she'd make a mistake and they'd laugh. He never did figure out where or how he'd known that, he'd just known it. Then, when he found out she had moved one street over from his own street, and they would be walking to school at the same time, he'd almost done cartwheels. Later, Sally said she didn't fall in love with him till they were in the eighth grade. He'd been heartbroken at that news but covered it up well. She loved him, and that was all that mattered.

Married for fifteen years now, and he loved her as much as he did that day in the seventh grade when she introduced herself. He hoped and prayed nightly that his two children would find mates as wonderful as their mother when it was their time.

Sally Pritchard Kelly was the wind beneath his wings. She was the reason he got up in the morning, the reason he was still sane considering the fact that he was a homicide detective. Because of Sally and the kids, he didn't carry his work home with him. When he walked in the front door of his mortgaged-to-the-hilt house, he was in another world. Worn, comfortable furniture waited for him. Sally always waited at the door for him, a smile on her face and smelling of a summer day. Always. He couldn't remember a single day in all the years they were married that she hadn't greeted him with a smile and a kiss on the lips. A real kiss that said she loved him, missed him, and now things were the way they should be because he was home. There would always be a warm meal in the oven if he was late. Didn't matter how late he was. Sally would curl up on the couch and wait. Sally was the constant in his life.

Prettier than a picture, he always said. He loved the freckles that danced across her nose, loved the crooked eyetooth she refused to have straightened. There wasn't one thing he didn't love about his wife because, in his eyes, she was perfect. At this point in his reverie, even if he was so tired he couldn't think straight, his eyes always misted up. He'd just curl up and die if anything ever happened to his beloved Sally. Well, that wasn't going to happen anytime soon; they had at least another fifty years to look forward to. Both he and Sally came from families where longevity was the rule.

Tick could feel his eyes start to droop again, so he pressed the stereo unit and turned up the volume. His and Sally's favorite song was burned on every inch of the CD, so he could play it over and over. "Mustang Sally." He started to sing along with Wilson Pickett at the top of his lungs, *"Ride, Sally, ride!"*

He was two streets away from where he lived on David Court when he saw the strobe lights shooting upward to the sky. Blue, red, and white just like it was the Fourth of July. But it wasn't the Fourth of July. He knew what the lights meant. Good cop that he was, he knew he was going to have to stop to offer any assistance if needed. Sally, the kids, and sleep would have to wait just a bit longer. He turned off the CD player and turned the corner, and his world came to a screeching halt. He saw the barricade, the yellow tape, the crazy arcing lights, the crowds of people, and too many police cars to count.

All parked in front of *his house,* in the driveway, on the lawn and sidewalk. He slammed on the brakes, threw open the door, and lunged forward. He heard his name being called from all directions, arms trying to reach him, someone trying to tackle him. He plowed ahead, driven by an energy he didn't know he possessed. And then he was in a vise grip, unable to move. The more he fought and struggled, the tighter the hold became. He looked up to see the face of the man holding him and was stunned to see his captain, tears rolling down his cheeks. "Easy, Tick, easy."

Tick ground his teeth together. He had to show respect to the captain. "Did someone rob my house? Where are Sally and the kids? Captain, I asked you a question."

"Tick . . . I . . ."

Rising onto his toes, Tick reared upward, loosening the hold his captain had on his arm. He sprinted forward as fellow officers rushed to prevent him from entering the house. He evaded all of them.

The house was deathly silent. The crime-scene personnel took that moment to stop what they were doing and stare at the man who looked like the wrath of God. "Where are they?"

Someone, he didn't know who it was, pointed to the second floor. Tick took the steps two at a time. It looked to him like there were a hundred people in his small upstairs. He bolted down the short hall to his bedroom. In his life he'd never seen so much blood. He saw her then, his beloved Sally, lying in the doorway leading to the bathroom. He knew it was her because of her nightgown and robe. And her wedding ring. There was little left to her face. How could that be gone? Those beautiful freckles dancing across her pert little nose were gone. Her throat was a gaping hole. Tick's knees buckled. Strong hands held him upright. "Ride, Sally, ride," he blubbered.

"Get him out of here. Have the ME look at him."

"Where are the kids?"

"Not now, Tick. Please," his captain said.

"Where are my kids?" Tick roared.

"In their room. Tick, please, let us handle this. I'm begging you, don't go there."

"Get the hell away from me. . . ."

Tick found them huddled together in the closet, which was full of toys and balls. There was blood everywhere. Too much blood for two tiny little creatures who once carried his life's blood. Now it was a river on a hopscotch-patterned carpet. He wanted to bend down, to scoop up his children, to hold them close, but they wouldn't let him. He wanted to run his hands through his daughter's curly hair, which was just like her mother's, but it was matted with blood, and he couldn't see the curls. He looked at his son and fainted dead away. He felt himself being carried someplace, heard voices he couldn't identify, then he felt something prick his arm. Ride, Sally, riiiide.

The Governor's Mansion
Tallahassee, Florida
August 2009

Thurman Lawrence Tyler checked himself in the mirror one last time. He adjusted his Hermès tie, examined the crease on the French cuffs of his custom-made shirt, brushed an imaginary piece of lint from his imported Italian suit, inspected the shine on his shoes, and smoothed a thick white errant hair in place before stepping into the foyer, where Elizabeth waited. At six foot one, he had an athletic build and sharp blue eyes that rarely missed a beat, and she thought her husband still as handsome as the day she had met him. Maybe even more so.

"Thurman, dear, you look as handsome as you did the day of our wedding." Elizabeth Tyler, his wife of forty-six years and right hand of Governor Thurman Lawrence Tyler, looked every bit the elegant wife of a dignitary. Perfectly coiffed blond hair, her grandmother's pearl earrings and necklace glowing next to her porcelain skin. A pale blue Chanel suit brought out the cornflower blue of her eyes. Both were tall, slim, and in excellent physical condition, and they appeared almost perfect as they scrutinized one another.

"And you, my dear, look like the innocent that you were." Thurman studied his wife for a moment longer. She'd aged extremely well, unlike many of her friends. Elizabeth was always careful to protect herself from Florida's punishing sun, never smoked, and rarely drank anything more than an occasional glass of white wine. She played tennis three times a week, had a facial once a week and her hair touched up every third Thursday of the month. Of course, he wasn't supposed to know this, so he pretended her blond locks were as natural as those of a newborn.

"You're too kind," she replied.

"Nonsense," he responded.

Without another word, he escorted her to the elaborate dining room where they had their breakfast. Each consumed two cups of coffee, his with skim milk and hers black. Both had one-half of a Florida ruby red grapefruit with one slice of homemade dry wheat toast. After they'd consumed their meal, they took their daily doses of vitamins with a bottle of mineral water imported from Switzerland.

Their morning routine was like clockwork and had been since Thurman was elected governor of the fine state of Florida almost eight years ago. With his second term coming to an end, both were preparing for the next step of their career—president of the United States. Yes, it was *their* career because Thurman never made a decision without first consulting his dear wife.

When they finished their meal, the governor went to his office, and Elizabeth went to hers, where she spent the morning going over the menu for an upcoming gala they were hosting. With nothing more on her agenda, she went to the personal living area that connected their offices. Knowing her husband would be occupied for the rest of the day with his lieutenant governor, she placed a phone call to her son, Lawrence. Hanging up after several rings went unanswered, Elizabeth called an old high school friend. They made plans to have lunch soon. Free time was rare, and she decided to take advantage of it and relax with a book. She'd spent her life promoting literacy and was very involved with the public-library system, but never once in all her years of reading had she told anyone of her love of horror novels. Today she planned to read Stephen King's latest.

Settling into a Queen Anne chair next to the window overlooking the garden, Elizabeth spent the next two hours immersed in her novel. Later, when she heard Thurman shouting on the phone to Carlton, she hid her book beneath the chair's cushion and hurried to the door, where she stood silently, listening to her husband's private conversation.

She and Thurman had done everything in their power to see that Lawrence never found out. It would ruin him and his father if the public got wind of this. Elizabeth thought she had done the right thing by keeping him. No, she *had* done the right thing. He was her son, the only child she would ever have. Whatever it took to ensure that he wasn't ruined by her and Thurman's past mistakes, Elizabeth would do it. After all, she was his mother, and if he couldn't count on her, then poor Lawrence had no one.

Every hope and dream they had ever imagined was about

to be destroyed. They had worked too long and hard for this moment. Elizabeth refused to allow anyone to ruin the future that was just now within their reach.

She'd made numerous sacrifices throughout her life in order for Thurman and Lawrence to be successful. Now that someone threatened her life's work, she wanted to fight back in anger; but that had never been her way, and she would not start now.

She went to her private office and sat down. She removed a sheet of creamy personalized paper from her desk. Lawrence would have to know this someday. If neither she nor Thurman were around to tell him, then a letter would suffice.

My Dearest Son,

If you're reading this letter then you must know that your father and I are no longer of this earth. There is something I have wanted to tell you since you were a little boy, but the time was never right. Then as you got older I thought it would be a disservice not to tell you, yet I could never find the right time. If you hate me or your father after reading this, know that I will understand and love you in spite of it. The first time I laid eyes on your father, I fell madly in love. . . .

Chapter 1

The 1,203 residents of Mango Key never knew what to call it or how to refer to it. For the most part, in the beginning, they called it a castle, then they switched up and called it a fortress. As it neared completion, they became puzzled at the high brick wall and the massive iron gates that sparked if they were touched and simply referred to it as that place at the end of the island.

The residents didn't know who lived in *that place,* but they speculated that maybe it was some aging film star who didn't want anyone to see their lost looks. Or perhaps it was some drug lord trying to hide out from the law since the only activity seen or heard came late at night.

The residents of Mango Key were simple folks and earned their living selling their mangoes, oranges, and grapefruit to the boats that came into the Key once a week, and they didn't really care about the phantom people who maybe lived or maybe didn't live in *that place.* They had never seen a soul in the light of day since *that place* had been completed five years ago. For the most part, they forgot that it was even there because it didn't affect them in any way.

In truth, there were 1,204 residents of Mango Key, but the additional resident wasn't a native, so the residents more or less ignored Patrick Kelly the same way they ignored *that place.* But that hadn't been the case when he had first arrived on Mango Key.

Even Patrick Kelly, known to old friends as Tick, although those friends were long gone, ignored the place, which was three miles down the beach from where he lived.

The reason he'd ignored the construction was because he was in a drunken stupor for the two years it took to build, and the third year, he was just more or less coming out of his stupor. And the least of his worries was someone building a house, a castle, a fortress, or *that place.* It simply held no interest for him; it was all he could do to get through one day so that he could go to sleep, wake, and struggle through the next. Today, seven years after the fact, he still had no interest in what he considered an abandoned structure he happened to see when he walked the beach, swam, or fished.

It was a beautiful August day on Mango Key. But then most days were beautiful except during hurricane season, and those exceptions usually lasted only a day or so. The sun was startlingly bright, warming Tick's body as he walked out of the ocean. He had his dinner in a net—a fish he couldn't name. Nor did he care if it had a name. He called all fish dinner. A few wild radishes, some equally wild onions, a few mangoes, and maybe an orange, and dinner was ready. A great diet. He'd dropped twenty-five pounds since arriving at Mango Key. He weighed 170 pounds, the same weight he'd carried when he was twenty-eight and in top form. Now pushing the big four-oh, at six foot two, he still carried the weight easily. He was brown as a nut, living in cutoffs and sandals. He couldn't remember the last time he'd worn a shirt. Maybe hurricane season last year, when the temperature dropped to sixty-five degrees.

Patrick Kelly, hobo, derelict, beach bum, drunk, former homicide detective, ex-father, widower, rich best-selling author, and recovering alcoholic.

Tick stopped two hundred feet from the place he'd called

home for almost seven years. His abode, that was how he thought of it, had been little more than a lean-to with iffy rusty plumbing and an even rustier generator when he arrived. It had stayed that way for close to three years, until he'd woken up one day and knew that his drinking days had to come to an end or he would die, which had been his purpose all along. But that particular morning, with the sun warming his bloated body, he'd taken his best friend, his only friend, Jack Daniel's, and dumped him in the ocean.

He wasn't sure now, but he thought he'd had the shakes, the crawlies, the hallucinations for a full week before he had shed all the bad toxins from his system. Then he'd reared up like a gladiator and taken a few steps into the land of the living. After which he took a few more steps and headed for the mainland, where he ordered all the lumber and nails he would need to redo his house, which he worked on from sunup to sundown. He'd made two more trips to order furniture, generators, appliances, a new laptop, a printer, scanner, cell phone, and anything else he thought he might need to make his life easier. The renovation took eleven months. He now had a skimpy front porch, with a swing and a chair. He'd christened the finished product with a bottle of apple cider. He'd even given his new abode a name. He called it Tick's Tree House because he'd rebuilt the structure on stilts. He loved it as much as he could love anything these days.

Tick headed up the steps that led to his porch and started to laugh when the parrot who came with the house began to squawk. At least he thought it had come with the house, but with his foggy memory, he couldn't be sure. He couldn't remember if the bird was in residence when he had arrived or if it came later. He marveled at the bird's vocabulary and couldn't remember if he'd taught it to talk or it learned from somewhere else. He called it Bird and had no way of knowing if it was male or female. Bird ruffled his feathers, and said, "You're late."

"Am not."

"Five o'clock."

Tick looked down at his watch. It was four thirty. "It's four thirty. Four thirty means I'm not late." Bird rustled his feathers, then swooped down and perched on Tick's shoulder.

"Five o'clock, time to eat. Five o'clock, time to eat!"

"No, Bird, it is not time to eat. We eat at six o'clock. I tell you that every day."

"Bullshit!"

In spite of himself, Tick burst out laughing. He wondered then for the millionth time who the bird had once belonged to. Obviously someone with a salty tongue. "Go on, Bird, I'll call you when it's time to eat." If anyone from his other life saw him dining with a parrot, they'd lock him up and throw away the key. He even set a place for Bird at the table.

Tick was sucking on a mango, the rich juice dribbling down his chin, when Bird's head tilted to the side. His feathers rustled as he flew out of the minikitchen straight for the front door. The hair on the back of Tick's neck went straight up when the parrot screamed, "Intruder! Intruder!"

Tick slipped off his stool, his bare feet making no sound as he backed up to the small cabinet where he kept his gun. Because he was a cop, he kept the Glock locked and loaded. It felt comforting in his hand. He never got company. *Never.* If one of the Key residents came around, they always rang the bell out by the oversize palmetto.

Bird was literally bouncing off the walls as he circled the small living room, whose door opened onto the little front porch. "Hey, anyone home besides that crazy bird?"

Tick blinked. He'd know that voice anywhere. It belonged to his twin brother, Pete. He jammed the Glock into the back of his shorts. "Enough, Bird. It's not an intruder!" The green bird squawked one more time as he settled himself on the back of Tick's favorite chair. Bird's eyes were bright as he watched his roommate walk over to the door.

They were the same height, the same muscular build, but there the resemblance ended. Tick was dark haired and dark eyed, thanks to his mother's Italian heritage. Pete was a redhead with blue eyes, thanks to his father's Irish heritage. "I was in the neighborhood," Pete said quietly.

"Bullshit!" Bird squawked.

"That's my line, Bird. C'mon in, Pete. How'd you find me?" They should be hugging each other, at the very least shaking hands or just doing brotherly things. Instead, they eyed each other warily.

"Nice place," Pete said, looking around. "That's a joke, Tick. What, eight hundred square feet?"

"More or less. How'd you find me?" Tick asked a second time. "It's been, what, almost seven, maybe eight years, and suddenly here you are."

Pete shuffled his feet. For the first time, Tick saw he was carrying his loafers and was in his bare feet. Maybe that was why they hadn't shaken hands. Yeah, yeah, that was probably the reason.

"I just got back two weeks ago. Yeah, I know I was supposed to write. You know me."

Tick motioned to one of the two chairs in the small room. He noticed that Pete favored one leg over the other. "What happened?"

"I got a little busted up on the rodeo circuit. Got a new hip and knee. Met up with this guy from Argentina, and he asked me to go with him to take care of his polo ponies. Seemed like a good idea at the time. Hell, I still think it was the best thing I could have done at the time. The guy paid me ten times what I was worth, gave me incredible bonuses. Everything was free, great lodgings, free food, my own Jeep. I banked every cent of my money.

"Listen, Tick, I didn't know about Sally and the kids. If I had known, I would have hopped on the first plane I could find. I went to see Andy, and he told me. Jesus, I walked around in a daze for almost a week. He wouldn't tell me where you were. Good old Andy wouldn't tell me. I couldn't believe it. He wouldn't tell *me*. I threatened him with everything in the book, and I gotta tell you, he's a hell of a friend and one hell of an attorney; he didn't give you up, Tick."

"You're here!"

Pete squirmed in his chair. He looked down at his shoes as though he wondered why he was still holding them. He bent over, winced, and set them on the floor. "Yeah, I did a little breaking and entering. Jeez, his office is a house on Peachtree. A ten-year-old could pick that lock. I looked in your file and found out you were here. So, here I am, a little late, Tick, but I'm here now. What can I do?"

Tick smiled. "I wish there was something you could do, but there isn't. I'm okay. You can go back to Argentina knowing I'm okay and don't need you or anyone else."

Pete leaned forward. "That's not quite true, now is it? You need Andy. I know he takes care of all your finances, I saw it in the files. Seems like you're doing pretty well for an ex-cop turned author. I'm okay with you not needing me, but don't start handing me bullshit, Tick. Jesus, I'm bleeding for Sally and the kids. I know the story, so you don't have to tell me anything you don't want to tell me. I can't go back to Argentina; my boss fell off one of his ponies and got stomped to death. I came back with enough money to go into business for myself. I even brought you a check for that five grand I borrowed from you." He reached into his pocket and pulled out a crumpled check. He laid it on the small table next to his chair.

"Keep it."

"Nah, it doesn't work like that. I always pay my debts. I found a bar and grill on Peachtree. Pop would have loved it. Andy's checking it out to make sure it's as good as it sounds. I have enough to pay cash and will have quite a bit left over. I have a realtor looking for some digs for me in the area.

And, I'm getting married in six months. I want you to be my best man the way I was yours when . . . you know."

Tick couldn't keep the surprise out of his voice. "You're getting married! You?"

"Hard to believe, huh? Yeah, I met her in Argentina. She was there on vacation with a few friends. She works for the State Department. Right now she's in England and will be back in six months, then she's quitting. She loves to cook, so we're going to buy the bar and grill together. She's willing to put in half the asking price. So, will you be my best man?"

A burst of panic flooded Tick's whole being. Standing up for his brother would mean he'd have to leave his nest. He had to say something to wipe the awful look off his brother's face. He shrugged. "Six months is a long time down the road." He hated the way his voice sounded, all shaky and squeaky.

Pete nodded as though he understood. "You might not want to hear this, but I'm going to tell you anyway. I went out to the cemetery. I took flowers. Said some prayers, talked to . . . Christ, that was the hardest thing I ever did in my whole life. I sat there on the ground and picked the flowers apart. So I went back and bought some more. They were pretty, Tick. I remembered how Sally had all those rose-bushes in the yard. I left a standing order for the flower shop to deliver every Saturday. I wanted to do so much more but, Tick, there wasn't anything else to do. If there's more I can do, tell me, and I'll do it."

Tick bit down on his lower lip. He should have done what Pete did. All those years and no flowers on his family's graves. He should have made arrangements to do what Pete did. Oh, no, it had been more important to put his snoot in a bottle and hide out. All he could think of to say was, "Thanks."

"You gonna talk to me, Tick? Do I have to drag it out of you?"

Tick finally found his tongue. "I'm sure Andy told you all the nitty-gritty details. After the funeral, which I really don't remember, I got in my car and started to drive. I honest to God do not know how I got here. I do know that I was in a stupor for about two and a half years. It's all one big blank. I woke up one morning and knew I was going to die. At first I didn't care. Then I did care. I thought about what Pop told us as kids when we did something wrong. He'd say, 'it's time to straighten up and fly right.' The village people must have taken care of me. I have vague memories of people standing over me. There always seemed to be food for me to eat. A boat comes once a week with supplies, so I have to assume I somehow made arrangements to get liquor delivered.

"I write books these days. Do you believe that? And, they make movies out of them. Who knew I could do that? Certainly not me."

Pete waved his arms about. "So, this is it? The end of the road for you? There's a lot to be said for peace and quiet and tranquillity, but to withdraw so totally, I can't believe that's a good thing. Don't you miss Atlanta and all the action? You had a lot of friends back there on the force. Everyone just said you fell off the face of the earth."

"I'm content. For now. Things might have turned out differently if they hadn't caught the punk who killed my family. They gunned him down right outside my house. I would have hunted him down and killed him myself. There's nothing back there for me now." His voice was defiant when he said, "I like it here."

"Yeah, I can see that. Kind of small, though. How about I stay around long enough to help you build another room on to this . . . stilt house? Remember when we helped Pop build a sunroom for Mom? I'm free as the breeze for the next six months. Let me help, Tick. I *need* to do something for you. If you're writing another book and need to concentrate on that, I can do it on my own. I was always better at the hammer-

and-nails thing than you were. Even Pop said so. A nice big room with wall-to-wall windows so you can see the ocean. Maybe a big fancy bathroom. By the way, do you own this place?"

"Yeah. I bought it a few years ago from the village. It's kind of complicated. Everyone in the village is related. Indian heritage. This Key is the result of some kind of land grant. One of the elders came out here one day, and he had this big stick. He asked me to follow him, and he kept dragging the stick; and then he said everything within the lines was mine. He held out his hand, we shook, and I paid him two thousand dollars. That's all he wanted. He signed his name on a piece of paper, and I signed mine. End of story."

All Pete could think of to say was, "Uh-huh."

Tick remembered that he was a host. "Want a beer?"

Pete's eyebrows shot up to his hairline. "You drink?"

"A beer now and then. I learned my lesson, I know my limitations. I don't crave it, if that's your next question. It's nice to see you, Pete. I mean that. I guess I wasn't very hospitable when you showed up. I didn't quite know what to do. I've been running from the past, then, suddenly, there you were, front and center."

Pete nodded. "No social life, eh?"

Tick laughed. "I guess what you're asking me is do I miss sex?" He laughed again. "I go into Miami every so often. I bought a cigarette boat. I see a lady there at times. She's one of those people who knows everything there is to know about computers. It's what it is. So, do you want that beer or not?"

"Yeah. Yeah, Tick, I do. Having a beer with my brother . . . it doesn't get any better than that."

Tick looked at his twin for a long minute. "You're right, Pete. And yeah, you can stay, and yeah, we can build the room. It will be like old times."

Pete let his breath out in a loud *swoosh*. "I didn't bring

anything with me. I'll have to go back to the Keys to get my stuff. You got some old shorts or old clothes? I'm sweating like a Trojan."

"I'll run you down there tomorrow," Tick said, tossing him a pair of khaki shorts and a threadbare T-shirt. "Bathroom is in there," he added, pointing to his left. "I'll get the beer, and we can sit on the porch. It sits two."

Pete guffawed. "I noticed."

And then it was like old times, two brothers who actually liked one another, talking about world affairs, women, work, and the weather as they shared a beer.

Then they were on the little porch, Pete on the swing, Tick on the chair, his feet propped up on the banister. "Tell me about the lady you're going to marry."

"She's great, Tick. You're going to like her. She's grounded. I know she works for the State Department, but that's all I know. She doesn't talk about what she does. I don't know if it's need to know or she just isn't comfortable talking about her job. She must be well paid because she has enough money to invest in our business. Her name is Sadie. Her real name is Serafina. She's Italian. Mom would have loved her. We call and e-mail. But there are times where she's off-line for weeks. She never gives me an explanation other than to say, 'it's job-related.' I learned to accept it. I've known her for three years. She's thirty-seven."

"I'm happy for you, Pete. I mean that."

"Do you want to talk about *it?*"

"No. It's not time yet. Maybe that time will never come. What color were the roses you took to the cemetery?"

"Yellow and some pink ones for Emma. Daisies for Ricky. The monument is nice. Andy took care of that. A mother angel and two little ones." His voice broke, and tears flooded his eyes. He swiped at them with the back of his hand.

Tick cringed. Everyone was doing what he should have done.

"Hey, let's take a walk on the beach. Show me how much of this glorious paradise is yours." Pete hopped off the swing and yanked at Tick's arm, jerking him to his feet. Then they were in each other's arms, hugging one another and pounding each other on the back.

"Sometimes life out-and-out sucks. It doesn't mean it won't ever get better, it just means you have to work harder at making it right. Hey, what about the bird? Do you have to put it in a cage?" Pete asked, hoping to drive the stricken look off his brother's face.

"When did you get so smart? The bird is a free spirit. He just moved in one day and decided to stay. I don't even remember what day or year it was. Suddenly, he was just there. We get along just fine, but he's a tad salty."

"When I was lying in a hospital doped to the eyeballs for my pain, I had a lot of time to reflect. A lot of time. Hey, I can tell when it's going to rain within three hours. If my bar and grill goes belly-up, I can probably get a job as a weatherman. You always gotta look at the positive. You got a bed for me, or do I have to sleep on the floor?"

Tick doubled over laughing. "That is an accomplishment. Not to worry, I have one of those blowup beds that come in a sack, and the only reason I have it is Andy keeps saying he's coming down here. Since he hates to fly, I don't see that happening anytime soon."

Tick looked up at the star-filled night in time to see a shooting star flash across the sky. He wondered if it was an omen of things to come. A light breeze ruffled his hair as he strode along. The ocean's warm water lapped at his feet and ankles. It was so soothing, he knew that if he ever left here, he would miss this nightly ritual.

A long time later, Pete said, "What the hell is *that?*" pointing to *that place.* "It looks like something you might see at the gates of hell."

Tick frowned. He hadn't realized they'd walked so far. A

full moon rode high in the sky, outlining the enormous building that stood like a dark avenging something or other. "I have no idea. The village people refer to it as *that place* at the end of the beach. As far as I know, it's uninhabited. I never come this far on my nightly walks and usually I go the other way. I've never seen anyone around the place or on the beach, at least I haven't during the day. Though I thought I heard someone crying once, I'm sure it was an animal. At night I think someone comes and goes, not sure why, never really cared to find out. It was being completed when I was just coming out of my drunken stupor. I never really cared enough to inquire, and, besides, who would I ask? I can tell you one thing, it cost a bundle to build. That's for sure."

"Are you sure it's empty?"

"No, but I never see anyone. I hear voices late at night sometimes if I'm out walking. No boats coming in. I'd hear a motorboat. The Coast Guard rips by five or six times a day. Usually the same boat. I can tell by the sound of the engine. And, when they start to approach that thing, they throttle back, so it's my guess they're keeping their eye on it. In order to get there on foot, you have to go past my place. I never see any lights, so I just assume it was built by some drug lord who got caught, and the place just sits there now because everyone is afraid to go near it. No one wants to get caught up in anything drug-related or whatever goes on there during the night."

"What do *you* think, Tick?"

"You know what, Pete, I try not to think about it. I have enough of my own problems without worrying about an empty building and the Coast Guard keeping an eye on it."

"Does anyone check on it?" Pete asked.

"You mean aside from the Coast Guard? Maybe the DEA, the DOJ; hell, maybe ICE has an eye on that thing. Aside from all the drive-bys I've heard, no one else has been poking around, at least to my knowledge. Why are you so curious about an empty building?"

"You live just down the beach from it, Tick. Those drug people shoot first and ask questions later. I would think with your background, you'd be a bit more curious."

"You trying to spook me, Pete?"

"Hell yes, I'm trying to spook you. You need to keep your wits about you. Jesus, there's not a soul to be seen except for you and me. If no one checks on you, you could be shot dead, and no one would know but that damn parrot, and I doubt you've taught him how to call 911."

Tick turned around and started back the way they'd come. "I think we're both tired, and it's time to go to bed. If you like, we can check it out tomorrow in daylight."

"Yeah, let's do that. You're right, it's been a long day."

Chapter 2

Kate Rush stood in the middle of the filthy room as she strained to see outside through the louvered glass windows that were a quarter of the way open, the handles to close them long rusted. Outside, sheets of rain blasted the building in hard-driving whacks of sounds. The palm trees, nearly bent in half from the ninety-mile-an-hour gale-force winds, slapped at the building, adding to the deafening barrage of sound. Visibility was zero. And it was going to be dark soon.

There were few things in life that frightened Kate Rush and, while she wasn't exactly frightened at the moment, she was uneasy. She'd been through a hurricane before and hadn't liked it then. And she sure as hell didn't like it now. Uneasy because the moldy, smelly building was empty of furnishings, her contact was a no-show, and a hurricane was raging just inches from where she stood. There was no place to sit, no place to hide or take cover. She'd been leaning against one of the mildewed walls for over two hours as she waited for her contact to show up. Her hand crept inside her jacket on the left side. The comforting feel of the Sig Sauer *almost* wiped away the uneasy feeling.

Little storm *my ass,* she thought as she remembered Tyler's words when he had called to tell her to meet him. She'd mentioned the word *hurricane*, which he'd pooh-poohed, saying, "We get these little storms all the time. This is Florida. Get used to it, Agent Rush." As if she didn't know this. She'd spent her childhood and teen years living in Florida. Of course, schmuck that he was, he'd probably forgotten that small detail.

So, she'd packed her bags, driven to Phoenix, parked her car in the long-term lot at the airport, and flown to Miami, where she'd rented a car and driven here through a hurricane. The big question was, where in the hell was her handler, the macho Lawrence Tyler, who was to meet her two hours ago? Hopefully in a ditch somewhere, never to surface again. Or, maybe, washed away out to the Gulf, never to surface again. Or stranded on someone's roof fighting for his life from the raging waters, only to be swept away, never to surface again. *Oh, be still my heart.*

Kate hated Lawrence Tyler. All the agents who worked under Lawrence Tyler hated him. If he threw himself a going-away party, no one would attend. Tyler was a sneaky, slick, obnoxious glory hound who used his agents to make a name for himself. He was the show horse, and the rest of them were the workhorses. She knew in her gut this assignment was a payback for the last confrontation she'd had with the nattily dressed special agent. She'd won that round, and Tyler had been transferred from the Phoenix office to Florida. But Tyler had a long arm, he knew how to kiss ass, and he had an all-powerful protector in his father, who just happened to be Florida's governor.

Kate fished around in her go-bag until she found the powerful Maglite she was never without. The bright light didn't help her mood. She shifted from one foot to the other as she listened to the storm outside. She ran the phone call from Tyler over and over in her mind. Tyler had said everything was NTK. Obviously, while he wanted her here, he wasn't about to tell her why until they were face-to-face. "Need to know, my ass," she muttered for the second time.

The long and short of it was that, for the snitch fee, one weasel had probably whispered something about some drug deal or something else equally rotten that was about to go down into another weasel's ear, who then whispered it into Tyler's ear, who then hit the ground running without checking the details—his usual MO.

As Kate leaned against the wall and listened to the hurricane outside, she wondered why she'd agreed to return to Florida after she'd spent twenty years of her life living elsewhere. She'd been days away from resigning and going to work in the private sector. Her resignation was typed and printed and in her purse. She'd given the DEA twelve years of her life, and because of people like Lawrence Tyler, she wasn't where she wanted to be. That was the bottom line. That, and the money sucked. She could make twice as much as she earned now with less danger to her person in the private sector. She had no social life, and at thirty-eight, her biological clock was ticking faster than she'd like; it was time to make some hard and fast decisions and stick to them.

Yet here she was. One last shot? Her swan song? Maybe one last time to get into Tyler's face? More than likely agreeing to come here was the stupidest thing she'd ever done. Not that she'd had much of a choice. The only way she could have avoided this assignment was to have handed in her resignation. Then again, maybe it was the fact that Tyler had said he might lend her out to the Coast Guard. *Why me?* she'd asked herself a hundred times since leaving Phoenix. She smiled at the thought that maybe Tyler planned on drowning her in the Gulf. An evil smile twisted her lips. He could try. Kate shined the beam of the light onto her wrist. Tyler was five hours late. "Which just goes to prove," she muttered, "if you want the job done and done right, send a woman to do it."

Two hours later, Kate's legs gave out, and she slumped to the floor. Not knowing if there were any rats in the abandoned building, she opted to keep the high-powered flashlight on, knowing she had spare batteries in her go-bag. Eventually, her eyes closed, and she dozed. From time to time she'd jerk to wakefulness to listen to the storm, which gave no indication it was abating. With no sleep the night before and traveling cross-country, she finally drifted into an uneasy sleep.

Hours later, Kate woke to an eerie quiet. Something had wakened her. Her hand immediately went to the gun in her shoulder holster. She looked around at the brilliant sunlight blasting through the louvered windows to see what it was that had pulled her out of her deep sleep. She crab walked, one eye on the doorway and the other on what she could see through the windows. She blinked at the elegant palms that were uprooted and piled in a pyre as though a bonfire were imminent. Crumpled aluminum lawn chairs were scattered over the narrow stretch of beach. A child's skateboard stood upright in the sand. An ice chest, the lid hanging drunkenly from one of the still-standing palmettos, lay on its side. She craned her neck and saw a motorcycle farther down the beach, the front wheel in the water, the back wheel buried in the sand.

Kate wheeled around; the Sig Sauer in her hand was steady, the safety off, when the door opened. Disgust whipped across her face when she saw Lawrence Tyler standing in the doorway. "A little late, aren't you?" she snapped. "Fifteen hours to be exact." Her hand dropped to her side, but she didn't holster her gun.

Lawrence Tyler was *GQ* handsome, with black hair that she'd happily noticed was thinning and clear blue eyes. Six-two, 170 pounds, and impeccably dressed, he was soft-spoken and as hateful as anyone she'd ever met. Classic nose, dimples, and a dentist's dream. Basically, Tyler was a wuss in every department except when it came to women. He was a deadly combination for the weak-willed women who were dumb enough to be taken in by his phony charm and good looks. She thanked God she wasn't one of them.

Tyler waved his hand toward the bank of louvered windows. "Hurricane. The roads were blocked."

"Amazing that I got through, isn't it, Lawrence? I've been hanging out here for fifteen hours. You had me fly across the country and threatened me with my job if I didn't get here on time even though there was a hurricane warning. You told me Florida was about to get a *little storm*, but you obviously were unwilling to venture out into this particular *little storm*." Kate saw the smirk on Tyler's face, and it stirred her to throw caution to the winds. "This is your revenge. This is all about your getting even with me for getting you transferred here. Admit it, and we can go on. Otherwise, I'm outta here."

Tyler looked around, distaste written all over his face. "You're being ridiculous, Agent Rush. Obviously, you are PMSing, so I'll overlook your little outburst this time. The only thing I expect from you is professionalism and doing your duty to the country. Threaten me again, and you go on report."

Kate bit down on her lower lip. She thought about the resignation letter in her purse, which she'd shoved into the bottom of her go-bag. Tyler had to pay for that PMSing comment. She debated pulling out the letter and ramming it down his throat. She could do it, too. Everyone knew what a *wuss* he was. He even got manicures. She realized at that moment how much she really hated the man standing in front of her. Still, she'd come all this way. The least she could do was hear him out before shoving her resignation down his throat or up his ass, whichever target presented itself first.

"Let's cut to the chase, Tyler. Why am I here? Why is this meeting taking place in this . . . this hellhole? There are hundreds of hotels in Miami. I know you set this up to spite me, no matter what you say."

"Your problem, Agent Rush, is that you're a drama queen. And you will address me as Special Agent Tyler and not by my last name. Is that understood?"

"It's understood," Kate said coldly.

"The reason, the only reason I picked you for this job is because you grew up in Miami. You lived here for eighteen years."

So the little shit remembered after all.

"You know the area, the people, you have friends here. You were the logical choice."

"The logical choice for *what?*"

"We have it on good authority that something big is going to go down on one of the Keys."

"When? What?" Kate asked.

"We don't know. It could be money laundering, it could be drugs, or it could be human trafficking. It could take as long as two years. Don't look at me like that, Agent Rush. You know how it works. We get in place, set up our surveillance, then wait it out. You'll also be working with the Coast Guard on a limited basis. There's a man we want you to watch. You'll be set up with accommodations that will give you access to the man in question."

"How did you come by this information, Special Agent Tyler? Which one of the Keys?"

"That doesn't matter. The source is reliable, that's all you need to know. The old maps call it Thunder Key, but these days it's known as Mango Key."

Was it all she needed to know? Nah.

Kate took a deep breath. This was where the rubber met the road. She turned around, picked up her go-bag, yanked out her purse, then reached in and grabbed her resignation letter. She whirled around, and said, "Let me make sure I have this right. You have a tip from someone who is more or less reliable who tells you something might or might not happen in approximately two years, and you need someone to babysit some man who lives on Mango Key. Do I have that all correct? Ah, yes. I can see by your expression that I got it right. Nah, I don't think so. Based on all of the above, I think I will pass on this gig, *Lawrence.*" In the blink of an eye, she thrust the resignation letter into his hand, turned, grabbed her bag, and was out the door and headed to where she'd parked her rental car. But it was gone, thanks, no doubt, to the hurricane, which just meant she'd have to hike to the hotel she'd checked into on arrival.

"Agent Rush! Stop right this minute!" Kate thought he sounded like a squealing wild pig caught in a rainstorm. She kept on going but did call over her shoulder, "Don't call me that again. I just quit. What part of that don't you understand?"

"You can't quit! I need you! The DEA needs you! You're an ace in this type of case. Look, I understand you're ticked off about yesterday, but these things happen. I said I'm willing to overlook the PMSing you're going through. Now stop, and let's talk this through."

Kate's eyes narrowed. She stopped in her tracks, dropped her go-bag, and got in Tyler's face. "Listen to me, you bastard. I despise you. For ten long years you've made my life miserable just so you could make yourself look good. I'm sick and tired of watching you take credit for other dedicated agents' work, my own included. I'd also like to know where you get all your money. That's a Hugo Boss suit you're wearing. I know how much a suit like that costs. You drive a Porsche. You have fancy digs. Where does the money come from, Lawrence? *Daddy?* The only reason you're still at the DEA is that your *daddy* is the governor of this state." She'd worked herself into such a rage she drew back her balled fist and coldcocked him square on the nose with all the force she could muster. "That's to remember Sandra Martin by, you son of a bitch!" Then her foot snaked out and found his groin. "That's for stealing Levinson's hard work and taking credit for it." She whirled around and kicked again, this time the blow landing deep in his side. He'd be peeing green for a week after a hit like that. "That was for Jacobson and how you put the screws to him." Then her fist shot out and landed in the middle of his throat. "That's for me and every other agent you screwed over. No witnesses, Lawrence. Now, if you'd been smart and had this meeting in some hotel or public place, you could sue me for assault and battery or have me brought up on charges."

"You bitch!" Tyler croaked, as he tried to staunch the flow of blood spewing all over his expensive suit.

"Goddamned bastard!" Kate said as she slogged through the sand to the road. She didn't look back.

Chapter 3

Kate strode through the Phoenix Sky Harbor International Airport as though she were on a mission. In a way, she was, to get home to her condo so she could shower and get some sleep. Now that she was unemployed, she had all the time in the world to do nothing but eat, plot Tyler's death, sleep, plot Tyler's death, dream, plot Tyler's death.

She felt grimy, angry, and tired. The smart thing would have been to stay in Miami, clean up, and get some sleep, but it didn't seem like an option at the time. If she had stayed, Tyler might have found her and done God only knows what. She'd opted to catch the next flight out of Miami and managed to get on board by the skin of her teeth by going standby.

Now all she had to do was pick up her bag, find her car, which she'd left in the long-term lot, and head for home. While she waited for her bag to come up on the carousel, she pulled out her cell phone and turned it on the way every other traveler was doing. She blinked when she saw the readout telling her she had twenty-seven messages. She knew they were all from Lawrence Tyler, so she snapped the phone shut and shoved it in her pocket. She felt giddy at the thought that she would never have to see or hear from him again.

Kate saw her olive green bag with the yellow ribbon on the handle. She reached down to grab hold of it, but a football type picked it up like it was a box of crackers and plopped it down in front of her. She smiled her thanks and headed for the nearest exit.

An hour later, she parked her car in the underground garage of her condo building. She took the elevator to the eighth floor and got out. The hallway smelled clean and fresh. Mrs. McDermott must have used her magic powder and vacuumed. Miss Dorothy, as Kate called her, was also responsible for the green plants by the elevator and in all the corners of the hallway. She watered and spritzed them every day, and they thrived under her care. Kate wasn't sure, but she rather thought Miss Dorothy was the one who had painted all the desert scenes hanging in the hallway. All in all, it was more than pleasant to step off the elevator to such splendor.

Kate opened the door, pushed her bag over the doorsill, and walked into the living room. She loved her condo, with the glorious view. She didn't have much furniture, but what she did have was bright and cheerful, each piece bought only after much agonizing. And it was all paid for. She never bought anything unless she could pay cash for it because she hated getting bills in the mail and tried not to live above the income her job at the DEA provided.

Kate looked around. Home sweet home. There was no sofa, but she did have a love seat and two deep comfortable chairs.

The love seat was a gorgeous pumpkin color and covered in a nubby hopsacking material. The two chairs were lemon-lime, in the same fabric. A beautiful, lush ficus tree reached almost to the ceiling. She should ask Miss Dorothy if she should consider cutting it back. Thank God she hadn't been gone long enough to really miss the place.

Kate's shoes flew here and there as she shrugged out of her

jacket, which also went flying to land half in the ficus and half on the floor. She continued to peel off her clothes as she headed for the bathroom.

When she was pink and puckered from the steamy shower and smelling like fresh strawberries, Kate stepped out of the shower and wrapped herself in her favorite robe, which felt like an old friend. Glancing at her reflection in the mirror—brownish-blond shoulder-length hair and clear blue eyes—she decided she wasn't a complete dud in the looks department if you didn't look too closely. She padded barefoot out to the kitchen, where she looked at the clock. She decided to break her own rule of never drinking until the sun was over the yardarm. It was five o'clock somewhere in the world. She poured a generous amount of white wine into one of her two fancy wineglasses and carried it out to the balcony. She loved sitting out there at that time of the day even though the opportunities to do so were few and far between. Since the sun was on the other side of the building, it was more comfortable than it was in the mornings. It was hot, but that was okay; the heat was dry, unlike Miami, where the humidity was almost a hundred percent.

Even though she'd closed the sliding glass doors, Kate could hear her landline ringing. Like she was really going to get up and go inside and answer it. Now that she'd resigned, she could do whatever she damn well pleased, and it pleased her not to answer her phone. She thought then about the messages on her cell phone. Those were for another day.

Kate leaned back and closed her eyes. She needed to think about her finances and how quickly she would have to seek employment. Her condo and car were paid for, thanks to a generous inheritance from her maternal grandparents. As she was the only grandchild, her grandfather had seen to her future. She had a healthy portfolio that could sustain her, according to Mitch, her broker, for ten years. She had an equally healthy 401(k) plan. She had close to thirty-six thousand dollars in her CMA account she could draw on for everyday living expenses until she decided what she was going to do. On top of that, she had a whole dresser drawer full of United States savings bonds that her father had left her, bonds she'd never cashed and were still drawing interest. Emergency money. She hadn't touched the money she'd gotten from her parents' life insurance policies because she couldn't bear to spend it. Despite her low government pay, she had four thousand eight hundred dollars in her personal checking account. Her life insurance, car insurance, and condo insurance, along with maintenance fees, were all paid up for the year. Ooops, she'd forgotten about the taxes on the Harbor Island beach house that had come to her from her paternal grandparents. That bill should be coming in soon. Maybe she should think about renting it out since she never went there. She could hire a management company to handle the details, including the credit check on prospective tenants.

A smile tugged at the corners of her mouth when she thought about the little two-bedroom Cape Cod house Grandpa Rush had built right on the beach during the last years of her grandmother's life. She remembered hearing her parents talk about how everyone laughed at the little house with the front porch. Some called it an eyesore, with all the fancy condominiums being built, but her grandfather didn't care. All he wanted was to make his wife happy during her last ailing years because she missed the home she'd lived in up north all her life until they retired to Miami. Kate clearly remembered her mother remarking that it had only cost thirty thousand dollars to build with him doing half the work. The land that little Cape Cod sat on was now worth more than a million dollars. She'd had offers over the years to sell it so it could be demolished so that some steel and glass edifice could be built. Like she would ever sell that little house. It didn't even bear thinking about. She loved the little house, with the window boxes and the diamond-shaped panes of glass. She had many memories from childhood in that house.

At least once a year, sometimes twice, she'd try to make it to Miami to check on it and just laze about and walk the beach. Sometimes, when a storm blew in, the water would come almost to the front porch. No, that house was her sanctuary, and she would never give it up. She thanked God now for her own wisdom in never selling it. She could go home and try to return to a normal life. It made more sense to sell the condo. She nodded to herself that she thought it was a good idea.

Satisfied that she was in good financial shape, Kate finished her wine and wished she'd brought the bottle outside. Then again, it wasn't wise to drink on an empty stomach. She fought the sleep that was threatening to overcome her, knowing full well that if she fell asleep, she would be up all night long.

The phone inside rang again. She ignored it as she wondered how long it would take someone to come knocking on her door. She couldn't help but wonder what Lawrence Tyler had told the Arizona office. She could almost hear it. "Rush got spooked because she was alone in a hurricane. She flipped out, took me on, and stormed out." She knew, just knew, he *wasn't* going to mention her resignation letter. He'd say she attacked him while still a DEA agent. It wouldn't matter that her resignation letter was dated. Or, would it? Would he be stupid enough to press charges? Of course he would because he was beyond stupid.

"Shit!"

Kate jumped to her feet and ran into the apartment, where she fired up her computer. She waited for it to boot up, then sent her resignation letter to her boss, Arnold Jellard, the agent in charge of the Phoenix office. She typed in a brief message that said she'd tendered her resignation to Lawrence

Tyler in Miami at 7:18 that morning. She added another line that said a hard copy would be delivered in person tomorrow. She read through the e-mail one more time and hit the SEND key. The relief she felt left her drained.

The wine bottle beckoned her. She grabbed it and headed back to her little balcony. The phone rang, then her cell phone chirped at the same time just as she slammed the slider shut. She was grinning from ear to ear when she settled herself and poured generously for the second time.

A long while later, when the wine bottle stood empty like a forlorn soldier, Kate tottered into the condo and went to bed. The clock on her nightstand read 5:45. She woke up twelve hours later to the sound of the ringing phone. She swung her legs over the side of the bed and laughed like a lunatic. She just knew her voice mail box was full, and her cell phone had probably exploded from all the calls coming in.

Like she cared.

Two hours later, dressed in jeans, running shoes, and a bright yellow T-shirt, Kate left her condo. In her car, she jammed a battered baseball cap that proclaimed her a fan of the Miami Dolphins on her ponytailed hair. She drove straight to a Starbucks drive-thru, got her order, and pulled out into traffic again.

With still enough coffee left in her cup for another five minutes, Kate drove steadily until she saw the turnoff for the field office, where she sat in the parking lot to finish her drink. She rolled down the windows to enjoy the bright sunny day Arizona was known for. In another hour, she would need the air-conditioning in the car. The big question was, where would she be in another hour?

Kate finished her coffee, crushed the paper cup, then dropped it into the trash bag she kept on the door handle. As much as she dreaded what was about to happen, she knew she had to get on with it. Sitting there contemplating her belly button wasn't going to get her anywhere. She reached over for her canvas bag and rooted around until she found her ID on a chain. She looped it around her neck, grabbed the bag, and got out of the car.

Kate looked at her watch. It wasn't nine o'clock yet, but the parking lot was deserted, and there was no one walking about. Normally that quadrant was a beehive of activity no matter the time of day or night. She couldn't help but wonder if it was some kind of omen.

The hum of traffic on the main road was steady, so people were out and about, going God only knew where. A formation of birds flew overhead in a V. Where were *they* going?

Kate licked at her lips, drew a deep breath, then yanked at the heavy plate-glass door. She marched across the lobby to the security desk, flipped her ID, and signed in. The guard nodded as she headed to the security checkpoint, breezed through, grabbed her bag—which had been duly noted as containing her Sig Sauer—off the belt, and headed for the elevator that would take her to the fourth floor, where she'd worked for so long. After today, she would never come back.

She was alone in the elevator, something that rarely happened. More often than not there was a gaggle of people inside. When the doors slid open, she stepped out into a hall that was blindingly bright from all the overhead fluorescent lights. She looked around as she shifted her bag to a more comfortable position on her shoulder. She headed straight down the hall to Arnold Jellard's office.

Kate frowned as she looked around. There was no sight of Josh Levinson or Roy Jacobson. Were they out in the field? She'd seen Sandra Martin's neat-but-empty cubicle, so obviously the third member of her team still hadn't been replaced. With Kate's departure, the team would be down to just Josh and Roy. The frown stayed put when she rapped on the glass door. The blinds were closed, which could mean one of two things: Jellard was with someone, or he was taking a break with his feet up on the desk, coffee cup in hand. When the knock wasn't acknowledged, she walked down the hall to the kitchen, where she knew there would be coffee and donuts. The only problem was, there was no coffee and no pink box of donuts.

Kate was so used to making the coffee that she fell into her old routine and scooped out coffee into the clean pot. She couldn't shake the feeling that something she knew nothing about was going on. She asked herself why she should even care. It was going to take a good five minutes for the coffee to drip into the pot. She might as well use the time to clean out her cubicle, not that there was that much to clean out. She'd never brought clutter to the office. For the most part, she could chuck everything if she wanted to. Tissues, an extra pair of reading glasses, a bottle of nail polish, some breath mints, and two stale power bars. She dumped them all into her bag, then looked at the corkboard, with all its Post-it notes. She ripped them down, then tossed them in the trash can. She covered her computer and used one of the tissues to wipe a few cookie crumbs off her little desk. Now her cubicle was as neat as Sandra Martin's.

Special Agent Kate Rush no longer inhabited this small space. Special Agent Kate Rush was now plain old Kate Rush.

Back in the kitchen, Kate looked around for her mug but couldn't see it. She opened one of the cabinets and reached for one of the complimentary cups the agency handed out from time to time. She rinsed it out, dried it with a paper towel, then poured herself a cup of coffee. Carrying her coffee, she walked back down the hall to Jellard's office. The door was still closed, the blinds drawn. She sat down on one of the two chairs next to the door and waited, but not before giving a loud, sharp knock to the door.

Kate told herself she would wait until she finished her coffee. If the door was still closed, she would slide the manila envelope under the door and leave. She was only there out of courtesy to Jellard.

"Screw it," Kate muttered to herself as she was about to take her cup back to the kitchen and leave. She was standing, her back to the door, when it opened. She whirled around. Arnold Jellard, a tall, barrel-chested man who looked like he could take on a grizzly bear and live to talk about it, stood in the doorway. Standing next to him was Lawrence Tyler.

Well, this isn't exactly what I expected.

Tyler offered up one of his truly evil smiles as he swept past her. Jellard's voice was as big and deep-timbered as he was. "You waiting for a bus, Rush?"

"No, sir," Kate said as she stepped past him. She looked at the two chairs facing the desk. Which one had Tyler been sitting in? She opted for the one on the right. She immediately started to rummage in her bag for her credentials, her gun, and the envelope with her resignation. She slid them all across the desk and stood up. "I guess that's it," she said.

Jellard stroked his snow white, well-trimmed beard. His blue eyes, the color of washed-out denim, sparked angrily behind his wire-rim glasses. His words cut her to the quick when he said, "I never thought you were a quitter, Rush."

Kate stood up, walked around to the back of the desk, and leaned over to kiss Jellard on the cheek. "I'm going to pretend I didn't hear that. See ya. Tell Josh and Roy I said good-bye."

The big man lumbered to his feet when he saw that his words had no effect on his former agent. "Where are you going? What are you going to do?"

Kate smiled. "I'm going back to Miami. Something about going home makes me feel good. I'll work on my thesis, and I've been tinkering with the idea of writing a cookbook. My grandmother's recipes. I've been wanting to do it for a long time. Now seems like it might be a good time. Just out of curiosity, what was Tyler doing here?"

Jellard stepped in front of Kate and closed the door. "His daddy found a way to give him my job. I'm being put out to pasture in two weeks. He was here to gloat. I wanted to kick his ass all the way to the Canadian border, but I didn't want to hurt my foot. I didn't know you knew how to cook."

Kate was speechless. She finally got her tongue to work. "I don't know how to cook, but I can learn. I learned how to be a damn fine DEA agent, didn't I? Are you being transferred, or are you retiring?"

"Got two more years to go. No way is that little shit going to force me out. I have two choices, Miami or New Jersey. I'm taking Miami. Josh and Roy already put in for transfers. I'm kind of hoping they follow me, but with those two, you never know. Maybe I'll drop by for a cup of coffee." Affection rang in his voice when he said, "I was jerking your chain a few minutes ago. I know you're no quitter. If it's any consolation to you, Kate, I would have done exactly what you did."

Kate nodded. "My door is always open, Jelly." The nickname Jelly was allowed only in private when they were just people, not agent and boss.

Her eyes burning, Kate left the office and took the elevator to the ground floor. She stood a moment and looked around. She didn't love this small field office. It was just a place where she checked in from time to time. She was a field agent. She corrected the thought: She used to be a field agent. She wasn't crazy about Arizona either. She hated the high temperatures and dry heat. No, she wasn't going to miss the place at all. What she would miss was the people she'd worked with, the few friends she'd made. She took one last look around, then waltzed through the door a man was holding open for her. She walked to her car, her cell phone in her hand. She scrolled down the numbers and hit Sandra Martin's. The least she could do was take her old colleague to lunch before she left Arizona. Plus, she wanted to tell her about her encounter with Lawrence Tyler.

Minutes and a few squeals of pure pleasure later, the two women agreed to meet for lunch at noon. Just in time for her to go back to the condo, pack her things, load up her car, and place a call to a realtor. She wasn't exactly sure at what moment she'd come to the decision to sell the condo. Not that it mattered. She was glad now she didn't have a lot of junk to pack up. She made a mental note to ask the realtor if she could sell the condo furnished. If not, she'd throw in the furniture or donate it to Goodwill.

Kate parked the car in the small lot behind Sassy Susie's, a small café that served homemade food and had the best coffee in the whole state. Sassy Susie, an aging spinster, made her own bread and desserts and, while the place was feminine-looking, the menu catered to men with huge appetites. It was said by those same men with the robust appetites that a person could get drunk on the aromas that wafted about the café.

Sandra was waiting by the door. The women hugged, laughed, then hugged again as they entered the café and were shown to their usual small round table. In other words, Sassy Susie considered the two of them regulars and treated them as such, which meant they were immediately served coffee and the homemade bread with fresh butter.

Kate looked across the table at her dear friend. Sandra, or Sandy as her friends called her, looked unbelievably happy. "There must be a man in your life."

Sandra giggled. "Yes and no. Let's just say I'm seeing someone. I actually have free time where I can make plans and carry through with them. He's a nice guy, but he's not the one for me. If he were, I think I'd know. So, how come you're dressed like you are in the middle of the day?"

Kate eyed her friend. She was so pretty—petite, dark hair,

incredible blue eyes, huge dimples, and a killer smile with flashing white teeth. She was also a martial arts brown belt. Cuban by nationality, she'd done her time in Miami before being transferred to Arizona. Like Kate, she hated Arizona, yet here she was.

Kate licked at her lips. "I quit. I'm moving back to Miami. I packed up my car this morning, and I'm leaving for Harbor Island right after lunch. I've had enough of this place to last me a lifetime. But the best part is, I got even with Tyler for you. I broke his nose for you. I kneed him in the groin for Levinson and kidney-punched him for Jacobson. It's a long story. He's replacing Jelly, thanks to his daddy. Jelly is taking his job in Miami. Guess Tyler whined enough about Miami that his daddy had to do something. Jelly seems to be okay with it all. He only has two more years, and he's not about to give it up. He can weather it. He promised to stop by for coffee."

"Oh my God! Tell me you're not kidding! You really decked that weasel? There is a God!" Sandy announced dramatically. "What about Josh and Roy? Did you tell them? They call once in a while. Damn, we were such a good team until Tyler ruined it."

Kate shrugged as she spread golden butter on a chunk of still-warm bread. "Jelly said they put in for transfers. I'm thinking he's hoping they want to go with him. Roy always said he was going to transfer out to ATF."

Sandy bit into her own bread and sighed happily. "I haven't been here since I quit and walked away. I really missed this bread. So what are you going to do, Kate?"

"Finish up my thesis. Write a cookbook."

Sandy laughed. "You don't know how to cook. I'm ahead of you, I finished up. You can call me Dr. Martin from here on in. I have résumés all over the place. Got a lot of replies and, believe it or not, one from the University of Miami. I'm taking my time. Not sure where I want to go. I miss being an agent, I'm not going to lie to you. I think I was meant to do that. I sent one to the FBI. I haven't heard back."

"Oh, Sandy, that's wonderful. I hope, for selfish reasons, you pick Miami. We could be roommates if you like, and I won't charge you rent. You know I still have that beach house on Harbor Island. We can split the utilities. Until you decide where you want to put down your roots, tell me you'll think about it." Susie appeared at the table, and the women gave their order. They always went with the special of the day, and today's special was pot roast, mashed potatoes, green peas, and a Southwestern corn medley.

"Here's my address and the phone at the house on Harbor Island. I'll write the directions on the back of the card. If you decide, just show up."

"Okay, I'll think about it. You make it sound . . ." She sought the right word, couldn't come up with one, so rattled off a long string of Spanish.

"I hope that means exciting and wonderful. More than likely it will be dull and boring, hot and humid, but we'll be right on the ocean. That's a plus that has no equal. I used to love going to sleep in my grandmother's house and hearing the ocean all night long."

"I think you just sold me. Are you sure, Kate? You're not just inviting me because you feel sorry for me?"

"God, no! By the way, do you know anything about Mango Key? Ooh, here comes our food."

"You mean Thunder Key?"

"Yeah."

"Not much. It's a private Key if I remember correctly. Some kind of land grant to some Indians. I should know, but I don't. Why?"

"Something is going on down there. But that's not my

problem. Right now I have to learn how to cook, so I can do a cookbook. Maybe I'll ask Susie for the recipe for this pot roast." Kate held up her glass of sweet tea, and said, "To women and the decisions they make on the spur of the moment."

"Yeah," Sandy drawled as she clinked her glass against Kate's.

Chapter 4

Eleven Months Later

Kate Rush sat on the front porch looking out at the ocean as she sipped sweet tea. She looked down into the glass and saw that the ice had already melted. She'd only been out here in the heat and humidity less than fifteen minutes, and already her drink was warm. July in Miami.

A quick trip to the kitchen, and she was back on her bright red Adirondack chair, staring out at the ocean. She was bored out of her mind. But she was now Dr. Kathryn Rush. She had no idea what she was going to do with that title. Nor did she have a clue what she was going to do with her life from here on in. She thought about her brilliant idea to write a cookbook and laughed out loud. A cook she would never be. Although she could now make a decent pot roast, she had to eat it and variations thereof for a solid week. She now hated pot roast. Sandra hated pot roast. When Sandy had moved out, she had been glad that she would never have to eat it again.

Kate gulped at the rapidly warming drink. Not only was she bored, she was lonely. Bordering on being a recluse, she knew it was time to make some important decisions. How ironic that just eleven months ago, almost to the day, she'd been sitting on her little terrace in Phoenix making the same kinds of decisions. Decisions she'd followed through on. Once again, it was time to do it all over. Back then, though, she'd had a plan. Right now, that minute, she couldn't see through to the next hour.

Financially, she was still sound. She'd been frugal, and for the five months that Sandy had lived with her, she'd contributed to the food bill and utilities. She envied her friend because in January she'd started teaching at the University of Miami. She'd bought a condo close to the university and a secondhand car, a Volvo, owned by a little old lady so she, too, was in good shape. She came to the Harbor Island beach house every weekend, and the two of them lazed about, walking on the beach, going out in the water in Kate's new Boston Whaler. Kate was tired of being a beach bumette. She needed a plan, a goal, incentives. Where was she going to find them? Within, she told herself.

Then, like always, she thought about Josh, Roy, and Jelly and wondered how they were doing. The last she'd heard was that Josh and Roy had joined Jelly in the field office in Miami. Even though it was only a short drive over the Seventy-ninth Street Causeway, the promised visit to drop in for coffee had never materialized. She'd been a little miffed at that. Surely, somehow, some way, they could have carved out an hour to visit an old friend and colleague. Out of sight, out of mind. She felt sad at the thought. Time to make new friends. Maybe if she found a job, she'd make friends at her place of employment. She grimaced at the thought. In six months, Sandra hadn't made any friends, saying it was a closed shop at the university, and no one was interested in adding new friends to their inner circle.

A smile tugged at the corners of Kate's mouth as she remembered how Sandy had said she signed up for every workshop Home Depot had to offer. She'd been convinced she would meet interesting people. She now knew how to spackle, paint, wallpaper, and lay tile and brick, but she hadn't made any new friends. The upside to Sandy's new knowledge was that the cottage sported fresh paint, some new wallpaper in the bathrooms along with new tile, and the walkway leading to the front door was neat and tidy, with brand-new brick and slate. And Kate had saved the money on the labor.

And there were no new men in either her life or Sandy's.

Kate looked at the remains of the tea in her glass—all water. She tossed it over the banister just as the phone inside rang. No one called her on the landline. Probably a telemarketer. Still, she was lonely enough to go inside and answer it. She could always tell the person on the other end to stop calling.

Inside, she picked up the phone and barked a greeting, daring the voice to be someone she wasn't interested in hearing from. "Kate, it's Arnold."

"Jelly! This is so weird, I was just thinking about you. Where are you? What are you doing? I thought you were going to stop by? How are Roy and Josh?"

The big man laughed, the sound booming over the wire. "Whoa. I tried for months to get out to the island, but I've never worked so hard as I have since moving here. I'm just coming out of court. Had to testify on a drug runner. Josh and Roy are standing right here, and we want to come over and have that coffee. We can talk when I get there. How about around six? We need to go back to the office first and clean up a few things. Dinner would be nice. Real nice. I'm sure you must be an expert by now. I can't wait to see how the cookbook is coming. You okay, Kate?"

Kate was grinning from ear to ear. "It's Dr. Rush these days, Jelly."

"No kidding! Congratulations. Have you seen Sandra?"

"She's Dr. Martin these days. I see her every weekend. Each time she comes, she asks if I've heard from any of you. I'll call and ask her to come over. I'll see you at six."

Kate hung up the phone, a huge grin in place as she clapped her hands. Company. She immediately called Sandy and left a message on her voice mail. Then she ran to the kitchen and opened the freezer to see six eye round roasts sitting side by side. She pulled one out, then the pressure cooker. "Oh, Susie, you would be so proud of my pot roast. It's just as good as yours!"

She could make it with her eyes closed. That she was sick of it didn't matter. The guys would love it, and she could pick at it the way Sandy would. She was excited now as she bustled about the kitchen getting things under way. The moment she was satisfied, she raced to the bathroom, showered, and changed into a white sun dress that showed off her tan. She was glad she'd gotten a haircut and had her nails done on Monday.

Back in the kitchen, she checked the refrigerator to make sure she had enough beer because the guys were beer drinkers. She had enough. She also had a frozen peach pie she plopped into the oven. The guys weren't gourmets, so they'd never know it was an out-of-the-freezer special.

Excitement coursed through Kate as she rushed around tidying up the living and dining rooms, where she had books and papers scattered everywhere. The guys were coming. How wonderful. The next few minutes were spent preparing the vegetables and potatoes. She was pouring fresh tea over a full glass of ice cubes when she stopped what she was doing when the realization hit her that she wanted to go back to being a DEA agent almost as much as Sandra Martin wanted to. Since they'd burned their bridges, the next best thing would be hearing the guys recount all that went on this past year.

The ATF was always looking for experienced agents, ditto for the FBI. She'd actually queried the DOJ, but when the Department of Justice called her to come in for an interview, she'd blown it off. Now with her doctorate under her belt, she knew she would be in high demand. Or was she flattering herself? Probably.

Kate shifted into a neutral zone and stared out at the ocean until she heard Sandy's car in the driveway. Sandy barreled up the slate walkway, jabbering as she reached the porch. "I can't believe they're coming. I'm so excited. Are you excited, Kate? Oh, God, are we having pot roast? Okay, okay, I know it's the only thing you know how to cook. It's okay. The guys will love it. I can't wait to hear what's been going on. Jeez, it's almost a year. Why now?" She deflated like a pricked balloon as she sat down in a lime green Adirondack chair. Kate did love bright colors. Painting the chairs had been their first project after Sandy's first class at Home Depot. Three more chairs were on the front porch, one bright yellow, one orange, and the other a beautiful sky blue. The chairs matched the colors of the flower-filled clay pots.

"How many times have we sat out here bitching and moaning about life?" Kate asked.

"Too many to count. Do you think they're coming for a reason, or is it just a social call? Eleven months is a long time without so much as a call. What do you think, Kate?"

Kate laughed. "What you're really asking is what do I *want* it to be? Why lie? We'd both kill to get back in, but that isn't going to happen. So let's just go with they're coming for dinner and let it go at that. If it's anything else, I think we'll both be surprised."

They heard the horn that started blowing a full block away. Both women ran down to the end of the driveway to wait for the Jeep Cherokee to swerve onto the driveway and park next to Sandy's car.

Arnold Jellard was out first, wearing shorts, T-shirt, and sandals. He looked like a beached whale. Josh Levinson was dressed in khaki shorts and a white Izod T-shirt. He was barefoot. Roy Jacobson wore long pants and a button-down short-sleeved shirt. All three men had military-style crew cuts and were heavily tanned.

The hugs, the squeezes were genuine, and the laughter was happy and joyous.

Sandy played hostess while Kate checked on dinner. She literally danced around the kitchen. She couldn't remember being this happy in a long time.

Tray in hand, with three Coronas, a lime wedge stuck in each bottle, and two glasses of ice tea, Kate made her way to the porch.

"Tell us what's going on. Do you miss us? What's up with Tyler? How do you like Miami?" Sandy never asked one question if she could ask three or four at the same time.

Jellard waved his arms. "We can't keep up with the drug runners. The money laundering is getting away from us. We've been working seven days a week for months. We're also shorthanded. Miami is great, but I hate the humidity. Tyler's daddy arranged for him to relocate to Los Angeles. Given the manpower shortage after the budget cuts, not only does he continue to supervise the office here in Miami, but also the Arizona and LA offices.

"Seems like the only place he isn't supervising is New Jersey. Don't ask me what they did to deserve that piece of luck. I suppose that if you have to work in New Jersey, you're entitled to luck on something. We've lost a lot of agents because of Tyler. But that's not my problem. We do our job, and I'm counting down the months till it's time to retire."

Josh Levinson laughed out loud at the expression on the women's faces. He was a good-looking guy with an aversion to marriage, but he'd had the same girlfriend for the past ten years. She was a professional model and had no more interest in getting married than Josh did. He was movie-star good-looking, with dark hair, laughing eyes, and a perfect smile. His body was okay, too, all 180 pounds of muscle. His six foot two frame carried the weight well.

Roy Jacobson was grinning, too. Shorter than his partner, with a receding hairline, wire-rimmed glasses, and a spare tire around his middle, he was happily married with five daughters, two sets of twins and one stray, as he put it.

Both men were the kind of agents you wanted covering your back, and they did it well because it was what they did. Once they'd been an exceptional team, each agent knowing the others so well they could anticipate one another's moves. Those instincts had saved all their lives on more than one occasion.

"One of these days, someone is going to pop the son of a bitch, and it will probably be one of our guys. I heard through the grapevine there is a petition going around. If he isn't removed, there is going to be a massive walkout. I heard a special task force has been initiated on the QT," Josh said. The other two men nodded to show they'd heard the same thing, which meant it was way past the rumor stage and absolutely a fact.

"Oh, be still my heart," Sandy cried dramatically.

Roy swigged from his bottle. "Don't get excited now. His old man is pretty damn powerful. He's one of those people who makes things go his way. Or, I should say, his son's way. He likes to brag that his only son is a big shot in the DEA. Don't ask me why."

"So, what are you working on right now? Can you talk about it?" Kate asked.

The silence that greeted Kate's question sat there like a hundred-pound rock. The two younger agents deferred to Jellard.

"Drugs, drugs, and more drugs. Money laundering is at an all-time high, like I said. It's just a long swim to Cuba from here. Yesterday, we had a visit from Homeland Security. Surprised the hell out of me, I can tell you that. Hey, Rush, what's for dinner?" he asked.

That told Kate Jellard wanted to change the subject. "Pot

roast. Sassy Susie gave me her recipe before I left. I perfected it. When you eat it, you'll think you're back there. And, of course, the peas and the Southwestern corn and peach pie for dessert. Anyone want another beer?" Three hands shot into the air.

"Relax, everyone, I'll get it," Sandy said.

The rest of the evening passed in a pleasant blur. The camaraderie was genuine and heartfelt. It was nine-thirty when Jellard finally got down to business. Kate recognized the look on her old boss's face. Her heart kicked up an extra beat as she licked at her dry lips. She risked a glance at Sandy, who she was certain was reading Jellard just the way she was.

"I'm here to make you an unorthodox backdoor offer. I'd like it to be otherwise, but I know the two of you realize how the game is played, so we have to go with what we can and cannot do. Just so you know, on paper you're both considered out-of-control hotheads. Tyler wrote up killer reports and made himself look like Agent of the Year. At least that's what his father's spreading around. He'd have to do a lot more ass kissing for anyone else to see him in that light, but blood's thicker than water.

"In any case, the way it was done makes it pretty hard to get it reversed. But with the task force looking into things, I'm confident that, even if he isn't canned, he'll no longer be supervising the Miami office. So I'm going to make you this offer. But first I need to know if you're interested. You both appear to have moved on, you have your PhDs now, and Sandy has what appears to be a fine job, while you, Kate, are following your dream of writing that cookbook you told me about. If you aren't interested, say the word, and we're outta here."

"Bullshit," both women said in unison.

"Lay it on me. I've been bored to death," Kate said. Sandy nodded in agreement. "Me, too."

Jellard's fist shot in the air, followed by Levinson's and Jacobson's. Then they were in a circle, pounding each other's backs.

"Just like old times," Sandy gurgled happily. "Now, tell us everything and don't leave a thing out in the telling. Anyone want another beer?"

"You can sleep here in case either of you have any thoughts of returning to downtown Miami tonight. No drinking and driving on my watch. I have plenty of space," Kate said.

"You sound like our den mother. We accept your offer and we'll also take another beer. My throat is going to get dry giving you all the details," Jellard said.

A light breeze coming in off the ocean stirred the ferns hanging from the rafters of the front porch. The paddle fans whirred softly to match the whispering breeze. Out in the distance, where the sky met the ocean, it was sparkly bright, the tide making its own music as it rushed toward the shore.

"This is like . . . I don't know, something almost ethereal," Jacobson said. "My wife would love sitting here on the porch, listening to the ocean and watching the stars. You sure, Kate, that you want to come back into the business? Give up evenings like this?"

Kate thought Roy's voice sounded a tad too anxious. The spill from the light in the living room bathed him in a golden color, but his features, she thought, were worried. "I don't have to think twice. This probably isn't a secret, but I will never make a cook. Pot roast is the only thing I learned how to cook. Since I can't cook, I'm not going to write a cookbook. At best it was something to say to make myself believe that perhaps I could do it. The bottom line is, I don't want to do it."

It was Sandy's turn, and she stepped up to the plate. "Maybe someday I'll be ready to teach, but this isn't the time. I knew that one week into the job. It won't bother me one little bit to hand in my resignation."

"Okay, ladies, then here's the deal. Last August, Kate,

when Tyler asked for you to come to Florida, he had a few clues as to what might be going down. He ran with the little he had and the two of you had your . . . altercation and his snitches dove for cover and nothing happened. But the same old crap that was simmering back then has now surfaced a year later. Tom Dolan, an old friend from Homeland Security, flew down here to talk to me yesterday. As much as it pains me to say this, I still have to say it. Tyler's informants had it right. Something is going to go down in the Keys, Mango Key, to be precise. It's not drugs either. Dolan thinks it's human trafficking, bringing in illegals to work for next to nothing, maybe even some prostitution. There's a huge amount of money involved. Is it dirty money? I have no clue. We all know informants give you just enough, and half of it is make-believe. You have to up the payout or wait till they're ready to tell you more. And even then, you have to cut through the bullshit.

"There's a guy who lives right on the beach on Mango Key. He was a homicide detective in Atlanta, and he's been there eight years. Lives in a house on stilts. We checked him out, tragic background, he lit out and ended up on Mango Key. He writes books and movie scripts. Keeps to himself. He's the guy Tyler wanted you to babysit, Kate. He had himself convinced, without checking, of course, that Patrick Kelly was the guy his squeals were telling him about. If he had checked, he would have found out some punk kid high on crack shot and killed his wife and two kids. After the funeral, the guy got in his car and ended up here. He spent a couple of years with his snoot in a bottle, then he cleaned up his act. The worst thing you can say about the guy is he's a recluse. Bought himself a cigarette boat and goes into Miami from time to time. That's the guy's life in a nutshell. There simply ain't no more.

"But down the beach from where he lives in what he calls Tick's Tree House is another . . . for want of a better word, another house, only it's not exactly a house. It's a compound of sorts. Some drug lord from Miami had it built, then the Coast Guard nailed him and the drugs he was running. Broke up the whole gang. But it's being watched. It's right at the tip of the Key and makes for easy access and an even easier exit. We can't find out who it belongs to. Seems like the private party who owned the land refused to sell it to the Indians when the rest of the Key was transferred from state control to them. And the records of its ownership over the years have proven impossible to follow. There is activity there but only in the middle of the night, and not every night.

"Tomorrow, I am going to Mango Key to talk to the elders there. It's a rather strange place, and how Mr. Kelly fits in with their rules and regulations is something I do not understand. We plan to ask the elders if they will lease a strip of the beach where we can put up a prefab building. We can have it up and operational in three days if they agree. I'm planning on asking Evan White from the Coast Guard to go with me to make my plea. We want you girls to move in and watch things. You'll be provided a cover, but as of this minute I don't know what it will be. You will be on the book, but it will be my book. I can pay for your living expenses, but you won't be getting a salary. When you officially go on the book, your pay will be retroactive. If I can't make it happen, you're right back here. You need to understand that going in. Jacobson and Levinson will be around a lot as your best buds, brothers, cousins, whatever they need to be." Both women nodded in agreement.

"And the cop on the beach? What's his role?" Kate asked.

"Gut instinct tells me the guy is just what he appears to be. He withdrew from something too painful to deal with. Tyler's spin on it is that he's into something up to his ears in order to get back at law enforcement for letting it happen in the first place. You pay your money and you take your pick. Personally, I think the guy just likes being alone."

"And what happens if, when we move in, he moves out because his privacy was invaded?" Sandy asked.

"This isn't about him. He's just there. This is about that compound and what the Coast Guard feeds you. I don't have to tell any of you how the guys swim in underwater on dark nights. Hell, probably half of them are SEAL aficionados. What that means is you're probably going to sleep during the day and stand guard all night. That's as much as we know right now. If you want out, now is the time to say so."

"I'm in," Kate said.

"Me, too," Sandy said.

"Then we have a deal, ladies and gentlemen."

Chapter 5

Tick Kelly walked down the steps from his house and looked around. The sun was just creeping over the horizon, the birds were chirping, the palm fronds dancing in the early-morning breeze. In another two hours it would be blazing hot, and the humidity would be creeping toward the hundred percent mark. In other words, a brand-new day. To do what, he didn't know. He'd finished his latest novel ten days ago, spent a week revising as needed, then, yesterday, he'd fired up his cigarette boat and headed to Miami, where he sent it off by FedEx, with a disk copy enclosed.

At the bottom of the steps, Tick looked around as he tried to decide which way he wanted to run, left or right. He opted for left before he did some limbering-up exercises. He'd been lax about his physical regimen the last two weeks, working around the clock to finish his book on time. If there was one thing he excelled at these days, it was tuning things out.

He started out slow, then his bare feet picked up speed. He knew every stick of driftwood, every chunk of coral, every lone bush or weed on his run. He looked over his shoulder to see if Bird was following him. He was. Normally, to Tick's amusement, he jabbered during the whole run. At times they actually carried on a conversation that made absolutely no sense at all. He'd tried these past years to ask the bird where

it came from, who his/her owner had been, and other interesting questions. There was no response from the parrot. *I'm
a cop, for God's sake. Ex-cop,* he corrected the thought.
He'd been a master at interrogation, but he hadn't been able
to break the bird; nor had he been able to clean up his "colorful" vocabulary. Bird was jabbering now about deep water,
then he let loose with something Tick had never heard before, "Shit happens." Tick slowed slightly so that the bird
was just above his shoulder. "Yeah, Bird, pretty much all the
time."

And then he saw it, a building on what he perceived as his
goddamn beach. How'd that happen? It wasn't there . . .
When had he last run? Two weeks ago, he decided. In ten
days, someone put up a building, and he was just now notic-
ing it? *What's wrong with this picture?*

"Told you man, shit happens. Deep water. This sucks. Boy,
does this suck!" Bird squawked. Then he let loose with another volley of words, "Bang! Bang! Bang! Get the girls! Get
the girls!"

His eyes bulging, Tick stopped and bent over, his hands on
his knees as he stared at what looked to be something like a
mini airport hangar. Caught off guard, Bird flew past, doubled back, and landed on his shoulder.

"Oh, shit, now I have neighbors. How come you didn't tell
me this was going on, Bird? You're supposed to be my look-
out. I appointed you to guard the portals of my domain, and
you damn well fell down on the job. Well?" Like the damn
bird was really going to answer him.

"You screwed up! You screwed up!"

Tick tilted his head to look at the bright-eyed bird on his
shoulder. "Was that an answer? Are you talking to me?"

"Listen! Listen, shit happens." Tick burst out laughing
and couldn't stop. He turned around and started to jog back
to his stilt house. Maybe after his coffee, he'd shower and
head into the village to see what if anything he could find

out about his new neighbor. He didn't want neighbors, didn't want his space invaded. Because he still thought like a cop, he wanted to know the who, the what, the when, and the why of everything. Nothing else would satisfy him. Cop school 101.

Back in his house ten minutes later, Tick headed for the kitchen to put on his coffee and fix his cereal. "What'll it be this morning, Bird? Cheerios or Fruit Loops?"

Bird ruffled his feathers and let loose with an ear-piercing shriek. Then he made another sound that one, if desperate, could take for laughter. "Nada. Zip. Zero. Bacon, eggs, pancakes, more, more, more!"

"In your dreams, my feathered friend. That crap will clog your arteries. Even birds must have arteries. The answer is no. Besides, you know we only eat bacon and eggs one day a week. The heart book says we can do that." Tick looked over at the parrot, who was perched on his chair, waiting for the breakfast he didn't want. His eyes were shiny bright as he watched his roommate get out two different boxes of cereal and a container of milk. He didn't make his move until the bowls were placed on the table, at which point he reared up, spread his wings, and flew low over the table, knocking the cereal boxes on the floor. His return flight sent the milk carton skidding across the table and onto the floor. Then he was airborne, lighting on one of the paddles of the fan, which had yet to be turned on. "Shit happens, man," Bird squawked.

"Son of a bitch!" Tick swore as he looked at the mess he had to clean up. Not knowing what else to say other than, "Bad bird," Tick started mopping up. And then he laughed. At least he couldn't say his life wasn't interesting from time to time.

"C'mon, c'mon, time is money," Bird said, ruffling his wings.

"Listen, you . . . you . . . bird. We need to talk straight here.

I want some answers. First off, are you male or female? Who taught you all this stuff? Where the hell did you come from?"

"Cuba."

Tick froze and looked up at the bird. "Did you fly here? What a damn stupid question. Or did someone bring you?"

"Boat. Deep water. Bang! Bang! Bang! Get the girls! Get the girls! Shit happens, man."

Tick digested this latest volley of words as he tried to decide if they meant anything. "You got a name, Bird?"

"Tick."

"That's my name. What is your name?" He'd asked this question a hundred times, and the bird would never respond.

"Pete."

"Pete is my brother. C'mon, Bird, what's your name?" Suddenly the question was the most important question in the world, and Tick didn't know why. "Tell me, or I'm going to turn on that fan, and you'll be nothing but feathers."

Bird sailed down gracefully and landed on Tick's arm. He stretched forward and pecked him on the cheek. He tilted his head to see how the peck was received. Tick stroked his colorful feathers and stood up. Bird settled himself on his chair by the table. "Bang! Bacon! Bacon! Bang!"

"Okay, okay."

And it was a new day, Tick thought as he bustled about the tiny kitchen. In his wildest dreams he could never imagine that he would cater to a salty-mouthed parrot who was smarter than he was. As he watched the bacon sizzle in the fry pan, he remembered the day Bird had seen him clean and oil his gun. That was the first day he'd said the words, bang, bang, bang, over and over. How weird that he knew guns made a "bang" sound. It was also weird that he knew what a cell phone was. That first time he'd almost gone nuts flying like crazy all over the place. He'd been in such a frenzy squawking, "Call me, call me, Jesus Christ, call me! Get the girls! Get the girls!" Then, when Tick had closed the cell phone, the bird had calmed down, but he was still jabbering about shit happening, getting the girls, and deep water.

In his gut, Tick knew the bird was trying to tell him something, but whatever it was, he wasn't getting it. Maybe in time. He fixed the bird's plate, not feeling foolish at all. He set the plate down on the table and stroked the bird's head. He really was fond of his only friend.

"You know what, Bird, I think it's time you earned your keep," Tick said, leaning back on the kitchen stool. "We have time on our hands now, my book is done, and I don't have to start a new one for a few months. So, it's easy-breezy time for us. I want you to fly down to that new place on the beach and check it out. Here's where we're going to see if you really are smart or if you've just been jerking my chain. Check it all out and report back in. You do a good job, you get ice cream for dessert tonight instead of mangoes. *Comprende?*"

"*Sí. Muchos gracias,*" Bird said.

Tick blinked, then swore. "WTF, you speak Spanish? Well, damn! Who knew? Okay, okay, I'm going to get a dictionary to brush up on my own Spanish, and maybe we'll get to the bottom of who and what you are and where the hell you came from. That's what we'll do for the next few months. I'll learn Spanish, and you, my friend, will learn some *decent* English."

Bird made the laughing sound again, then flew out of the kitchen to his favorite perch on top of Tick's small television set. He tucked his neck down into his wing and went to sleep while Tick cleaned up the kitchen. At night, he slept on the shower rod in Tick's bathroom.

An hour later, dressed in new khaki cargo shorts and a new white T-shirt that said he was a member of the Sierra Club, Tick strolled into the village and went right to the house of the man who had sold him his parcel of land. He knocked on the door and waited for someone to open it. The elder was short on words and long on expression during the few times he'd had conversations with him. The door opened, and Tick stepped back. He was never invited in, but that was okay. He didn't need any new friends.

Tick got right to the point. "You told me no one would be living on that strip of beach where I live when you sold me the property. There's a building there now. Why? Who is it?"

"I had no choice, Mr. Kelly. One does not argue with the government. It is not a wise or judicious thing to do. It is temporary, I was told. I did not sell, I leased that little parcel. I will honor my contract with you. The building is what I believe they call prefabricated. It is written that it will be dismantled when their time has expired."

Tick clenched his teeth. "How much time did you give them, and who are *they*?"

"One man was from the DEA and the other was from the Coast Guard. I only know that two women, who I believe are DEA special agents, will be living in the temporary quarters. They told me nothing else. They did, however, ask about you. And they wanted me to agree not to tell you anything about them. I refused. They didn't like that one bit. I told them nothing other than that I sold you the land and that you repaired, at great expense to yourself, the existing building. They assured me the residents would not interfere or trespass on your privacy. I told them if that was to happen, they would have to dismantle the building and relocate immediately, government or not. That also is in the agreement all three of us signed. I am sorry that you are upset."

Tick shrugged. He was not about to pick a fight with this old man, who had gone out of his way for him and who had been nothing but kind. He would have extended his hand to shake the elder's, but the man's hands were clasped behind his back. Tick nodded and started to walk away, then turned around and came back. "Do you happen to know, sir, how I ended up with that parrot? Or where it came from?"

"I have heard that it belonged to someone in *that thing* at the end of the Key. I am told parrots are very loving, loyal birds and extremely loyal to their owners. Supposedly their vocabularies are phenomenal. And that they bring good luck. I would assume when the people who lived there were arrested, the bird was left behind, but I do not know this for certain." The elder allowed himself a small smile before he turned to enter the house.

"Well, I'll be damned," Tick muttered to himself as he walked through the small village, nodding to the women who were bustling about. He stopped once, to buy a sack of mangoes and a bucket of oranges, before continuing on his way home. He knew how he was going to spend the rest of the day. On the Internet and making calls to some friends back in Atlanta. He wondered how many sites there were for parrots and what kind of information he could garner. Maybe he could find an online Spanish class while he was at it, brush up on his Spanish. Maybe he'd get that CD that he heard the CIA and FBI used to train with.

Even though his sack and bucket were heavy, Tick's steps were lighter and faster the closer he got to home. He had a purpose now, a goal.

Back at the house on stilts, Tick poured himself a glass of orange juice, gulped it down, rinsed out his glass, then looked for his boat keys. He snatched them up, checked to make sure he had his wallet, and left. There was no sign of Bird when he walked down to his dock. He grinned to himself, hoping the parrot had paid attention, if that was possible, and was checking out his new neighbors. The computer and what he'd planned could be done when the sun went down. He told himself there was no hurry these days to do anything he didn't want to do.

Tick took a moment to admire his cigarette boat the way he always did when he set foot on the dock. The boat was his only real purchase since coming here to Mango Key. He always got a good belly laugh when he rolled into the marina in Miami. A cop with a cigarette boat! Everyone in the world knew cigarette boats were the drug runners' boat of choice. The reason for the belly laugh was that no one knew he was a cop. While he wasn't on the payroll of the Atlanta PD, he was still on the books. Next to his name and badge number it said he was on extended leave. And that was the way it was going to stay.

Tick climbed into the *Miss Sally,* named after his wife, and fired up the boat with a big roar, wondering if his new neighbors were watching. Like he gave a good rat's ass what they were doing. He recognized the lie he was trying to feed himself as he headed out to open water. Once a cop, always a cop. Didn't matter if he wrote books, drank himself into a stupor, or packed a gun. The bottom line was he was a cop, and at one time he'd been a damn fine one. His instincts were kicking in now and telling him something was going to go down on his turf, and he didn't like it one damn bit. He'd bought and paid for peace, quiet, and tranquillity. Anything interfering with those things would have to be dealt with.

Secretly, though, he admitted to a small thrill of excitement that perhaps *something* was going to go down that he would be privy to, at which point he would have to decide if he wanted to engage or to keep on pretending to be a full-time writer, when in truth he only wrote when the mood struck him. Oftentimes he didn't write for months; and then, when his editor reminded him that his manuscript was due, he'd work around the clock.

The bottom line was, he was a cop.

Thirty minutes later, Tick shoved all his reveries to the back of his mind, cut back the engine, and the *Miss Sally* sailed up to the dock, where he tossed the mooring lines to a young boy who was brown as a berry and whose black hair shone like coal in the bright sun. He smiled, his teeth glistening in the noonday sun. "How long, Mr. Kelly?"

"Two hours. Three at the most. No joyriding, Tobias."

"I hear you, Mr. Kelly." The boy winked at Tick. "The narcs are out today. They were cruising all night. Must be something going on somewhere. They're going to smell this little treasure a mile away."

"Just don't let them dirty up my boat. Tell them I kick ass and take names later."

"I hear you, Mr. Kelly." The boy laughed uproariously at Tick's words.

Tick was grinning as he strode down the pier and onto dry land. Tobias would deliver his instructions verbatim if the narcs came around. He stopped a minute to get his bearings as he decided which way he wanted to go and what he wanted to buy.

Tobias settled himself in the cigarette boat, the engine idling as he tried to figure out just who Patrick Kelly was. The man had been the topic of many discussions at the marina, but so far only speculation reigned. He was some hotshot rich guy from up north pretending to be a beach bum. He was a drug runner who was too smart to get caught. And the one he liked the best was Kelly was running away from his wife, who was trying to steal all his money, and Mango Key was where he was hiding out.

Tobias knew Kelly had to be someone special to be living on Mango Key because everyone in Key West, probably the whole state of Florida, knew that the elders on Mango Key never let anyone on the Key who didn't belong. To live on Mango Key you had to be Indian and part of the family. Patrick Kelly was not Indian; therefore, he did not belong. For sure he wasn't part of the family. Tobias knew for a fact Kelly was Irish and Italian because he'd asked him one day.

He tipped good, and that was all Tobias cared about. That and taking the *Miss Sally* for a bit of a spin before he docked her. He craned his neck now to see if Kelly was within eyesight. He wasn't. He backed the boat out, hit the throttle full force, and off he went, flying over the water, the wake behind him three feet high. He didn't care one bit that he would have to dry down the boat. These few minutes were like ecstasy to the young man.

On dry land and meandering down the road, Tick strained to see Tobias playing with his boat. He laughed to himself. When he was seventeen or eighteen, the age he figured Tobias to be, he would have done the exact same thing just for the thrill of it. "Get with the program here, Tick. You came here for a reason, so get to it," he muttered to himself as he stepped up to an ATM, punched in his code, then the amount of money he wanted. He looked around to see if anyone was watching before he jammed the cash into the pocket of his cargo shorts and smoothed down the Velcro closure.

Five doors down, Tick stopped at a hole-in-the-wall store with massive iron gates that were lowered at night. He walked in, looked around as though he were in a supermarket choosing melons for the day. He picked up a knife that looked like it could skin a bear, a switchblade, night-vision goggles, and assorted other heat-sensing apparatuses that spies used in their trade. He carried all his purchases to the counter, which was filled with so much junk the clerk had to ring up each item as Tick handed it to him. When all his merchandise was tallied, he asked for two hundred feet of nylon rope, then whipped out his police ID and got a box of clips for his gun.

"You going alligator hunting?" the old man joked.

"Something like that," Tick said. "Box it up, seal it good, and take it down to the marina. Ask for Tobias and have him put it in my boat." Money changed hands, and Tick was back outside in the bright sunshine.

Tick kept walking until he came to the bodega where he usually bought his groceries and walked into the dim interior that smelled of ripe cheese and sausage. He handed over his grocery list, paid for everything, and gave the same instructions to the little old lady in the sparkling white apron. "I will send Manuel to deliver the groceries, Senor Kelly."

Tick walked out into the bright sunshine a second time and looked around for another ATM. He hit it again, pocketed the money, then headed to the nearest bait, tackle, and dive shop. He walked around the cluttered fish-smelling store, breathing through his mouth. Cash in hand, he walked up to a middle-aged guy who was so leathery-looking his face could be mistaken for a road map. A bad road map. He rattled off what he wanted, and added, "Two of everything. Pack it up, seal it good, no markings on the boxes, and take it to the marina and tell Tobias to load it on my boat." Money changed hands. As he counted out his change, Tick knew he would have to hit up an ATM for a third time if he wanted to eat a decent lunch. He asked where the nearest ATM was, and the leathery-looking guy pointed to his left.

Tick pocketed his money for the third time, then crossed the busy street to his favorite restaurant, not that there were that many to choose from. He liked sitting outside under the orange and green umbrella sipping at the hot Cuban coffee. He opened the menu and pointed at the pictures. Basically it was the same food he could have gotten back in Atlanta at any Mexican restaurant but better. With the temperatures in the midnineties and climbing, it was too hot for coffee. He waited for his Corona and gulped half of it before he settled the bottle on the rickety iron table. He raised a finger to indicate the waiter should bring another bottle with his food.

Tick was people watching as he played a game with himself. Who, what, where, when, and why? So many people. All with secrets. He didn't know how he knew this, he just did. When he felt a light touch on his shoulder, he whirled around, his hand automatically going to his side for his gun, which wasn't there. He looked up to see who had dared touch him in such a public place.

"Pete! What the hell are you doing here?"

"You sure you want to know?"

"Well, when you put it like that, maybe I don't. Can you give it to me in degrees?"

"Degrees? Yeah, yeah, I can do that. What'd you order?"

"I have no idea. I just point to the pictures. The menu is in Spanish, and the little bit I know doesn't include Cuban menu items. You want the same thing?"

Pete nodded. Tick turned around, pointed to his brother, and yelled, "The same for him, and a Corona.

"Articulate, little brother."

Chapter 6

"Nothing earth-shattering, Tick. Just needed some time off, away from the bar. It's doing extremely well, by the way, but I'm married to the place. I was going to come down sooner, but I wanted to make sure my people were as good as I thought they were. The saloon business is the easiest in the world to rip off. Then Andy told me the trial he was working on was postponed when something in the basement of the courthouse blew up, and they had to shut down the entire building. You know nothing goes on in Atlanta in July, so he volunteered to work the bar while I came down here. Trish is doing the kitchen. Their kids are at camp until school starts in August. Win! Win! It was an offer I couldn't pass up. So, here I am."

Tick stared at his brother, his dark eyes full of questions he had no intention of verbalizing. He waited, hoping his brother would see fit to confide in him the way they had when they were younger. Pete looked away and stared at the people walking by in their bright-colored tourist outfits.

Pete turned back to face his brother. "I caught an early flight, came standby. Man, I hate the Atlanta Airport. It took me longer to get through security than it did to fly here. Do you believe that?" Tick shrugged since he hadn't been near an airport in eight years, and it was all Greek to him.

"Yeah, it's a mess at *any* airport. When I got here, I went straight to the marina and asked your buddy Tobias if he could run me out to Mango Key, and he said you had just pulled up and pointed to the *Miss Sally*. He said you probably came in for supplies and would have lunch before you headed back. He pointed me in the right direction, and here you are. But, something happened before I found you. I stopped at this outdoor place about a block and a half from here for a cup of coffee," he said, pointing off to the left. "Someone left a copy of the *Miami Herald* on the table, so I was reading it and drinking my coffee when I heard these guys talking behind me. There were three of them. At first I didn't pay any attention, but then I heard them mention Mango Key and the cop who lived on the beach. Since you're the only cop living on Mango Key, my ears perked up."

So did Tick's. He looked around to see who was sitting at the occupied tables, then leaned forward. "What did you hear?"

Pete lowered his voice. "Not much. Even I knew they weren't just guys out for a cup of coffee. They were law and order, what branch I don't know, but you could just tell they weren't local or tourists. They were dressed like tourists but wearing jackets. That made me think they were packing heat. No one wears a jacket in Key West. They said they had to keep an eye on you, and they weren't sure about buying into the story that you were some kind of shitty writer trading on your life experiences."

"They actually said that?" Tick blustered indignantly.

"Yeah. I thought about jumping to your defense, but I wanted to hear more, so I just kept pretending I was reading the paper. They really didn't say much else. They talked about two chicks, Kate and Sandra. No last names. And they were really getting off on some asshole, that's their word, not mine, named Tyler, whose daddy is the governor of Florida. Two of the guys were probably late thirties, early forties. The third guy was way older, maybe early sixties. He seemed to be the one the other two deferred to. That's it, Tick. So, what do you think? Do you know those guys? Does any of it ring any bells for you?"

Though intrigued over Pete's story, Tick shook his head just as their food arrived, and the small tables around them started to fill with chattering tourists. Off to the right, a group of locals were strumming on banjos, making conversation impossible. The brothers began to eat. They finished in record time and set out on their walk back to the marina.

Halfway to the marina, Pete veered to the left to a pushcart selling snow cones. He called over his shoulder, "You still like strawberry?"

"Yeah, a double-decker," Tick called back as he meandered over to a bench under a tree that was so big it would take a dozen men to wrap their arms around it.

Pete held out the snow cone like it was a golden chalice. "Kind of like old times, huh? Remember how Mom would give us ten cents when we were little, and we'd run to the corner to get the cones. You always ate yours so fast and got a brain freeze."

"And your cone always melted before you could really enjoy it because you tried to save it. What's wrong, Pete?"

"Am I that transparent, big brother?"

"Yeah."

"Sadie dumped me. I should have seen the handwriting on the wall when she didn't make it back in six months like she promised. She said it was work-related, so I couldn't make a big deal out of it. Then the calls and e-mails started to taper off. Damn good thing I did my financing without waiting for her. Even back then, I think I had a premonition. I'm not sure about this, but I think Andy knew it wasn't going to happen because he told me to go ahead with the financing, and we could add her later if she still wanted in. Then she called me two weeks ago to tell me she was marrying some British diplomat. Just like that. It was all over in a minute. So, yeah, I'm kind of bummed. I swear, Tick, I thought she was *the one*. Do you have any idea how stupid I feel? How come I didn't see it? Guess I wasn't good enough. Ex-rodeo roustabout, saloon keeper, that kind of thing. Can't compare to a British diplomat," Pete said morosely.

"Don't be so hard on yourself, Pete. I learned a long time ago never to sell yourself short. Like Mom always said, everything happens for a reason. Accept that Sadie wasn't the right one. And, you did see it, you just chose to do nothing about it. You're doing okay, right? If you don't need her financing, get over it and move on. Life is too short for the would-haves, the could-haves, and the should-haves. Move on."

Pete slurped the last of the blueberry juice out of his paper cone, his lips as blue as the coloring in the hot-day treat. He wiped his mouth on his sleeve the way he used to do when he was a kid. Tick did the same thing. "Yeah, like you did?"

"That was a low blow, and you know it. That's like talking apples and oranges. Sally died," Tick said flatly. "Sadie married some British diplomat. I rest my case."

Suddenly contrite, Pete said, "I didn't mean it like that, Tick."

"I know you didn't. Come on, let's head back to the boat. Jesus, it must be one hundred and ten degrees. The humidity is unbearable. When we get home, I'll make us a big pitcher of ice-cold lemonade, and we'll sit on the porch. You can bring me up to date on Atlanta, and I'll bring you up to date on Mango Key. How's that sound?"

"Pretty damn good. Can you make the lemonade the way Mom made it, real sweet and tart, with the lemon peels in the pitcher?"

"You know it, bro," Tick said, slapping his brother on the back. It was the signal from childhood for both to sprint forward and race the other to the marina. Tick won by a hair.

Both men were laughing as they climbed aboard the *Miss Sally.* Tobias waited until Tick checked his purchases to make sure everything was intact before he released the mooring line. He waved happily, the hefty tip Tick had slipped him deep in his pocket.

The short ride to Mango Key was exhilarating, the ocean spray bathing both brothers as they roared through the water at close to ninety nautical miles an hour. "Don't go getting the idea that I speed like this all the time, I don't. I don't need the Coast Guard hauling me in and breathing down my neck. I just wanted to cool us off," Tick said, easing up on the throttle. Off in the distance, he could see one of the Coast Guard boats on its daily patrol. He eased up even more on the throttle, making it easier to be heard.

"What's that?" Pete asked, pointing to the structure down the beach from Tick's house on stilts.

"That, Pete, is my new neighbor. Short-term, I'm told. I think they're feds, probably DEA. I checked it out earlier this morning with the town elder. It's a prefab building. I wouldn't want to swear to it, but I think the men you heard talking this morning might have something to do with what's going on. What that is, I have no idea."

"What about *that thing?*"

"I guess it's still there. I haven't been down that way in a few weeks. The last two weeks, I was working around the clock. I woke up this morning and saw that damn prefab, and it pissed me off. If it stays up longer than a month or so, I'll be looking for other accommodations."

"Damn, Tick, are you *ever* going to come out of this self-imposed exile? Eight years is a hell of a long time to be so alone. It's not healthy, and you damn well know it. You have to get back among the living. I'm not saying you have to go back to being a cop or even come back to Atlanta, but you need to . . . to socialize. Talk to people other than that damn parrot. How about coming back and helping me run the bar? We could expand, do all kinds of things. You could still write. Will you think about it?"

"No. I'm quite happy here. Look, Pete, I can't go back to Atlanta. Not now, not ever. Don't try throwing that cemetery business in my face either. My family is in my heart, so they're with me every hour, every minute, every second of every day. I don't need a place to go to. I just have to put my hand over my heart and Sally, Ricky, and Emma are with me.

"See that flash, Pete?" Tick said, changing the subject.

"Yeah, what is it?" Pete asked as he shaded his eyes to see better in the bright sun.

"It's someone in the prefab building looking at us with binoculars. Look away, don't let them see that we noticed."

"Do you think they're interested in you in particular, or are they watching the other boats or maybe just the water? They have a boat that's half on the sand and half in the water. What the hell does that mean? Dumb as I am on all things maritime, even I know you don't beach a power boat."

"It means they aren't seasoned boaters. There's no dock. Off the top of my head, with just a quick look, it appears to be an old Boston Whaler. Good boat. Maybe there's something wrong with it, or it's just there for show. It's probably outfitted to outrun this boat. Appearances can be deceiving, Pete."

Pete snorted. "That's the cop in you talking. See! That's what I'm talking about. You can no more hang it up than you can stop breathing."

"Shut up, Pete, I don't want to hear it."

Tick cut the throttle and allowed the *Miss Sally* to slide up next to his dock. Pete hopped out and secured the boat. Tick handed up the packages, then both men stood for a few minutes, looking down the beach. The sun was still glaring off the binoculars, which meant Tick's neighbors were still watching them. He shrugged. "They must be novices or just plain stupid. I don't like people spying on me. Do you like people spying on you, Pete?"

"Hell no!"

"Then maybe when the sun goes down, we'll go for a walk on the beach and tell those fine people we don't like being spied on."

Pete sucked in his breath. Now *that* sounded like the old Tick. "Sounds like a plan. You said something about making lemonade."

Both men hefted the cardboard boxes onto their shoulders as they made their way down the dock, then to the deep sand that would lead them up to the house. They made two more trips before they hit the beach for a swim to cool off.

Ice-cold lemonade, two comfortable seats on the porch, and Bird for entertainment were their rewards.

While the brothers were sipping their lemonade, probationary DEA agents Kate Rush and Sandra Martin were grumbling about the incredible heat in the metal building they were living in. "They saw us spying on them," Kate fumed. "I just know the sun glinted off the lens. I saw them both looking right where we're standing. Talk about dumb."

"You can't be sure," Sandy said, trying to soothe her frustrated friend. "Look, both of us are just cranky. We've been up all night seven days in a row, and nothing has happened. I'm beginning to think this is all one of Tyler's stupid bids for another promotion, and Jellard somehow got sucked in. Nothing is going on. *Nothing.* The guy was probably buying supplies, at least that's what it looked like to me. I saw celery sticking out of one of the boxes. He has to eat, and he also has to buy toilet paper and paper towels. It's the other guy we should be asking about. Who is he?"

"I can't be sure, but the cop's profile says he has a twin brother. Maybe it's him. Damn, I don't remember it ever being this hot," Kate said, wiping at her forehead with a tissue from the pocket of her shorts. "Let's go for a swim."

"Sounds great. Tonight, if it doesn't cool down, I'm going skinny-dipping." Sandy laughed as she moved off to one of the cubicles separated by folding partitions. "I really hate this place, Kate. Do you hear me, I really, *really* hate this place."

Kate grimaced. "I hear you, Sandra. Hey, we can always quit and go back to what we were doing before we signed up for this gig. By that I mean being miserable and missing this cockamamie life."

Minutes later, Sandy whirled and twirled in her brand-new sky blue bikini. She looked spectacular and knew it. "Do you think those two guys will be spying on us?" Not waiting for an answer, she said, "Let's give them something to drool over. We can let the water sort of, kind of, carry us farther down the beach, closer to that crazy-looking house in the trees."

Sandy gaped at Kate. "Well, damn, Kate, what's with the tank suit? They're going to think you're hiding something in that suit." At the stunned look on Kate's face, she hastened to say, "Whoa, I didn't mean that the way it sounded. You look like dynamite. Why not show it off a little more? One-piece suits are so not in, Kate. Don't you look at the fashion magazines? Trust me, tank suits are long gone."

Kate shrugged. "I'm just more comfortable in a one-piece. The truth is, I've never worn a bikini and don't own one. Look, it's not like we're trying to entice that guy and his brother or whoever he is. We're just going in the water to cool off. Period. End of discussion. C'mon, I'll race you to the water. Last one in stinks! Oh, God, what was *that?*" Kate dived to the ground, her face smashing into the sand.

Sandy, who'd hit the sand at the same moment, raised her head and looked around. "It's that crazy-ass parrot that has been dogging us is what it is. I bet he belongs to that guy up the beach," she said, getting to her feet.

Bird, his eyes bright, was perched on a piece of driftwood, eyeing the two women. He tilted his head, and said, "Oh, baby! How's tricks. Bacon and eggs. Pretty boy! Bang! Bacon! Bang! Bullshit! Hello, Dolly, hello, Dolly!"

"What the hell!" Sandy exploded. "It talks! That damn bird talks! I bet that cop sent it here to spy on us. Say something, Kate, and say it *right now*!"

"You're right, it talks! You want to send a message back to his owner, assuming the guy owns the bird? It could belong to someone in the village, you know. Think about it. What would be your message?" She started to laugh then and couldn't stop. "You have to admit, Sandy, it's a great pickup move." A second later, Kate hit the water, her strong arms propelling her forward, Sandy in her wake.

Tick yanked at his newly purchased binoculars on the cushion where he was sitting and brought them up to his eyes. He watched both women dive into the water. But what really drew his attention was Bird, perched on the driftwood. He passed the binoculars to his brother, who was grinning from ear to ear. "Strong swimmers. *Very* strong swimmers. Extraordinary breast stroke. Olympic potential. And there's Bird in the thick of the action. Is he due to report in soon?" Pete asked with a straight face.

Tick grinned. "Go ahead and laugh. Bird knows what he's doing. I sent him there to spy, and that's exactly what he's doing. What he will report is another story entirely. I think I'm going to put him in my next book. I can see it now, *The Case of the Foul-Mouthed Parrot.*"

Pete lowered the binoculars to take a better look at his brother to see if he was putting him on or not. Nope, he looked serious as hell. Then he laughed. When he calmed down, he said, "So, clue me in on all that stuff you bought in Key West. You preparing for war or what?"

Tick shrugged. "For the most part everything I bought was stuff I used to pack around in my car back in Atlanta. I more or less just replaced everything. Except for the Uzi and the other guns. I wish to hell I knew what happened to all that stuff and my car."

"Why are you bullshitting me, Tick? You didn't carry scuba gear and oxygen tanks in the trunk of your car. What's up with that?"

Tick slapped his bare feet down on the porch floor. He reached over for his brother's glass and headed inside to get a refill. "Strictly recreational, Pete," he called over his shoulder.

Pete snorted. "Recreational, my ass," he muttered. He knew in his gut the two of them would be out in the ocean on the first dark night, trying to figure out what was going on down the beach. His heart kicked up a beat at the thought. At least Tick appeared to be coming out of the fog he'd been living in. He said a silent prayer that whatever was happening down and around them would affect his brother only in a good way and not send him into a funk.

When Tick returned with two fresh glasses of the ice-cold lemonade, Pete said, "Looks like I might be sticking around a little longer than I thought. Unless you don't want me here. If that's the case, say so now."

A sudden breeze whipped through the palm trees in front of the porch and ruffled both men's hair. "Why would you think that, Pete?"

"That's a question, not an answer. I think it's because you never seem happy to see me, and I admit this is only my second visit. I've taken into consideration that I'm a reminder of your past, and that I bug you. I worry about you. Andy worries about you, and your cop friends worry about you. They come by the bar all the time and talk about you. Don't worry,

I never said anything. Bartenders are just listeners, kind of like priests in a weird kind of way. You wouldn't believe half the shit people tell me. A total stranger. For some reason, people feel safe confiding in bartenders."

Tick was only half listening. He was trying to come to terms in his own mind about what he would do if Pete up and left. Then he would truly be alone, and he'd had enough solitude to last him a lifetime. It was finally time to admit it. Maybe his problem was he loved too hard, too deep. Maybe a lot of things. He had to say something, and he had to say it now to wipe off what he was seeing in Pete's face.

"I don't want you to leave, Pete. I've been in a deep hole for a very long time. I'm just starting to make my way up and out. The best thing that could have happened to me was your showing up last year. I think you know, but if you don't, I want you to know that if you were in trouble, no matter where you were, even Atlanta, I'd be there as fast as I could. It's important for me to know that you understand that. I'm trying, Pete. I really am. Maybe not hard enough in your eyes, but for now, it's the best I can do.

"Maybe I am a coward in your eyes. I did cut and run. At the time, it seemed like the right thing to do for me. I don't expect you to understand because you weren't walking in my shoes at the time. Which by the way, I lost along the way. I really liked those shoes, too. Funny how I remember that, and the rest is just a blur. I'm glad that you're here, I really am, Pete. I guess that's why I bought two of everything even though I told the guy at the dive shop I liked to keep spares. I guess, in my subconscious, I had decided to call and ask you to come down.

"You know what I've been thinking?"

"Hell, it could be anything with you, Tick. What?"

Tick laughed. "I think I was meant to be a beach bum. I love it here. I like what I do. Yeah, I miss being a cop. But I like writing, too. If I tried to do both, one or the other would suffer. I've seen to my future, yours, too. I don't know if Andy told you about that or not."

"What do you mean?" There was an edge to Pete's voice that Tick didn't pick up on.

"I set up a trust for you a few years ago. Don't look at me like that. I have more money than I can spend in my lifetime and no one to share it with. I wanted you to have what I have. Sally always worried about the future on a cop's pay. College, things like that. The future was important to her. You know what cops make in retirement. I didn't want Sally to have to work, but she did anyway because we needed her salary. I guess what I'm trying to say here is I love you, and I don't want you to have to worry about your old age. I'm telling you, Pete, stop looking at me like that, or I'm going to knock your ass right off this porch."

Pete settled back in his chair. His voice was soft, almost gentle when he asked, "Is that the God's honest truth, or did you do it because I got off the rails and couldn't find my niche?"

"Nah. You were doing what you wanted to do. I always admired that free spirit in you. You know what they say— when God is good to you, you have to share. That was a litany of Mom's. Who else can I share with but you? You're my twin brother, for God's sake. We were joined at the hip for more years than I can remember. You gonna fight me on this, Pete?"

"Hell no! I'm going to enjoy spending all that money you busted your ass earning by scribbling away your time. I just hope to God I'm not too old to enjoy spending it when the time comes. What do I say? Thanks?"

"That'll do. Lookie there, here comes Bird. Let's see what he has to say."

The parrot flew onto the porch, dipped his wings, then settled on the banister, his eyes bright. He made his laughing sound and ruffled his feathers again. He waited.

Tick looked at Pete. "See, this is the part I can't figure out. Sometimes he just jabbers a mile a minute. Other times I think we're having an actual conversation. I know he's smart, I just don't know how smart. I told him to spy on those women.

"So, what did you find out, Bird?"

"Put on your big-girl panties and deal with it."

Pete looked at Tick, then at the parrot. "Did he just say what I think he said?"

"Yeah. Sometimes he says a whole sentence. Other times, just a word, or he repeats the same word over and over. He likes to cuss, too."

"What are they dealing with, Bird?" Tick asked, leaning forward, his voice perfectly pitched so as not to throw off Bird, who was staring directly at him.

"Bullshit. All bullshit. Bang! Hello, Dolly!"

Tick shrugged. "What did you see, Bird?"

"Girls. Big-girl panties."

Pete let loose with a loud guffaw. Tick grinned.

"Hot! Hot! No sleep. Sleep. Big boys sleep! Hey, Tick! Bang!"

Tick got up and opened the screen door. Bird flew in and went straight to the bathroom, where he perched on the shower rod. "He's tired now. Maybe when he wakes up, he'll talk some more. What do you think?"

"What I think is I'd like to see those big-girl panties." Pete guffawed again as he brought the binoculars up to his eyes. "They're getting out of the water. Both of them are damn fine-looking women. There are two of them, and there are two of us," he said, lowering the binoculars and leering at his brother. "I think it's time to decide how you want to play this. What say you, bro?"

Chapter 7

Los Angeles

Lawrence Tyler stared out the window at the twinkling lights that seemed to be coming to life, one by one. The parking lot, three floors down, was almost empty at that hour. He craned his neck to see the four corners of the lot. All he could see in the dusky evening was his bright red Porsche and a clunker of some kind that probably belonged either to the janitor or the cleaning lady. He should have left an hour ago, but the truth was, he had nowhere to go. Oh, he could go back to his town house, but then what? Watch the news? Get a rental video? Cook? Take a shower and go to bed? It wasn't like he had a bushel of friends here in the City of Angels. In the beginning, he rather thought he'd have starlets knocking on his door. Such a foolish notion on his part.

Tyler could see his reflection in the plate-glass window. He was still wearing his jacket, shirt, and tie. He should have shed the jacket hours ago, should have rolled up his sleeves and jerked his tie loose. Dress for success had always been his motto. No, that had been his father's directive, which he followed because he always did what his father told him to do. It didn't matter that he was almost forty-one. Forty years old with a receding hairline. His father had told him months ago to get hair plugs, then pointed to his own luxurious mane of silvery hair. He'd responded that he'd look into it. It would certainly give him something to do for a few weeks.

Lawrence Tyler, "never call me Larry," walked back to his desk and sat down. His computer was still on, turned to his e-mail account. There were no new messages. Earlier in the day he'd sent out close to thirty e-mails, and so far, no one had responded to him. He'd suspected there would be no responses when he sent them out, but he'd done it anyway. It rankled that his father, of all people, hadn't responded. The others he could understand. The others made no secret of their dislike for him, but his father was supposed to love him. Yeah, right? The old man didn't know the meaning of the word *love*. Neither did his mother. He was just something they pulled out every so often to show off to their political friends. He was always introduced as, "My son, who is a DEA agent." Before one of what he thought of as "show-off meetings," his mother always called and told him what to wear. Then she'd end the conversation by saying he should go to a tanning bed so he would look *alive.*

One of these days he was going to get a goddamn tattoo and have his ears pierced. That would certainly make *them* look *alive.* Then he'd buy a motorcycle, a Ducati, and roar up to the governor's mansion with his new hair plugs. The thought was so ludicrous, he laughed out loud.

He looked around at his spacious office, at the Jackson Pollock paintings on one entire wall, all thanks to his old man. The black-and-white photos were the photo ops that had been arranged by his father, important people with whom Tyler needed to be seen to further his father's political ambitions. And every time he moved from one location to another, he had to lug the damn pictures and paintings so he could hang them up in case his father decided to pop in for a visit—something that as yet had never happened.

Each time he was reassigned, with more nominal authority

but less operational control, his mother sent a decorator, and in twenty-four hours he had a suite befitting the son of the governor.

Tyler bit down on his lip. He wanted to cry, but big boys didn't cry. That was what both his parents had instilled in him at an early age. He wasn't sure he knew how to cry anymore. He'd shed so many tears in his early years, when they sent him away to all the different schools he'd attended. He couldn't remember a night when he didn't cry himself to sleep even into his late teens.

Damn, now he was tripping down memory lane again. It was happening too much of late. Tyler gave himself a mental shake, turned off his computer with a loud, "Screw you, Dad," and grabbed his briefcase. He turned off the light, locked his door, and made his way out of the building to the parking lot.

He unlocked the door, climbed behind the wheel of his Porsche—another must-have according to his father—and just sat there. He wondered whether, if he was driving a Honda or a Taurus, anyone would invite him to join them after work. Probably not, since he was so far above them, he couldn't relate to bellying up to the bar for a beer. Thanks again to the warning his father had instilled in him—do not fraternize with the help. He winced at the thought of wearing a baseball cap or blue jeans. He owned one pair of sneakers, which were fifteen years old, and a sweat suit of the same vintage. From the days when he pretended to be a running enthusiast.

The Porsche growled to life. Everything was about pretending. He was sick of it. Did his father and the people he worked with really think he didn't know what was going on? He knew there was a task force investigating him, knew he'd be expelled, and *expelled* was the right word, from the DEA, and there wasn't a damn thing his father could do about it. The media would be all over it like fleas on a dog. His fellow agents would open up, and he'd be a laughingstock. Mummy and Daddy might even have to leave the country. Such shame on the Tyler name. Maybe he should just go to the governor's mansion and shoot them both. The thought so appalled him, he almost choked on his own saliva.

Forty minutes later, Tyler roared into his assigned parking spot at the town-house complex where he lived. He got out, locked the door, and was halfway to his front door when he heard his cell phone ringing. "Crap!" The word shot out of his mouth like a bullet. Damn, he'd tossed his cell phone into his briefcase before he left the office because he wasn't expecting any late-evening calls on his work cell. He fumbled at the latch on the case with shaking hands. It was rare to get a call at that hour of the evening. Maybe it was his father, who would be pissed to the teeth if he didn't answer. One, son or not, did not ignore the governor. Ever. His wrath was legendary, and . . . the governor *never* called back.

Inside his town house, which shrieked of being professionally decorated, again by his mother, Tyler finally wrestled his cell phone from the junk he toted around with him day and night. He scrolled down to see the number of the caller. It was a number he didn't recognize. Probably a wrong number. He sighed with relief that the call hadn't been from his father.

He looked around at the room he was standing in because that's what he did each time he entered the town house. The decorator, who had never met him, must have thought he was some kind of outdoor macho man who liked to hunt and fish. Probably because that's what his mother would have told the decorator. He hated the dark leather, the earth-tone carpet, the hunting prints on the wall. He liked vibrant colors, bare floors, and fabric-covered furniture. He even liked green plants as long as he didn't have to water them.

Tyler looked over at the bar and decided a drink was in order. The bar was stocked with manly liquor: scotch, whiskey, gin, rum, and vodka. He was a white-wine drinker.

He uncorked a bottle and poured until the exquisite crystal glass was filled almost to the brim.

Still dressed in his suit, he sat down in one of the leather chairs and sipped at the wine. He finally yanked at his tie, then swiveled his neck from side to side to undo the kinks. *What the hell kind of life is this?* Every nerve ending in his body was twanging in protest. For one crazy minute he actually thought about digging his sweat suit and sneakers out of wherever they were to go running. The thought was so outrageous, he just shook his head in disgust.

He was no longer sipping at the wine in his glass the way he usually did. He was gulping at it, a sign that things were out of control. There was no way to unring the bell, to go back in time. No way to right the wrongs he'd done. He knew he was just weeks, maybe even days away from being fired. *Fired!* No one in the Tyler family had ever gotten fired. Never. The Tylers were the ones who did the firing.

Back at the bar, Tyler shed his jacket and pulled off his tie. He poured a full glass of wine and drank half of it before returning to the hated leather chair. He was about to flop down when he changed his mind and headed back to the bar, where he grabbed the wine bottle. He placed it on the coffee table, directly in his line of vision. If he was going to soul-search, he would need some false courage.

The glass steady in his hand, Tyler leaned back into the supple leather. It was all wrong. His life was wrong. He was tired of pretending, sick of the way he'd taken credit for others' work, sick of the lying, sick of the covering up, sick and tired of his parents' meddling in his life. Sick and tired of not being able to cut it. Sick and tired of being hated by his superiors and fellow agents even though he deserved their hatred. He wondered, and not for the first time, if there was any way he could get back on track. At forty, how hard could it be to start over without his father the governor paving the way?

Damn hard, he decided. They'd check his records. People in law enforcement had loose lips. Maybe if he told his father he wanted to transfer out of the DEA and go to the FBI or the ATF, he could pull it off for him, at which point Tyler would work his ass off to become the man he always wanted to be. He'd do it by the book this time, his book, not his father's.

An hour later, Tyler looked at the wine bottle and was surprised to see that it was empty and realized that he was drunk. He could hear his mother now. "For shame, Lawrence! A drunkard in the family is totally unacceptable."

"Well, Mummie dearest, tell that to someone who cares. And to my father and his White House aspirations," Tyler mumbled as he made his way to the kitchen. He should probably eat something. One of the rules in law enforcement was always eat, you never knew when you'd eat again, especially if you were in the field. The refrigerator was full; his day lady always saw to it that there was cold chicken, cold ham, cold roast beef. The drawers held fresh fruit, vegetables, bacon, eggs, muffins, and there were all sorts of desserts in the freezer. From time to time he wondered who ate it all because he dined out three times a day. His day lady probably fed her family on it. Not that he cared because she was a nice Mexican lady with a large family. He knew she was illegal, and he hadn't done a thing to change her status. She was just trying to take care of her family the only way she knew how. He would have given her cash, but she was too proud to take money for nothing. He knew he was breaking the law by not reporting her, but he simply didn't care. Maybe he was more human than he thought. He closed the door and looked around at the gleaming kitchen. Maybe he'd move out and give Talaga the town house. The thought made him warm all over. Now, wouldn't that just kick the governor's ass? He started to laugh and couldn't stop.

Time to go to bed.

Still laughing and sputtering, Tyler stripped down to his

T-shirt and boxers, brushed his teeth, removed his contact lenses, and crawled into his sweet-smelling bed. He scrunched up his pillow as tears spilled from his eyes. He felt like a lost little boy again as he fought the tears. Eventually, he slept, his tears drying on his cheeks, his dreams invaded by gunfire, shouting, smoke, and racing automobiles.

Hours later, as he battled his dream demons, the landline next to his bed rang, a long, jangling sound that made him sit bolt upright. He tried blinking as he struggled to see the time. Three A.M. Six o'clock in the East. He looked at the caller ID and saw the readout said, WIRELESS CALLER. NUMBER UN-KNOWN. Well, at least it wasn't the governor. Probably another wrong number. He picked up the handset and mumbled a greeting.

The voice sounded whiskey soaked, gravelly, as though it was disguised somehow. Tyler blinked again when the voice said, "Agent Tyler?" Work-related? Another crazy tip he would have to pay attention to. Or not.

"This is Agent Tyler. Who is this? It's three o'clock in the morning in case you can't see the time wherever you're calling from. Where did you get this number? It's unlisted. If this is DEA business, call the office in the morning."

"Who I am isn't important. It also isn't important how I came by this number. There is nothing sacred at the telephone company these days. I am very aware of the time, Agent Tyler. It is DEA business, and I will not be available when your office opens in the morning. I also know I can call your twenty-four-hour hotline, but I chose not to do that."

"What do you want?" Tyler asked, his voice hard and strong. He took a moment to wonder where his gun was. In his briefcase, of course. It was supposed to be on his nightstand. What a stupid thought. Was he planning on shooting a hole in the telephone?

"We spoke a year ago, Agent Tyler. Right before the hurricane hit Florida. Do you recall that conversation?"

"I remember. I also remember it all turned out to be a joke on me."

"Yeah, that's how I read it at the time. You sure do move around a lot for an agent. I told you to pay attention and do something about the situation on Mango Key. You didn't listen to me. They've had a whole year to do what they're doing."

"What the hell are you talking about? Who are *they?* And what are *they* doing?" Tyler clenched his teeth as he waited for a reply. *Damn Kate Rush.*

"Listen, Agent Tyler, I know your days are numbered at the DEA. I know you blew it. There aren't any more strings for your daddy to pull. You know what else I know?" Not bothering to wait for a response from Tyler, he said, "I know that lady who works for you is illegal. With one phone call, I can have her and all her brats deported. I know you like sweet-smelling sheets, and I know you have a pair of boxers with little hearts all over them. You also have a pair with lightning bolts on them. Not that I care, mind you. I'm just saying, I know things. Now, do you want to listen or not?"

Tyler looked around, his eyes wild. Someone had sneaked into his house, *touched* his belongings. "Fine, fine, you broke into my house. You went through my things. Why? Why me? What are you getting out of this, or are you just out for cheap thrills? You do anything about my housekeeper, and I will hunt you down like a wild dog, and what happens after that won't be pretty." Jesus, did he just say that? Obviously he did because the unknown wireless caller laughed, a creepy, evil sound.

Tyler's mind raced. *I know this voice,* he thought. *I've heard it before somewhere, and not just from his previous call. Who? Where would I have heard it?*

"Pretty brave talk for a guy who's never in the line of fire. The reason I'm calling you is you're the only agent who has deep pockets. By the way, I know to the penny what's in your bank account. I want money. I don't want it for nothing. I'm willing to give up what I know in exchange. And just so you know how serious I am, I know your deep dark secret, the one your daddy doesn't know. Just tell me if you're interested or not."

Tyler started to shake. Who the hell was this guy? Was he interested? Damn, he knew the voice. If he could just tie it to a real live person, he'd have something to go on. He surprised himself when he said, "How much money are we talking about? What exactly do I get in exchange for it?"

"You get your reputation back. The governor will be proud of you. You won't have to slink out of the DEA with your tail between your legs. Your colleagues will look at you differently. In time, they might even come to like and respect you. And best of all, your secret remains safe. A hundred grand should do it."

Tyler laughed. "Just like that, a hundred grand. You must be smoking something illegal. What's the guarantee the information is solid? By the way, this is blackmail."

"Agent Tyler, there are no guarantees in life. You buy the poke, you open it, then you do your share. Call it whatever you like. I have something to sell, and if that includes your secrets, and you're willing to buy, then, hey, it's a simple sale. Just for the record, I'm just a conduit. You really should think about my offer because that task force is closing in on you. Two weeks, tops, and you're out on your ass. I'm going to give you till noon. And then I'll call you for your decision. Go back to bed, Agent Tyler, and have sweet dreams."

Tyler held the phone to his ear until he heard the dial tone. Maybe this was all a bad dream. He pinched his arm. Nope, he was wide awake. He fell back on the bed and stared at the ceiling. Tears rolled down his cheeks. He felt like he was seven years old in that fancy school they'd sent him to, the one where he had to wear white socks, saddle shoes, shorts, and suspenders over a starched white shirt. Just like the von

Trapp kids from *The Sound of Music*. For days, for weeks and months, he'd tried to figure out a way to run away to join the circus, where people would care about him. Why he thought people in a circus would care about him he had no idea. It didn't matter because even back then he'd been a gutless wonder.

Tyler sat up and swiped at his eyes with the bottom of his shirt. He might as well get up. He'd never fall asleep now. His head buzzed like a beehive as he trotted out to the kitchen. Talaga always left the coffeepot ready to go. All he had to do was press a button. He'd never made a pot of coffee in his life.

He sat down and tried to think. The wireless caller's voice, disguised or not, was somehow vaguely familiar. He rubbed at his temples as though that would somehow magically make a name surface. Was the caller primarily a blackmailer or an informant? The first time, when he'd called a year ago, he hadn't tried to blackmail Tyler. A hundred thousand dollars was a boatload of money. But, as everyone knew, blackmailers never let up. They kept coming back again and again.

The coffeepot pinged, the signal that it was ready to be poured. He yanked open the dishwasher, pulled out one of the heavy DEA complimentary cups, and filled it to the brim. He'd taken it from the office back in Phoenix to a mall, where he had his name stenciled on it. It made him feel important. He looked up at the dishes in the cabinet to see only fine bone china, thanks to his mother. Itty-bitty cups that held about two swallows. He was sick of that, too. He'd gone out of his way to buy paper plates and napkins, and that was what he used on the rare occasions when he made himself a sandwich or a salad.

As he blew on the coffee and sipped at it, Tyler let his mind race. Who the hell was that guy? For all he knew, it could just as easily be a woman using some kind of disguising device. Criminals used them all the time. *And, why me?*

Yeah, yeah, I'm the one with the deep pockets. Obviously, the caller knew something pertinent. He wondered what would happen if he hopped a flight to Miami to check on things, which was his right to do since he was technically Jellard's boss. Maybe he'd look up Kate Rush's address and stop in for a visit. He owed her an apology. The big question was, did he have the guts to follow through and actually do it?

His coffee was cool enough now to gulp at it. He liked strong coffee even though at times he felt like his eyeballs were standing at attention.

He needed to pull a rabbit out of a hat, and he needed to do it soon since his unknown caller had stressed the time frame of the task force working against him.

Like I needed a reminder.

Tyler went to his computer, his coffee refreshed. He logged on, booked an airline ticket, paying for it with his own credit card. He booked a 6:00 P.M. flight. He needed time to do some shopping and a few other things both before and after he was home for the noon phone call. Satisfied, he went to MapQuest and started to type.

It was eleven o'clock when his housekeeper handed him the neatly folded clothing she'd just taken out of the dryer. Her eyes were full of questions, but she said nothing. Her English was sketchy, so Tyler made flapping motions with his hands to show he was going on a trip. He went over to his desk and opened an envelope that contained his emergency stash of cash. He pulled out enough bills to pay her for a month. Then he added an extra hundred-dollar bill. The housekeeper's eyes filled with tears as she hugged him. She hugged him so hard Tyler knew it was how a mother's hug really felt. He almost swooned. He shoved two more hundreds into her hand. She cried harder. She gripped him harder as she cried, jabbering away in English and Spanish.

Finally, it dawned on Tyler what his housekeeper was saying. "No, no! I am not firing you. I'm coming back." He pulled away and took her out to the kitchen, where he showed her the calendar and marked off when he would be back. The woman went limp, and if Tyler hadn't caught her, she would have fallen to the floor. She started to bless and hug him again. For the first time in a long time, a very long time, genuine laughter erupted from Tyler.

Now it was time to get dressed in his new duds. MapQuest had given him a direct route to a used-clothing store, where he found worn jeans, shirts, and a tattered Florida Marlins baseball cap. He found a pair of sneakers that actually fit and matched an equally tattered windbreaker plus four other equally worn sets of clothing.

As he dressed, he thought he would feel squeamish about wearing someone else's used clothing, but it just felt like clean clothing. The fact that everything fit was a bonus. The baseball cap was the hardest. He plopped it on his head and looked at himself in the mirror. He thought he looked like a regular guy on his way home from a construction job.

Perfect.

The phone rang. Tyler's gaze flew to the digital clock on his nightstand. His unknown caller was right on time. The digital readout said it was twelve o'clock.

Tyler picked up the phone, and said, "This is Lawrence Tyler."

"How you doing, pal?"

"Let's get one thing straight right now, I am not your pal. I've thought over your proposal, and I've decided to decline. That's as in screw you, don't call me again, and if you even think about trying to blackmail me, I will make you wish you'd never been born. Are we clear on my response, Mr. No Name?"

The crackly disguised voice on the other end of the phone

waited a few seconds before he said, "Big mistake, Agent Tyler."

"Mistake or not, that's my answer. I'm going to hang up now, and I want to warn you not to call me again." With shaking hands, Tyler broke the connection. He hated that his knuckles were bone white. He licked at his dry lips. Was it a mistake? Maybe. Only time would tell. What was it his old nanny used to say? Don't cry over spilled milk or something like that. Overall, his tone had been hard and cold, and in the end, he thought the call had gone well.

Tyler looked at the Rolex on his wrist. Damn, he'd almost forgotten about the watch. He rummaged in his bag for the Timex with the leather strap he'd bought in the drugstore on the corner. He dropped the Rolex into the drawer in his night table.

A glance at his new watch told him he had roughly four hours to get everything together before he had to be at LAX. If he allowed himself some extra time, he could grab something to eat at the airport before going through security.

Maybe he could pull *this* off on his own. He wasn't exactly stupid. Just cowardly. Well, this was where the rubber met the road, and there was no time to be either stupid or cowardly.

Tyler headed back to his home office and sat down at the computer. All he needed was a plan and a hell of a lot of luck.

Chapter 8

It was three o'clock in the morning local time when Lawrence Tyler checked into a Holiday Inn in Miami. He'd parked his Ford Mustang rental in the lot and lugged his own bag into the lobby of the hotel. He was simply too beat to drive all the way to Key West. He wished again that he'd been able to get a flight directly to Key West International instead of Miami, but booking a reservation at the last moment wasn't the best way to secure a seat. He'd get up early and drive to Key West. By three-thirty, he was sound asleep in the queen-size bed with the orange bedspread.

From long habit, Tyler woke at six without the aid of an alarm clock or a wake-up call. For a moment he was disoriented, wondering where he was until he noticed the orange bedspread with the big yellow flowers on it, and it all came back to him. He hopped out of bed, showered, shaved, and dressed in the same clothes he'd arrived in.

Downstairs, he took the time to avail himself of the inn's complimentary breakfast and coffee, which he swigged down at the speed of light. He checked out and was on the road by seven-fifteen.

On the long drive to Key West, he let his brain go into overdrive as he plotted his course of action when he arrived. He stopped once for a bathroom break and fresh coffee.

Tyler climbed back into the Mustang to continue his 120-mile trip down US Highway 1 to the Keys. It was a beautiful, hot sunny day, and he drove with the windows down, the radio playing some golden oldies that didn't bother him at all. He wasn't into jive and rap or any of the other funky stuff that passed for music these days. He absolutely loved the music of the fifties. That was the one and only thing he and his father had in common. Music for some reason always allowed him to think things through and come to a resolution of sorts. In short, music calmed and soothed his soul.

As he tooled along, his thoughts took him in all directions. If he could just remember who the phone voice belonged to, it might help him a lot. With the clock ticking on his case, he knew he was going to have to act quickly to sort out what was going down on Mango Key and at the same time be aware that it could be nothing but a hoax and a blackmail scheme. He'd never gone undercover as a solo agent before. Agents always worked as a team or as a group. What he was doing was totally outside the box, not to mention breaking the rules, and he had no idea if he was made of the right stuff to pull it off. He admitted to a certain amount of fear, yet he felt exhilarated at what he was about to do.

His thoughts took him to Patrick Kelly, the cop who lived on Mango Key. He'd read the man's dossier and it was now committed to memory. He was ninety-nine percent certain Kelly was just who he said he was, a former homicide detective in Atlanta who had dropped out of the mainstream because of a personal tragedy. But he might have observed activity if there was indeed any. Tyler's last call before boarding his flight to Miami had been to the Coast Guard, and while they were doing their daily patrols, they had nothing to report in regard to any strange or illegal activity.

So was the tip last year a hoax? What about the recent call? He had to admit he wasn't one of those agents who had a sixth sense or was tuned to all things criminal, but this time his nerves were twanging all over the place. Then again, his twanging nerves might have something to do with the DEA trying to oust him. He knew he was a little late entering the game, but if there was a way to backtrack and prove himself, he was going to do whatever he could to make it happen. If he was successful and got fired for his efforts, at least he'd be able to live with himself.

Suddenly, traffic slowed, and Tyler slammed on his brakes. The SUV behind him braked with a loud screech, stopping within a hair of his rear bumper. Tyler craned his neck to see if he could spot anything in front of the long line of cars, but most of the vehicles were SUVs, and it was hard to see over their tops. Either an accident of some kind or a car had broken down in the middle of the road.

Tyler climbed out of his car as a dozen or so other lookie-looks trying to see what the problem was climbed out of theirs. It was an elderly bearded man, who bore a striking resemblance to that macho writer who'd lived in Key West, who clued them in from nine cars up that a pickup had broken down. While they waited outside their cars, the people chatted among themselves, including Tyler in their conversations. He was one of them. He liked the feeling and joined in, talking freely about the heat, the road, the pipeline that carried the water supply to Key West. He was told to go to Sloppy Joe's, Ernest Hemingway's favorite watering hole, to eat and enjoy the view. Also he was told of the upcoming Sloppy Joe's Thirtieth Annual Papa Look-alike Contest on July 22–24. That explained the bearded old man.

Kids scampered around, and dogs in the backseats howled their unhappiness at not being allowed to join in. Tyler loved it all. He listened to glowing details about Key West's spectacular sunsets and the quaint bed-and-breakfasts.

Tyler turned when he felt a hand on his arm and saw a pleasant freckle-faced thirtysomething woman asking what was going on. She smelled like warm sunshine and vanilla. She was wearing jeans, a cherry red tank top, and a baseball cap. Great tan and no makeup. The girl-next-door type.

Tyler pointed ahead, and replied, "That guy up there said a pickup broke down. It looks like they're trying to push it to the side although there isn't all that much room. It might be a little while."

"Oh, well." The woman shrugged. "I'm on vacation, so I'm in no hurry. How about you?"

"Yeah, me, too," Tyler lied with a straight face.

"Your first time to Key West?" the pleasant woman asked.

"No. I've been here before. I'm staying at the Southernmost Point Guest House." Was she flirting with him the way he looked? He decided she was. "Have you been here before?"

"My first time. Actually, it's kind of a vacation and work trip all rolled into one. I teach tenth grade at J. P. Stevens High School in Edison, New Jersey. We're going to be studying famous authors when school starts in September, so I thought who better than Ernest Hemingway? Nancy Holliday," she said, holding out her hand to be shaken. Stunned, Tyler stuck out his hand, surprised at how solid her handshake was.

"Nice to meet you, Nancy. Currently, I live in LA, but I get around a lot with my job. Looks like traffic is starting to move. Nice meeting you."

Nancy Holliday smiled and lit up Lawrence Tyler's world. "Maybe we'll see each other again. I understand Key West isn't all that big. You know, small world, etc." She laughed again, and Tyler grinned.

"Tell you what, I'll meet you at Sloppy Joe's tomorrow

around eight if you aren't busy. Hey, we better get moving," he said when horns started to blow.

"Okay," Nancy called over her shoulder as she sprinted toward her car.

An hour later, Tyler turned left off the highway onto Duval Street, headed to the Southernmost Point Guest House, where he'd made an open-ended reservation since he didn't know how long he'd be staying. It would be his home base. He assumed that Nancy Holliday wasn't staying at the same place since she hadn't said anything about what a coincidence. He didn't want anyone watching his comings and goings. He knew, though, that he'd do his best to meet up with her at Sloppy Joe's tomorrow if it was at all possible.

There was a bounce to Tyler's step when he parked his rental, yanked out his duffel and laptop, and made his way into the guesthouse. He registered under his own name and was shown to his room, which thank God had its own bathroom as well as an Internet connection. The room was huge, neat, and cozy. It would work. *Oh, if my parents could only see me now,* he thought. The thought made him laugh out loud.

Tyler unpacked, laying out his used clothing in one of the lavender-scented drawers. For a moment he thought he was back in his own town house with his own dresser drawers, which Talaga lined with what she said were lavender-cypress drawer liners.

He fired up his computer and sat down to read his e-mail to see if the boat he'd reserved would be ready in another hour. He used his cell phone to check in with the Coast Guard and was told there was still nothing to report. He shrugged as he brought up Google Earth and zeroed in on Mango Key. He wished now he'd made a trip down earlier to check out the Key in person. Well, he was here now. The big question facing him was, did he check things out in the daylight or wait for darkness? The boat he'd requested would have running lights, but he'd have to notify the Coast Guard if he was going to take to the water in darkness. "Always cover your ass," he mumbled under his breath. But then again with the cover of darkness, he could move at his own pace, do what he needed without fear of discovery.

Screw the rules.

He also needed to check out the cop on the beach. A straightforward house visit should do it, he told himself. Face-to-face, he'd get a measure of the man, then make his decision as to whether he was who he appeared to be on paper.

Tyler never fooled himself, at least not in private. He knew his one strong point was his ability to have total recall of events and occurrences. He remembered every single word he'd ever read. He remembered every little nit-picking detail of cases he'd worked on even years ago. His father had always been surprised at his phenomenal memory, with his mother saying he inherited his memory from her side of the family, which was all bullshit as far as Tyler was concerned.

He hit Google Earth again and homed in on the structure at the end of Mango Key. But before he sat down to study the pictures that were popping up on his computer, he raided the minibar under the television stand. He withdrew a bottle of Evian water and drank half the bottle in one gulp. He was back at the computer within minutes.

Tyler studied the huge structure, surrounded by a high brick wall, from all angles as he tried to figure out what it was going to be used for. Mango Key was the perfect place for all manner of illicit enterprises, and one couldn't forget it was a mere ninety miles by water to Cuba. He gulped the last of the water and leaned back to think, his mind racing a hundred miles a minute.

If he could only remember what it was about the voice of the unknown caller, disguised or not, that made him think he knew who it was. Sooner or later, when he was least expecting it, something would come to him. He was sure of it. His thoughts still churning, he glared at his cell phone, which had the audacity to pick that precise moment to ring. He looked down at the caller ID and winced. He clicked it on. "Tyler," he said succinctly.

"Mr. Tyler, please hold for the governor," a flat-sounding voice said coolly. Like he had a choice? As far back as he could remember, he'd never refused to take a call from his father. Not when he was still a force in the house of representatives, nor since he became the governor of Florida. His stomach muscles crunched into a knot as he waited to hear his father's voice, wondering what he'd ask of him this time.

The voice, when it came through, was booming, just like the man himself. It was full of authority and cheerfulness. To a point. "How's it going, son?"

Tyler sucked in his breath. "Depends on what you mean by *it*, Dad." Was the old man finally going to get around to telling him he knew his ass was on the line, that he was soon going to be an *ex*-DEA agent? Not likely. He was probably already pulling and yanking strings behind the scenes to make sure it didn't happen. Someone should tell him this time around, no matter what he did, it wasn't going to work.

"You DEA agents are all the same," the voice boomed. "Overworked and underpaid. Where are you, son?"

Tyler's antenna went up. His father had never asked him where he was on an unsecured phone before, so why now? Unless he had someone watching him. To what end? Lie or not lie. He opted for the high road, and said, "Circumstances being what they are, I'd rather not say over *this* phone, Dad."

His father's voice still boomed, but it seemed to Tyler that it had lost some of its luster. "That serious, eh?"

"Afraid so, Dad. Company phone." Something was up with his father. He knew this particular number wasn't secure. Tyler focused on a vase of fresh purple flowers on his nightstand. He wondered what they were called. He just bet Nancy Holliday would know what they were. *Now, where did that thought come from?* "Is there anything in particular that you wanted?"

The voice still boomed. "Just staying in touch with my only son. However, I did want to ask if you would be joining your mother, me, and Carlton over the Labor Day weekend. I thought we might go sailing on the *Chesapeake*. Make a day of it, have a picnic on board, a few drinks, see the fireworks they shoot off at the harbor."

The last thing he wanted to do was go sailing with his parents and Carlton, his godfather, whom he'd despised from day one. Nor did he want to picnic or watch fireworks with them. He wondered if the old man knew he'd be out in the cold by Labor Day. Probably, he decided, and that was the reason for the invitation. Probably wanted to negotiate another trade-off.

"Sorry, Dad, can't make it." An inner voice warned him not to make an excuse, but he was sick and tired of the lies, tired of being his father's lackey. *Sorry, I can't make it* would have to suffice. "Listen, Dad, I'm being paged. Gotta run. Tell Mother hello for me."

Sweat dripped down Tyler's cheeks. He swiped at his face with the sleeve of his shirt. What the hell was *that* all about? His father had the ability to surprise him still.

Something suddenly pinged at his memory, but he couldn't quite bring it to the surface of his mind. No matter, it would come to him eventually just the way the identity of the unknown caller would come to him. It always did.

Tyler walked over to the window and looked out. If he wanted to, he could go to the marina now and take out the boat he'd rented, but he hadn't notified the Coast Guard. One phone call would be all it would take. But should he do it? Second-guessing himself had always been one of his major problems once he joined the DEA. Before he could change his mind, he grabbed his canvas bag and left the room. He called the Coast Guard on his way to his car.

July in Key West was hotter than the fires of hell. Residents strolled the streets in flower-printed shirts and worn-out flip-flops. Didn't they realize how silly they looked? Obviously not, he decided. On a whim, he illegally parked in front of a tacky tourist shop. Inside, he purchased clothes like all the tourists wore. He would fit right in. He kept his temper in check as he made his way, mile by mile, to the marina. The high temperature and equally high humidity weren't helping matters. He couldn't wait till he was out on the water to cool down. He regretted now that he hadn't bought some shorts and some sandals, normal-looking clothes he wouldn't be embarrassed to wear. Maybe he could pick some up on the way back. Or he could head back to Miami and purchase them there, where he wouldn't stand out as much as he suspected he was going to stand out here in Key West. He'd manage.

He was experienced on the water, almost as good as the governor. If his father knew he had to take a shitload of Dramamine because he'd never acquired sea legs, he'd never hear the end of it; but what his father didn't know wouldn't hurt either of them. He'd sailed every summer and had his own sailboat at the beach house. But he preferred power boats, to his father's dismay.

His eyes searching for the landmarks the owner of the marina had provided, Tyler found his way to the lot, where he parked his rental, climbed out, and headed for the ramshackle office that boasted that they carried top-of-the-line Jet Skis, catamarans, and cigarette boats to rent. Next to the office was a souvenir shop, where they stocked beachwear, sand in a bottle, plastic palm trees, and what seemed like a hundred shelves filled with suntan oil. He sauntered into the shop, his gaze going in all directions to see if anyone was following him. He didn't see anything or anyone that looked suspicious, so he walked inside. Maybe he was flattering himself that someone was interested in him. The blast of cold air shocked him. He actually found himself shivering.

Fifteen minutes later, he had three pair of shorts that looked distressed and three T-shirts that said he "hearted" Key West. He bought two pairs of Ray-Ban sunglasses and another baseball cap, which said Miami Dolphins on it. If he dipped it in the ocean water, it would be perfect. Once he hit the water, he could throttle down, snip off the tags, and change his clothes. Two pairs of rubber flip-flops, and he was good to go. He paid for his purchases with cash. No sense leaving a trail for anyone to pick up.

When he signed for the cigarette boat he'd rented, he paid in cash but used a phony credit card for security, a card he'd used many times on different cases. It matched a phony driver's license. Who was he kidding anyway; no one would be looking for him. For someone to be looking for him, he'd have to be important, and that was the one thing he wasn't. At least according to his colleagues at the DEA. He was nominally in charge of the Miami office. He should be there issuing orders, but no one, not even the custodial staff, would speak to him, so he'd opted to go out on his own. Then, he asked himself, *What the hell am I doing here hoping I'm incognito?* Almost as if in answer to his question, his cell phone rang. He looked down to see the number of the caller. He swallowed hard. UNKNOWN CALLER. UNKNOWN NUMBER. Answer or not? He opted not to. Whoever the bastard was, he'd call back. He was sure of it.

Key in hand, Tyler jogged his way to the waiting cigarette

boat, which would take him out to open water. He leapt on board and checked things out. Satisfied that the boat was going to get him back and forth, he opened his canvas bag to check the contents. All the tools of the trade, even his gun. He was good to go. He liked the idea that a map of Florida and all the different Keys was under hard plastic on the side of the dash. Along with a navigation chart.

A scraggly looking teenaged boy released the boat from its moorings, and Tyler backed away from the dock. The boy waved. He waved back.

He was on his own. He admitted to a small thrill of excitement at what might lie ahead of him in the days to come.

Chapter 9

Kate Rush swiped at the sweat dripping down her face from the blistering midafternoon heat. She looked over at her partner and grimaced at her angry countenance. Should she try to mollify Sandy or should she start to bitch the way Sandy had been bitching all morning? "I'm going for a swim to see if I can cool down a little. If you see that crazy parrot attacking me, call the Coast Guard."

"Are you out of your mind? I'm going with you. Whoever the hell said that skimpy air-conditioning unit would keep us cool is off their rocker. It's hotter inside this tin can than it is outside. One more day, Kate, and I'm outta here if something doesn't happen. I mean it this time. Do you hear me, Kate? I really mean it."

Kate knew her partner meant it because she felt exactly the same way, but since she was the leader of this two-woman team, she had to act accordingly. She reached for a bright green and yellow beach towel and slung it over her shoulder. "By something happening, do you by chance mean your suggestion that we hike down the beach and invite our two male neighbors to a weenie roast? I said I'd go along with the idea if you *really* want to do it. Do you?" As a diversion it wasn't much, but it would have to do for the moment.

Sandy reached for her own beach towel. "Well, yeah," she drawled. "At least it's something to do. By the way, do you see that boat that's just sitting out there?"

"I'm one step ahead of you. The guy is fishing and reading a book. He's probably some local who just wants to get away from his nagging wife, and he's killing two birds with one stone. He's fishing, which is what guys tell their wives, and he's probably reading some horror novel about how to kill your pain-in-the-ass boss, who makes your life as miserable as your wife makes it. Anything else you want to know?" Kate asked sweetly.

"I think that about covers it, Ms. Rush. I'd race you to the water, but it's just too damn hot. Listen, Kate, I am serious about leaving here. You know I'm no wuss, but this is beyond the call of duty, and we aren't even getting paid."

"I know, I know. We can fall back and regroup later when the sun goes down. I'm surprised we haven't heard from Jelly today."

Sandy bristled. "Think about it, *Ms. Rush,* why should he call us? We're on the scene, nothing is going on except we're slowly getting cooked to our bones, so why should he waste his time with a phone call just to hear us bitch and moan. Get real here. And another thing. You haven't seen hide nor hair of Roy or Josh, have you?"

A moment later, she ran into the water and was lost to sight. She came up and shouted, "I think my core temperature just dropped twenty degrees. This is heaven. I might never come out of the water. I might even sleep on the beach tonight and get bitten by sand fleas, and then I can legitimately pack in this gig and head back to civilization."

Kate rolled over on her back and closed her eyes as she floated by Sandy. "Then we can't have a weenie roast on the beach, and you won't get to meet that redheaded guy."

"Who said I wanted the redheaded guy?" Sandy asked lazily.

"I know you, Sandra Martin, and I know your taste in men, Sandra Martin," Kate singsonged, before she rolled over to slip beneath the water. When she came up for air, she said, "The guy out there in the boat is watching us. No binoculars, but he's staring right at *you*. Don't even think about it, Sandy; it's too far to swim out there."

"There goes the Coast Guard on their daily patrol. Oh, look, they're pulling up alongside that guy. If he's still there after they leave, we'll know he's just another local or some dumb tourist thinking this is fun."

In spite of herself, Kate laughed, the sound tinkling over the water. "If you want, I can recite a litany of mistakes the Coast Guard has made over the past five years. Remember Rule Number One, which is, 'Nothing is what it seems.' Always investigate."

Sandy was now on her back as she stared at the two boats. "I like Rule Number Two, which is, 'Ignore Rule Number One.' What else should we make for our weenie roast? Maybe I should clarify that statement, and say, what should *I* think about preparing? We have some steaks in that thing that passes as a refrigerator. We could roast some potatoes. Doncha just love them when you pull them out, and they're all black and crusty?"

"Why don't you bake a pie. Men love pie. Ooops, that's right, we don't have a real stove, and no oven," Kate added playfully.

Kate's sarcasm did not go unnoticed by Sandy. "You are determined to rain on my parade, aren't you?" Not bothering to wait for a response, she stared out at the two boats. Even from that distance she could tell that the Coast Guard boat had cranked the throttle. They were moving off, so that had to mean the guy checked out and was now back to reading his book and tugging on his fishing line. *Coincidence?*

The bright orange ball of the sun literally sizzled on the water. Kate couldn't ever remember the water being this warm in all the years she'd lived in Miami and all the years she'd vacationed in the Keys. Overhead, the sky was cerulean blue, the few clouds marshmallow white. Absolutely beautiful if only it weren't so hot. With the back of her hand, she swiped at the seawater dripping down her cheeks. God, how she hated the heat.

"We should head back to shore and do our walk down the beach if you're ready, Sandy. But . . . we put on some clothes. Agreed?"

"You're no fun, Kate Rush," Sandy said as she started to tread water. "Hey, look, there's that parrot."

"And that means what?" Kate said, as her feet touched down on the burning-hot sand. "Forget the damn parrot and check out the guy in the boat. I'm thinking we should call Jelly and report in. Maybe he can run a check on the boat. From this distance, I can't see if it has a name on it or not. Might be the guy's own boat if he's a local. If it's a rental, there will be a record."

"It means the bird is spying on us. Remember it talks. I think you're right. I'll call Jelly and see what if anything he wants us to do. You okay with that, boss?" Sandra asked, deferring to Kate's seniority.

"Go for it. I'm going to change. God, I'm sweating already. Didn't the weatherman say rain at some point today?" she called over her shoulder, but Sandy was already punching numbers into her cell phone and ignored her.

By the time Kate emerged from behind the dressing screen, Sandy had hung up and was yanking at the straps of her bathing suit. "He's going to check it out. What are you wearing?"

"Clothes that cover my body. I suggest you do the same thing." She looked down at the cutoff jeans that had become shorts and a sleeveless tank top in sunny yellow. She pulled her hair back into a ponytail. With her tan, she didn't need makeup, but she wouldn't have applied any regardless. She could hardly wait to see what Sandy was going to wear.

"Didn't you ever hear of enticing men with your body? Men will give up anything when they think . . . never mind. Okay, here I come!" Sandy shouted three minutes later.

Kate gasped. This had to be a first for Sandy, who liked to show off her assets and was up on the latest fashion. Knee-length plaid shorts and a white tank top that showed off her tan. Her hair, too, was pulled back and held in place with a scrunchy. "You happy now? I look like a damn tourist who bought all her vacation wear at Talbots. On sale. From their catalog."

Kate grinned. She loved to ruffle Sandy's feathers. "I guess that raises the question, why do you even have an outfit like that?"

"For an occasion such as this," Sandy replied flippantly. "C'mon, let's get this show on the road."

"In a minute. I want to check out that guy on the boat one more time. I want you to go outside, do some calisthenics or something so he's looking at you. I want to see him with the binoculars and don't want his attention focused on this building. Talk to the parrot or something but move up the beach toward where the guys are. I want to see if he follows your progress while I check him out."

"Done," Sandy said as she walked through the door. Bird greeted her with a resounding, "Put on your big-girl panties. Bang! Bacon! Oh, shit! Panties are purple!"

Sandy burst out laughing. "You, my friend, are a dirty old bird! You need to clean up your vocabulary. Say nice things like, Sandy is beautiful. Kate is a plain Jane. Or, how about this, you lamebrain bird, Sandy is a hot chick? Tell me about that guy down the line. What's he like? Tell me about the brother. Are they hotties? C'mon, I won't tell anyone you sang like a canary. Damn, I crack myself up sometimes."

"Secrets! Oh, boy, secrets! Hot chicks, red-hot chicks. Wak, wak," Bird screeched.

Sandy whirled around as she pretended not to look at the guy in the boat. What was taking Kate so long? She scuffed the superhot sand with her bare foot and found a ratty-looking cracked shell. She stared at it, then shoved it into her pocket just as she heard the metal screen door to the hut slam shut. Kate loped over to where she was standing.

"What did you find out?" Sandy demanded.

"Maybe nothing, maybe something. Guy definitely is not a fisherman. He doesn't have any buckets of bait on that boat. There's no bait on his hook. Saw him check it. He's reading some thriller. At least it looks like a thriller, and the author's name is Loomis. Either he's a slow reader, or he likes to read the same page over and over. He didn't flip the page the whole time I was watching him. The way his head was tilted, he was watching you. He's wearing sunglasses, but damn if he doesn't look familiar. For whatever it's worth, I do *not* think he's a tourist or some guy trying to get some peace and quiet. Hey, he could be a superspy, or he could just be some dumb schmuck out there piddling around hoping to pick up some hot babe in a string bikini water-skiing. But my gut is telling me he bears watching."

Sandy frowned. "But you're leaning toward him being something other than what he's trying to portray, right?"

"Yes. We'll keep our eyes on him to see if there's any change. I can't get over how he reminds me of someone. Oh, well, sooner or later it will come to me. Oh, oh, I almost forgot, the name of the boat is *Sooner or Later.* It doesn't look new, kind of battered and tacky actually. I think it's a rental, so Jelly will probably come up with something on it fairly quick. Now, let's see what those guys are all about, so we can get back to what we do best—which at the moment is zip. Tell me again why we're checking out these guys other than you want to hit on the redheaded one. By the way, where's that damn bird?"

Sandy looked around and shrugged. "Probably waiting at his digs to welcome us. He sure is a salty old bird."

Kate sighed. What she called her belly-sight was kicking in, which meant something was out of kilter. She hated it when she couldn't figure something out. Was it the guy out on the boat? Was he there to check out the cop and his brother? Where in the damn hell did that bird figure into things? *Sooner or Later.* Who did the guy in the boat remind her of?

"Okay, we're almost there. Let's get our act together. I'll take the lead since you get tongue-tied around men. You know you really have to get over that hang-up of yours. It's been proven that women are superior, so start acting like you believe it. Two minutes tops. We invite them. If they say no, we leave. If they say yes, we still leave. We can pick their brains around the fire. A little beer or wine loosens the tongue. We're just being neighborly and have no ulterior motives. They don't know who we are, so we're safe. Any holes in anything I just said?" Sandy asked.

Kate grimaced, her eyes on the boat in the water. "Yeah, one really big hole. The guy is a cop, for crying out loud. What makes you think he didn't go to the same guy, the leader of this damn Key, and ask who we are? Jelly had to give it all up. The cop, in case you haven't figured it out, is a *resident* of this Key. No one is going to hold out on a cop. We're renters, squatters, or whatever you want to call us. I can almost guarantee they know who we are, so let's just dispense with any cover story. We're here. They're here. You are inviting them to a weenie roast. I don't want to come across as a fool and have to backpedal so that has to be the end of the story. Agreed?"

"Yep."

Kate licked at her dry lips. Damn, she should have put some sunscreen on before they left the hut. Her stomach was tied in a knot, and she hated the feeling. Sandy was right, Kate thought, she never did well meeting men in a social setting. For sure it was one of her worst hang-ups. One-on-one with a gun in her hand, she had no equal. She steeled herself when they got to the property line, which was marked off by palm fronds. She looked up into the stilt house and was impressed with the architecture. "Hey, anyone home?" she called.

Two heads leaned over the banister. "Just us," a voice called out. "Come on up and have a glass of lemonade?"

Sandy looked at Kate and wiggled her eyebrows. A hissing whispering was going on. It was obvious that one of the two wanted company and the other one didn't. Before they could change their minds, Sandy started up the sturdy-looking steps that led to the small front porch. Kate was right behind her.

The parrot was going ballistic, screaming about purple panties and bacon and squawking, "Intruder! Intruder! Bang you're dead! Get the girls! Sandy's hot! Real hot!"

"Sandra Martin," Sandy said, holding out her hand. "The bird is right, I am hot. I mean, I'm . . . you know, *warm* from the heat. This is my friend, Kate Rush. We're hanging out down the beach. We came to invite you to a weenie roast, but we also have some steaks and some pretty good wine."

"Pete Kelly. This is my brother Patrick. Just call him Tick. And this noisy creature is Bird."

"Sandy is hot! Bang!"

"Just ignore Bird; he has no social skills," Tick said as he gave the two women the once-over. He liked what he was seeing and relaxed a little. "How about some lemonade or a cold beer?"

"That would be nice, but no thanks. We have to get back.

You know, to prepare and all," Kate said, knowing full well her face was probably beet red. "Interesting house you have here. Did you do the work yourself?" she asked, not caring one way or the other what his answer was going to be.

"Actually," Pete said, "we worked on it together. Would you like a tour?"

"Yes," Sandy said.

"Not right now," Kate said.

"Maybe some other time when you have nothing to do," Tick said coolly.

Kate nodded, turned, and started to walk down the steps, Sandy in her wake.

Sandy turned around when she got to the bottom of the steps and called over her shoulder, "So is it a yes or a no?"

Pete leaned so far over the banister, Tick had to reach out to grab his shirt. "We'll be there. What time?"

"When the sun goes down. You'll see the smoke. Feel free to bring the bird," Sandy shouted.

When they were out of earshot, Kate grumbled, "You had to do that, didn't you?"

"What? *What?*"

"We said in and out, offer the invitation, and what do you do? You say, yes, you want a tour. No, we did not want a tour. A tour would make us look nosy. Don't you get it, Sandy?"

"Yeah, I get it. You were uncomfortable around the cop, and I saw he was just as uncomfortable. He was really *looking* at you, Kate."

"Oh yeah, well guess who else is looking at us? Don't look now, but our buddy on the *Sooner or Later* is watching us. Just keep walking, and act like we paid a social visit to those guys. And, according to you, that's what we just did. I bet five bucks that guy stays out there until it gets dark. Or if he sees us building a fire, he might call it a day."

"Okay, okay. What did you think of those guys? I think Pete looks *real* interesting. I'm also thinking he just might be my type."

"Well, Sandy, I got so hot and bothered with the one called Tick, I just had to get out of there before I decided to jump his bones because I just can't help myself sometimes."

"Well, damn, girl, you sure are full of surprises!" Sandy said in awe.

Kate blinked. "And you believe me?" She gave her friend such a shove that she fell to the sand, at which point Sandy reached out for Kate's ankle and toppled her into the sand.

Back in the stilt house, Tick and Pete watched the two women tussling on the sand.

"I've never seen a catfight before," Pete hissed.

"Yeah, Pete, when two women do what those two are doing, it's a diversion. Probably for our benefit or for the benefit of that guy sitting out there in that boat. Didn't anyone ever tell you women are devious? And sly? Not to mention manipulative, as well as ornery and sneaky."

"For someone who's been living like a hermit for the past eight or so years and who was married to a saint, one has to wonder how you know so much about women." Pete sniffed.

"I didn't say I was an authority. Do you see that guy out there in the boat? He's been out there a good long while. Coast Guard stopped by to check him out. Doesn't mean he's clean, though. What do you say to taking out the *Miss Sally* and scaring the shit out of him? After we cruise around a bit of course. I think I recognize that boat, *Sooner or Later.* It's from that ragged marina in Key West. I'm almost sure of it."

"Count me in," Pete said, jamming his baseball cap more firmly on his head. "By the way, do you have anything to take to the party tonight? Mom always said you should never show up empty-handed."

"Yeah, Mom always did say that. Having said that, I'll hold your hand. That should do it, don't you think?"

Pete started to laugh. Tick joined in as he pocketed the keys to the *Miss Sally*.

"You want to make it look more real?" Tick asked.

"Sure. What do you want to do?"

"Pete, when was the last time you went waterskiing?"

"Never. When was the last time you went waterskiing, Tick?"

"Never. I'll buzz us over to the marina and rent some water skis. I'll drive, and you can pretend to ski. We can try to find out who the guy is with the rental boat at the same time. We've both been snow skiing, so how hard can water-skiing be?"

"You just want to see me make a fool of myself for those damn women on the beach. I know you, Tick. You are insidious. I don't mind being your guinea pig because Mom liked me best."

"She did not!"

"Did so."

It was an age-old battle neither one of the twins ever won.

Chapter 10

Lawrence Tyler stared across the shimmering water, which was starting to turn choppy. A sailor all his life, he knew a storm was coming, probably within the hour by the look of the darkening sky and the chop of the water where his boat rocked a little more than gently. He checked his fishing line by tugging at it. What he knew about fishing wouldn't fill a thimble. Not that he had any firsthand experiences with thimbles.

He was angry. No, angry was the wrong word. He was *pissed*. How dare that asshole Jellard go around him and bring Martin and Rush into the mix! He should have him up on charges the minute he got back to dry land. It would serve him right if that affected his pension. Jellard should know better than to pull a stunt like this.

But with the investigation into his own record going on, it was more than likely that virtually all his authority had been stripped away, and he had become strictly a figurehead, which meant Jellard could do whatever he damn well pleased. *But Rush and Martin?* He knew for a fact they hadn't been reinstated. Seeing them here in work mode had to mean they were off the book. He could really get Jellard fired for that. If anyone would listen to him, that is. But he didn't have absolute, ironclad proof of anything. However slim the odds were, the pair could be on vacation.

The boat rocked wildly. Tyler looked off to the east and saw dark clouds gathering. He thought they looked ominous. It was definitely time to head back to shore. Then he looked toward the shore. He was farther out than he had intended. His stomach rumbled. He'd forgotten to take the Dramamine. Shit. If he was lucky, he'd keep the contents of his stomach intact at least until he managed to dock this piss-poor excuse of a boat.

The two unauthorized agents were watching him while he watched them, and he knew in his gut they couldn't place him. He also knew by now that they'd placed a call to Jellard to check out the *Sooner or Later.* At best he had a few hours until his cover was blown. A few more hours after that, he would have to go *deep,* as agents were fond of saying when they wanted to disappear and still work a case anonymously. He closed the book he'd confiscated from the marina's lending library, which consisted of tattered dog-eared books people had left behind. He pulled up his unbaited line and tossed it on the floor of the boat. He turned the key in the ignition. He was about to open the throttle when his cell phone chirped to life. He flinched when he saw the Caller ID. UN-KNOWN CALLER. UNKNOWN NUMBER. Should he answer it or shouldn't he? Tyler glanced up at the black clouds, which were rolling in at a speed that unnerved him. He felt the chop of the water as it slapped against the *Sooner or Later.* Before he could think twice, he clicked on and identified himself. "Tyler," he said briskly.

"Special Agent Tyler, you'd better turn that boat around and head back to shore. A storm is rolling in, and it won't be pretty. By the way, didn't your daddy tell you fishing is an art? The first rule is you need bait. There's no bait on your hook. Those people on the beach know you don't have a bucket of bait on board." The voice clucked his tongue in disapproval. "Dead giveaway, Special Agent Tyler."

Tyler felt his stomach start to grind as his gaze raked the open water. There were no boats other than the two Coast Guard cruisers moving up and down the waterway. No one was on the beach. Where the hell was this guy? "I thought we were clear when you called the last time. Piss off, buddy. You want to blackmail me, go for it." Brave words from a coward. He let his gaze rake the water again. Where the hell was the jerk hiding? Was it possible he was holed up in that mausoleum at the tip of the island? He directed his gaze to the monstrosity but saw nothing out of the ordinary.

"Okay, so I came on a little strong. I'm not going to yank your chain, Special Agent Tyler. I have information, and I want to sell it. I help you, you help me. Let's talk. With the info I have, you could very well be the next head of the DEA, administrator of the Drug Enforcement Administration."

The dark clouds were moving almost at the speed of light. He had to get to shore. If he let the throttle out, he wouldn't be able to hear on the cell phone. He was surprised he even had reception out here. "Bullshit. If you can see me, then you know I need to get back to shore. I'm hanging up now. I wouldn't make promises like that either," Tyler added. *Where in the hell have I heard this voice?*

Ten minutes later, Tyler did some fancy maneuvering and backed the *Sooner or Later* into her slip. The same skanky kid reached for the mooring line as he leapt up to the dock. He tipped him ten dollars. Tyler looked around like he didn't have a care in the world as he made his way to the rental car he'd parked in the lot. He used up another fifteen minutes driving to the bed-and-breakfast where he was staying. Just as he pulled into the small parking lot, rain poured from the sky. His cell phone chirped again.

Though only late in the afternoon, it was darker than night. Thunder and lightning ripped across the sky. A little Florida shower? He wasn't sure. It might turn out to be a killer storm for all he knew, or it could just be a typical late-afternoon heat shower of the kind Florida was famous for. All he knew for certain was that he was safe and sound and his goddamn cell phone was ringing and the caller was unknown.

Tyler settled himself on one of the white-wicker chairs on the porch and clicked on the phone as the rain continued to come down in torrents. Overhead, the paddle fans fought with the whipping wind. The beautiful graceful ferns hanging from the beams whirled faster than a whirlybird. "What is it you want?" he said into the cell phone, not bothering to identify himself.

"You look nice and comfy on the porch. I always like to watch a wicked storm myself. But to answer your question, I want money. But I don't want it for nothing. I want to trade what I have for money, but then I already told you that. You know, buying and selling, and you wound my pride when you refer to it as blackmail. I see it as a win for both of us."

Tyler's mind was racing a mile a minute. He sure as hell needed a win, right now. He decided to play along to see what he could get. "I need to see something. You have to be aware that, right now, given my current position, I have no access to the kind of money you're talking about. That means the money you're wanting for selling me information has to come from my own personal funds, and like I said, I'm not buying a pig in a poke. This, Mr. Unknown Caller, is where you either put up or shut up. What's it going to be?" *That sounded pretty good,* Tyler thought smugly.

The unknown voice cackled with laughter. "Can't say as how I blame you. How about this . . . the house, that big ugly thing at the tip of Mango Key, is being renovated or, at the very least, cleaned up. Company is coming shortly. Actually, the guests are about seven months late according to my intel, but with things being what they are, I think you will understand once you know what's going on. By the way, those clowns on the beach have no clue. People have been going in and out of that fortress for weeks now."

Tyler chewed on his lower lip. *How does this guy know this shit?* "And you know this . . . how?"

"I'm one of those people who watch and listen. Can't make any money watching and listening unless I have a buyer interested in buying the information I've stored in my brain."

"That's not enough incentive," Tyler snapped. "What's going down?"

The unknown voice cackled again. "Now, you see, that's what you're going to be buying from me. Do we deal or not? Oh, one more thing, I was just funnin' with you when I said I was going to spill your secret. I know you're not gay even if you have friends who are. That was just to get a rise out of you to prove to you that I know everything there is to know about you. I know things about you, Agent Tyler, things you yourself don't even know."

A zigzag of lightning lit up the sky, and moments later Tyler literally jumped out of his chair when a boom of thunder erupted overhead. He moved then, slamming himself against the wall of the porch and sucking in his breath. Hail the size of a nickel pelted the steps leading to the porch. One by one, the ferns hanging from the rafters shot outward like rockets, propelled by the wind rushing through the right and left sides of the porch. The paddle fans sparked, telling him the power was out. *A transformer probably blew out at the corner,* he told himself. For a few seconds, he thought it was the end of the world. His heart, beating trip-hammer fast, finally slowed. He inched his way to the door and went inside. He called out, but no one responded.

Ten minutes later, he could see that the sky was starting to turn lighter, but the rain continued to river down on the guesthouse. He thanked God he'd had the good sense to head to shore when he did. He looked down at the phone in his hand, knowing the connection was dead. He wasn't sure how he felt about that at the moment.

Feeling his way along the dim hallway, Tyler inched his way to the stairway that would take him to his room on the second floor. It wasn't that he was frightened, but discretion, as everyone knew, was the better part of valor. Besides, he was thirsty, his throat and tongue bone dry.

Safe in his room, with the door locked behind him, Tyler opened the minifridge and pulled out a bottle of Evian water. In two gulps he finished the bottle. Then he reached for a frosty bottle of cola. This he sipped as he reclined in the deep, comfortable chair by the window. He sighed mightily as, the rain still slashing at the windows with tropical force, he started to consider his immediate options. He sighed again and, within seconds, drifted into sleep, the relentless heat and sun of the day taking their inevitable toll.

Back on the beach at Mango Key, Agents Rush and Martin stared out at the storm as they huddled together inside the metal hut. "This is worse than that hurricane I went through last year. I wonder where that bastard Tyler is," Kate said.

"He's probably back in California, dining with his flavor of the month under some cactus plant with a fan circulating hot, dry air all over him. I was really looking forward to that weenie roast. Wonder what the Kelly brothers are doing."

"The same thing we're doing, only they're probably guzzling beer. Those winds are pretty ferocious, and I haven't seen hail like that in years."

"You know, Kate, this would be the perfect night for something to happen at that house on the tip of the Key. A boat or boats could be docking as we speak. I haven't seen any lights on the Coast Guard boats, so I assume they aren't out there in open water. Drug runners and smugglers live for this kind of weather, as we both know."

Kate pondered Sandy's words. She did have a point. "When this storm clears up, and it will eventually, what do you say to a little B and E down there. There won't be a moon tonight, so if we're careful, we just might be able to penetrate the building."

"Great idea. We should have done that when we first got here. Can't imagine why Jelly wants us to wait it out. Since we aren't on the payroll, we *really* don't have to follow his orders. And since there's no official law enforcement on this Key, I think we might just pull it off. If something goes awry, we just say we were operating independently and not involve the DEA. The burden of proof will be on them, whoever *them* turns out to be, to prove we're *official* DEA, which we both know we aren't at this particular moment in time. What's the worst thing Jelly can do to us? Fire us? When you're in the field, you take every opportunity that presents itself. I'm okay with trying to scale that outer wall."

"Then we'll do it," Kate said forcefully.

Farther down the beach, the Kelly brothers were also watching the storm from their nest in the oversize stilt house.

Pete's voice was jittery when he said, "Do you get storms like this very often?"

"No, not like this. I haven't seen a storm that produced hail like this one is doing since I've been here. It should cool things off a few degrees," Tick said, as though he were explaining what he was going to prepare for dinner.

"Is this the beginning of a hurricane?" Pete asked, his voice still jittery.

Tick laughed. "Hardly. It's just a bad storm because of the unusual heat. It will be over soon. Scaredy-cat," he teased. "You always were afraid of storms when we were kids."

"Yeah, yeah. Do you think it had anything to do with our house being struck by lightning? As I recall, you were over at Bobby Mitchell's house when it happened and didn't go through that am-I-going-to-die-or-not thing."

"Yeah, that's probably it. Still, don't you think you should have outgrown all of that?" Tick continued to needle his twin.

"Well, yeah, but we're sitting in a goddamn stilt house, and everyone with a brain knows lightning strikes the highest object. This house is pretty damn high."

Tick just laughed. "Listen, I have an idea. Since this damn storm prevented us from screwing with that guy on the *Sooner or Later,* what say you that around midnight, if the storm is over, we head down to *that thing* at the end of the Key. No moon. No boats on the water. We can go in underwater. We have all the equipment."

"Won't the Coast Guard be running their boats? I would think a black night like this would be perfect for drug runners."

"You're right, it is a perfect night for all things illegal. But we'll be underwater. I think it's safe to say the weenie roast is off. Unless those women plan on cooking the wieners with a butane lighter. No dry wood anywhere once this rain lets up. Two more hours, and it should let up. And then a steady drizzle until morning. What's your hip telling you?"

Pete forced a laugh. "The same thing. I was really looking forward to a little social time."

Tick almost laughed. *Almost* because laughter didn't come easy these days. He'd almost said he, too, was looking forward to the weenie roast. *Almost* because it just wasn't in him ever to give his brother the edge. On anything, and that included attending weenie roasts.

The brothers shifted their conversation to other topics: speedboats, the high cost of fuel, the war in Afghanistan, the price of mangoes, and the nightlife in Miami compared to the nightlife in Key West. "No comparison," Tick said with authority.

When they'd exhausted all available mundane subjects, Pete brought up the building at the end of the Key. "What's your opinion, Tick? What's the cop in you saying?"

"I don't think it's drugs even though this is the perfect spot for it. You asked for gut, and that's my gut talking. Hell, this is a smuggler's paradise. It could be anything, and like I said, Cuba is just a few miles away by water.

"About a month ago, the Coast Guard picked up two cigarette boats in the middle of the night. It was like the Fourth of July out on the water. Strobe lights, bullhorns, whistles, gunshots. Woke me up. Smugglers bringing in illegals. Didn't make it to US soil. Saw on the Net the next day that there were over two hundred minors on board. The Coast Guard catches one batch, and two more are in the wings waiting to take their place. It's like Plans A, B, and C. It's almost like they know the first batch is going to get caught, so they bide their time, then bring in the stringers, who magically make it through. I'm thinking that's what is about to go down. You'd be surprised at how many women are smugglers. This Key is the most logical place for it to happen since, in my opinion, there is no real law enforcement here other than the Coast Guard."

Pete digested all the information his brother had just imparted. He leaned back and closed his eyes as he thought about what the coming hours would involve and what his own role would be. Watching Tick's back, no doubt, the way Tick had watched out for him when they were growing up. He admitted to a small thrill of excitement.

A long time later, Tick spoke out of the blue. "So, Pete, which one of the women did you set your eyes on?"

Pete bolted upright, his eyes popping wide. Those words were the last thing he had ever expected to hear from his brother's lips. He decided to play it cool and be noncommittal. He shrugged. He wondered if that would be the end of it. It wasn't.

"So you're saying neither one rang any bells. That's pretty hard to believe, bro."

Still playing it cool, Pete said, "Why's that?"

"Well, you always liked the ladies even back in our sandbox days. I remember you putting the moves on Patty Baker when we had our sixth birthday party. She smacked you as I recall." Tick guffawed at his own words.

"Yeah, I do remember that, and I also remember you told her I wanted to kiss her. One of these days, I'm gonna make you pay for that. I'm off women, too much trouble."

"Ha! Come on, which one?"

Pete heard something different in his brother's tone. He could tell he really wanted to know. "The dark-haired one seemed nice. What did you think?"

"I thought she might fit your criteria. You need to get over what's her name."

Pete bristled. "Her name was Serafina."

"Whatever. You know what, I think I'm going to take a nap since we're going to be out and about later this evening. I like to fall asleep with the rain hitting the roof. You used to like it, too, if I remember correctly."

"Sounds like a good idea. So, should we set the alarm, or does that internal clock of yours still work like magic?"

"It works. We'll get up around eleven and head on out after that. It'll be well after midnight by the time we get all our gear together and swim down and around the tip. Sleep tight, bro."

"Yeah, you, too. Where's Bird?"

"In the shower, where else? He doesn't like storms, and he's scared to death of thunder. I don't know why I think this, but I think he equates thunder with gunshots. You know how he's always saying 'bang, bang'? In a way it makes sense. The dark-haired one, eh? Her name was Sandy in case you forgot." Tick laughed like a lunatic as he made his way into the house.

Chapter 11

"Are you sure you want to do this now, in this weather?" Sandy asked Kate, while the two of them dressed for their evening adventure—dark shorts and T-shirts.

"Of course I'm sure. I don't know why I've waited this long to investigate that monstrous place. It's not like Jelly is here looking over my shoulder. Besides, these storms never last long. The worst of it will be over by midnight."

"True, but what do we tell our neighbors if we just happen to bump into them at that ungodly hour?"

Kate tied her hair up in a ponytail. "I doubt they'll be out traipsing around the beach at midnight. If we're lucky, they drank too much and are both snoozing away, dreaming about hot chicks in teeny bikinis. And if we do happen to 'bump' into them, we simply tell them the truth. We're working. Remember, Jellard told the elder or whatever the heck they call him that we were agents. Jelly was pretty sure the elder would report that to the cop ASAP. I don't think we have anything to worry about where he's concerned."

"Yeah, but Jellard said the cop was an ex-drunk, too. He didn't look like a drunk to me. But then again, what does a drunk, ex or not, really look like? What about that crazy bird?"

Kate shook her head. Leave it to Sandy to ask stupid questions.

"Jelly said the cop was dry. And what about the bird? If he shows up, we give him something to talk about."

Sandy clucked her tongue. "I get it. You feed the bird information, hoping it'll get back to them, is that it?"

"Yep, you got that right. I'll just make sure the info is . . . enticing."

"I like it. Feel free to mention something about my interest in the redhead. That way they'll know up front."

"I can't believe you. We're getting ready to break and enter, possibly endanger our lives, and all you think about is that . . . *man!*" Kate motioned toward the beach.

"Somebody has to think about our future. We're not getting any younger."

Sandy was right, but it wasn't the time to concern themselves with their love lives or lack thereof. "True, but we don't know them. For all we know, they could be gay."

"No, they're not. I can spot a gay man a mile away. My gaydar is always right on the money. The dark-haired one was married before, remember?" Sandy stated seriously, as though this were the most important conversation she'd ever had.

"And that's supposed to make a difference how?" Kate grimaced.

"I wonder about you, Kate, I really do. Let me spell it out for you. If the man was married, chances are pretty slim that he's gay."

"Whatever you say. Right now, those two are the least of my concerns. Jelly said he was sure the cop is who he claims to be, and I agree. I didn't see anything suspicious at his place, nothing to indicate he was anyone other than a man who seems to want nothing more than a bit of peace and quiet."

"Not that we went inside to investigate further, no thanks

to you, I should add. He sure as hell isn't getting any peace and quiet with that whacked-out bird of his, but I agree he seemed normal, whatever that is these days."

"True, but that's not our business, at least not now. Let's get over to that . . . compound. Something sinister is going on there, I can feel it in my bones. If that jerk Tyler thinks he's going to discover what it is before we do, he's got another thing coming. And you're positive Jelly identified him as the guy on that ragged excuse for a boat called *Sooner or Later?*"

"Absotively, posilutely sure," Sandy added.

"I can't believe the little weasel has actually been spying on us. Probably doing big Daddy-o a favor. There's something about that bunch that isn't right despite their public image of one big happy family." Kate stuffed a mini Maglite in her pocket, along with her cell phone and a small bag of tools given to her by Jelly. She slipped a Sig Sauer, one she had purchased after turning in her government-issued firearm, in her ankle holster. As an afterthought, she rubbed mosquito repellent on her face, arms, and legs. She was going prepared.

"You think you'll really need that?" Sandy asked, indicating the gun strapped to Kate's ankle.

"I'm not willing to risk it. You should be packing, too. Who knows who might be watching, just waiting to jump our bones, and I don't mean it in the way you think I mean it, so wipe that smirk off your face. You better use some of this, too," Kate suggested, tossing the bottle of insect repellent to her.

The bottle hit the floor with a thud. "No thanks, Kate. You're just no fun anymore," Sandy teased.

"And you're just a barrel of laughs yourself. Look, let's get this over with. I want to have something to report to Jelly when he calls tomorrow. I'll figure out how to omit the breaking-and-entering part. Seriously, take your gun, Sandy."

We don't know what or whom we're likely to run into, and I don't mean our hot-looking neighbors either."

"At least we agree on that," Sandy replied. "You're human after all."

"I never said I didn't think they weren't attractive."

"No, I don't believe you did."

"Come on, *Sandra,* let's get our butts in gear. If we keep this up, it'll be morning before we're out the door."

Sandy strapped her shoulder holster on. She slipped on a dark blue windbreaker to hide the gun.

"You'll suffocate with that on," Kate admonished.

"Then I'll suffocate, I'm getting used to it. I'm not strapping an ankle holster on. What if it gets wet on the way over?"

"Shit, Sandy, let's stop with the twenty questions! It isn't going to hurt a damn thing if the gun gets wet. I don't plan on going for a midnight swim unless I have to. I'm leaving now. You can come along or not."

"Okay, *okay!* I'm in on this, too."

"Then move your ass. I don't want to spend all night in that godforsaken place, do you?" Kate demanded.

"I haven't been there yet, so how would I know? They could have all the amenities we're lacking in this metal shell that's supposed to be livable. Like a bathtub and a real shower. And an air conditioner that actually cools."

They'd both known going into this gig that the accommodations weren't going to be ideal, but Sandy hadn't stopped complaining. They had to make do with a handheld shower attachment connected to a freestanding sink for showering, and the window-unit air conditioner did little more than circulate hot air. Sandy was right. Their accommodations stank, but Kate knew this might be her last case as a bona fide DEA agent, on the book or not. She wanted to prove to Jellard, and to herself, that she still had the guts to do whatever it took to see a case to its end, win, lose, or draw.

Kate knew that Jelly had taken a huge risk when he asked them to go undercover while under the radar. She would not make him regret his decision. Besides, complaining about their lack of amenities wouldn't look good on her or Sandy's record if something more came of this opportunity. It would be looked at, they're women, they were born to complain, that kind of thing.

"Then don't forget to pack a bath towel and shampoo. Seriously, Sandy, we're working here, not lazing around at some luxurious spa. Now come on, or I'm going without you."

"All right," Sandy said.

Both women checked their guns for ammunition, then each added an extra clip/magazine for good measure. Neither knew what they were likely to encounter.

With no visible moon, the darkness concealed them as they made their way to the stretch of beach directly in front of their quarters. The night air was balmy, the humidity still near the hundred percent mark. A light rain continued, the only evidence of the earlier storm. Even though it was close to midnight, the warm breeze sweeping in from the Gulf did little to ease the oppressive heat.

Sandy slapped at her legs. "These bugs are the size of moths. I can't believe how many times I've been bitten since we've been . . . marooned. If this keeps up, my legs are going to look like a leper's."

Kate shook her head. "You should've used the repellent like I told you. This area is a natural habitat for bugs."

"Isn't that just grand?" Sandy replied. "Anyway, you stink. Scent travels, you know that. That's why I didn't use the repellent. What if we see our neighbors? I don't want to smell like I've bathed in chemicals."

Kate laughed. "We don't have a bathtub, remember? I may stink, but I don't have ugly red bumps all over my legs. I told you, it's highly unlikely we're going to run into our neighbors. Like I said, if they're smart, they've had one too many and called it a night." What she really would've liked to do herself, but she was on a mission, and personal comfort wasn't considered a high priority on a stakeout, sanctioned or not.

"I'm not taking any chances. It's not every day we're stuck on a beach with two hunks. I'm going to do whatever I can to make sure the odds are in my favor," Sandy snapped.

"Since when did you become so gung ho on attracting men? It's not like you haven't had your share."

Sandy swatted Kate's arm. "You make me sound like some two-bit bimbo."

"I didn't mean it that way. Sorry. You can have any man you want, so why this redheaded guy? What's so special about him?"

"There's just something about him, I'm not really sure I even know what it is. Yet. I could see it in his eyes when he looked at me. He felt it, too, I could tell."

"Whatever 'it' is will have to wait, Sandy. We have a deal with Jelly, and I, for one, intend to keep my word, men or no men."

"And you think I'm not? Shit, Kate, what kind of person do you think I am? I know what we signed up for, and I intend to see this to the end, same as you. But there's nothing wrong with a little male incentive to get the juices flowing."

Kate laughed again. Poor Sandy, she needed a date. Badly. And soon.

"All in good time, my friend, all in good time."

"Yeah, a good time. That's exactly what we both need," Sandy added, as they carefully made their way to the compound stationed at the end of Mango Key.

"Enough. No more talking. From here on in we'll use hand signals until I say it's clear. We don't have a clue what we're about to encounter. Are you ready?"

Sandy ran her hand along her right side, making sure her gun was in place. "I'm ready."

"Then let's go. I want to find out what's really happening at that . . . *place.*"

Feeling like an eel in his wet suit, Pete adjusted the band on his diving mask, then pulled it back to sit atop his head. He checked his equipment. Fins, snorkel, regulator, dive watch, tank of compressed air.

"We won't need the regulator or the tank since we're not going that deep," Tick said.

"I'm not taking any chances, bro. I've never done this before, remember? I'm not so sure we shouldn't have rented those skis you mentioned. At least we'd be above the water."

"You'll do fine, Pete. I'm no expert myself. Let's just take the snorkels and masks. We can get by with them. We can stay close to the beach, we'll swim out just far enough so we're not easily spotted. No one in their right mind is going to be out fishing or doing who knows what this time of night. If we were skiing, we'd be spotted for sure."

Pete breathed a sigh of relief. "True. That'll work for me. I don't have to tell you, I wasn't too enthused about diving or waterskiing. Keep me above the water any day."

"Yeah, I can see you're still a wuss," Tick needled. "Think you'll need a life jacket, too?"

"Kiss my ass," Pete shot back.

"I think I'll take a pass on that, bro," Tick said. For the first time in a very, very long time, he felt good. Really good. As in let's-kick-ass-and-take-names-later good. Good as in he wondered about the woman who called herself Kate. Visions of her romping on the beach filled his head. She was hot, even hotter than her friend. Somehow Tick knew that she was as totally unaware of her knockout looks as her partner was totally aware of her own attractiveness.

"One of these days, I'm really gonna kick your ass, you know that?" Pete shot back with a grin.

"When hell freezes over. Get your gear so we can get started. The sun'll be up before you're out the door. And remember, once we swim ashore, no talking. You follow me, stay close so you don't get into any trouble. When and if I see it's clear, then I'll decide our next move. If—and I don't see this happening—but if for some god-awful reason it does, if we encounter trouble of any kind, I want you to hightail your ass back to the house. Call Joe; he's the island elder. Tell him what's going down. He'll know what to do from there. You sure you're okay with this?" Tick asked, suddenly serious, more serious than he'd been for a long time. This wasn't a game, and he wanted to make sure Pete understood the rules.

"I wouldn't be here if I wasn't. No cowboys and Indians. We're not kids. I know this is serious shit, Tick, and I'm good with all of it," Pete assured him.

"If you're sure, then let's go. Remember, you follow and do as instructed or else," Tick reiterated.

"I heard you the first time. Let's go before I chicken out," Pete joked. "Why the hell do I have to wear this? I feel like I'm being strangled by a boa constrictor," he added.

"Warmth."

"In this heat? I'd think that would be the last thing we'd have to concern ourselves with."

"Then you know what to do?" Tick asked as he attached equipment to various parts of his body.

"You haven't changed one bit, *ass face*. I won't think. That's what you wanted to hear, isn't it?"

"I see the ponies didn't kick all the horse sense out of you. This is good. Now shut up. And yeah, that's what I wanted to hear. Despite the warm weather, once we're in the water, you'd be amazed at how fast your body temperature drops."

"Looks like I'm not going to find out either. Let's get out

of here before I choke to death in this damned thing," Pete said.

"Deep water! Deep water!" Bird croaked from his perch.

"Is he coming?" Pete asked, pointing at Bird.

"He's my right-hand bird. Of course he's coming." Tick directed his attention to Bird, perched on the back of the kitchen chair. "Go to *that thing,* Bird! See what you can find. We'll be there in fifteen minutes."

Pete shook his head. "I never thought I would live to see the day that you, Mr. Police Officer, best-selling author, would be talking to a damn parrot. What's worse, you expect him, or her, whatever, to understand you. Nope, I never thought I'd see the day."

Tick turned off the living-room lights on their way out. He left the front-porch light on just in case Pete would need it as a guide if he had to return to make a phone call, though Tick hoped that wouldn't be necessary. He knew that he could feel his way back to the house if push came to shove.

"Get the girls! Get the girls!" Bird squawked.

"See? He knows what's expected of him before he's even asked. Unlike some people I know, right, Bird?"

"Bullshit! Bullshit!"

Both Tick and Pete doubled over with laughter.

"Bird, it's time to go to *that place* at the tip of the island. Listen up and wait for us when you see us getting out of the water. You got that?" Tick asked seriously, though his grin was as wide as the ocean.

"Outta here, outta here!" With a flutter of wings, Bird flew off the back of the chair and out the front door before either Tick or Pete could say another word.

Carefully, they inched down the steps. Tick was the first to speak. "I've never heard Bird say that before. I swear he's more intelligent than some of the residents here on the island. I wonder who trained him. And why?"

"Unless Bird tells you himself, or herself, I guess you'll never know. I have to admit, I'm surprised that he or she actually understands and follows orders. Maybe it's time to put Bird on the road. Make some big bucks off a show like that," Pete said thoughtfully.

"Don't make plans for my pet. He's not going anywhere except where I tell him to go," Tick snarled to his brother's back.

Pete flipped him the bird.

Waddling like two penguins in their wet suits, with their diving gear sticking out every which way, Tick and Pete looked like sea creatures from a bad B-rated 1950s movie as they entered the water.

"We'll walk out about fifty feet, then if the water's deep enough, we'll swim out another hundred yards, give or take a few. From there we'll head east, which will put us directly in front of *that thing*. Remember, once we're onshore, no talking. Stay behind me, and don't do anything unless I tell you. Just in case you don't know this, sound carries over water."

Exasperated, Pete shook his head. "Okay, *Dad*. I think I'm old enough to follow a few simple instructions."

"Old enough, yes. Smart enough, I'm not so sure," Tick razzed.

"Hey, you better watch your mouth."

"Just kidding, bro, just kidding."

Without another word between them, the two men waded into the water until it was waist deep. Securing their snorkels and masks, they swam away from shore, heading into unknown territory.

Chapter 12

Wearing the pink and yellow shirt patterned with bright green parrots and palm trees, his new distressed shorts, and flip-flops, Tyler knew no one would recognize him in what he thought of as his new-island-tourist garb. He discarded the Miami Dolphins cap, choosing instead the white baseball cap emblazoned with the word parrothead in bright orange print above the bill. He figured it had something to do with Key West and Jimmy Buffet, but didn't give a damn because he wasn't about to let anyone see him like this, or at least anyone that mattered. What would Nancy Holliday think if she saw him all decked out in flowers and birds? Something told him she'd like him no matter what he wore.

He parked his rental behind the marina, took his cell phone from the dash along with his night-vision goggles, his Glock, and a set of binoculars. The night air was steamy, tinged with the odor of rotting fish. He glanced around at the older homes, some of them nothing more than shacks, all without central air-conditioning, and he wasn't sure if they actually had plumbing or not. He wondered how anyone could possibly live here in this heat without all the amenities he had in his Los Angeles condo. In Phoenix, the heat had been dry, nothing like the sweltering, dank air in Florida. It could be worse. At least he hadn't seen any alligators slithering around the marina. Yet.

Fifteen minutes later, under a moonlit sky, Tyler expertly maneuvered the *Sooner or Later* from its slip at the marina. No one saw him as he idled slowly down the inlet of water leading out into the ocean. God help him if his father were to see him dressed like this. He smiled at the thought of it. Hell, he might wear this to Christmas dinner this year.

The pitch-black skies accommodated his plans for the night. For that he was thankful. He knew if he couldn't see *them,* meaning those sneaky bitches, Kate Rush and Sandra Martin, then they couldn't see him. He planned to extinguish the lights and cut the engine as he neared the tip of Mango Key. He had a plan. Sort of.

Tyler steered the sleek, albeit *older* model boat out into the open water. When he saw there were no other boats within sight, he bumped the throttle up to its maximum speed. The boat danced over the tops of the whitecaps at a dangerously high speed. He didn't care, he was experienced on the water, a fact that even his father would agree on. Though, if asked, Tyler was sure his father would take all the credit for teaching him even though they both knew that wasn't true. His skill could be attributed to summers spent at the beach yacht club with various instructors and hours upon hours of practice.

With enough miles between him and the marina, Tyler pulled back on the throttle, shutting down the engine. He cut the running lights. The only visible light was a single yellow glow coming from a house on Mango Key. Talk about desolate.

Waves slapped against the sides of the boat as it rocked from side to side. "Damn, I'll puke if this keeps up," he muttered to himself.

While Tyler was an avid sailor, he'd never acquired sea legs. Another weakness, he knew, but it is what it is, and he couldn't do a damned thing about it other than remember to take a Dramamine. Of course he'd been in a hurry when he'd raced out of the bed-and-breakfast, and now he knew he'd have to suffer the consequences. He took a deep breath, hoping to calm the waves sloshing around in his brain, but all it did was make him light-headed. He sat down, closed his eyes, and visualized the beach, with all its white *flat* sand. He knew the place at the tip of the island was within swimming distance, but until his nausea subsided, he opted to remain in the boat. Besides, this was as far as he'd planned on going. When he thought about the plans he should have made, he laughed. Here he was once again playing the role that was expected of him. Loser with a capital L. What the hell did he hope to accomplish other than spying on Rush and Martin? Did he actually think he was going to shoot his way into that damned castle, or whatever the hell it was, rescue or arrest whomever he found, then sail back to the marina? No. He hadn't planned that far ahead. All he wanted was something, some kind of *proof* that something illegal was going down in that fortress, something other than suspicions from his so-called informant, his blackmailer.

He didn't have the instinct that most DEA officers developed during their careers. All he had was his daddy's name and an attitude to go along with it. He would have to wing it like he usually did, and he knew what that led to. Zero. Zilch. Nada. Something had to be going down at that fortress, or he would be forced to return to Miami with his tail between his legs, a common sight. He'd find out what the hell was going on; maybe then he'd earn a few brownie points with his father and the powers that be, and his critics would think twice about that goddamned task force that wanted to kick his ass to the curb.

Then there was the blackmailer. A part of him hoped he'd just bump into his blackmailer and get it over with. Whatever *it* was. Taking another deep breath, Tyler decided he'd head back for dry land in order to rethink his lack of planning.

Swallowing back the nausea for a second time, he was reaching for the key when a loud smack against the side of the boat caused his heart to hammer. "What the hell?" he whispered. Nervous, he swallowed several times before he found the courage to stand up and peer over the side. Probably a stingray. He'd seen some that were the size of a car tire. Leaning over the boat, his gaze raking the surrounding water, he saw nothing lurking in the dark waters of the ocean. He sat down again and was about to click the key to the start position when he saw something swoop in and out of the water.

Reaching for the night-vision goggles, he strapped the contraption to his head, then scanned the water around him. About fifty feet ahead he saw something leap out of the water, then dive beneath the surface. A few seconds later Tyler saw something surface again, and he realized what he'd seen . . . *fins*! Someone was actually in the water swimming. Who in their right mind would be out in the ocean this time of night? Swimming? At least he was in a boat. He strained to see ahead, his night-vision goggles turning the water a murky greenish tint. The figure was at least a hundred feet ahead. Tyler almost fell over the side of the boat when he saw another set of fins swoop out of the water. There were two idiots in the ocean! Knowing he was outnumbered, he waited another minute before cranking the boat's motor. He could be out of there in minutes, but curiosity got the best of him. Who the hell were those two, and what were they doing here at this time of night? He'd told no one of his plans—if you could call them plans. Hell, he wasn't even sure what he'd expected to find when he'd hightailed it out of the marina. Surely this was just a coincidence, two lone people, swimming toward the mansion at the tip of the island? Bullshit.

He'd bet his last dollar they weren't tourists out for a midnight swim.

It wouldn't surprise him in the least if it were Rush and Martin trolling the waters, looking for a way to screw him over. The pair would go to any lengths, especially Rush, if she thought she could overshadow him in any way. In view of his current delicate position with the DEA, it wouldn't take much to accomplish if that was her ultimate goal.

Raking his gaze across the water, he spied the two swimmers in scuba gear as they clomped toward the beach. Grabbing his binoculars for a closer look, Tyler observed the duo. Whoever they were, they weren't Rush and Martin. They were too tall, too broad-shouldered. Definitely not women.

Briefly, he wondered if the two had any connection to the blackmailer. Though why they'd follow him out on a night like this, he hadn't a clue. Placing the binoculars on the floor, he removed the night-vision goggles, then reached for the binoculars again.

For the life of him, try as hard as he would, he couldn't put a name to the blackmailer's voice. Maybe these two would remove their gear, and he could get a closer look, possibly nudge his memory a bit.

Tyler adjusted the binoculars, zooming in for a close-up. Because it was so dark, he was only able to view their silhouettes. Try as he might, he couldn't get a good enough visual to identify the swimmers. But why the wet suits and snorkels? Their masks were arranged on top of their head. Where were their tanks, buoyancy vests, all the normal gear one would need to actually go scuba diving? Tyler concluded they must've come from somewhere on the island. He remembered the cop. Maybe he'd gone for a midnight swim, but who was his partner? Tyler knew the cop lived alone, but something didn't feel right.

Lowering the binoculars, he decided to get back to the

marina as quickly as possible, then he'd rethink his plans, which, in Tyler-speak, meant he'd think about actually *making* some plans. Tyler cranked the boat, no longer caring if the two men saw him or not. He figured if they wanted to do him harm, they'd had their chance. Pulling back on the throttle, he zoomed across the water at maximum speed. Even though he knew that his days as DEA chief in the Miami district were numbered, Tyler was still the boss. So what if he considered himself in *deep?* No one other than he, and obviously his blackmailer, knew his whereabouts. He still held a position of authority, and he planned to take advantage of it for as long as possible. Arnold Jellard had some explaining to do.

Kate lifted her right hand high in the air, indicating to Sandy it was safe to move forward. Sweat trickled down her neck, settling at the base of her spine and soaking the waistband of her shorts. The heat and humidity were almost unbearable and made worse by the rain. Insects the size of bees swarmed around her but didn't touch her skin. Sandy, on the other hand, couldn't stop smacking herself. Kate wanted to say, "I told you so," but knew it'd have to wait, as they had more pressing matters to deal with. Like trying to figure out how they were going to scale an eight-foot-high brick wall. The gates were electrified, and there was a security system she'd have to dismantle. Whoever had once lived here, and perhaps still did so, wanted to make damned sure no one could get inside.

Behind her, Sandy awaited further instruction.

"I think it's safe to whisper. One of us is going to have to climb this fence if we want inside. Wanna toss for it?" Kate asked.

"I suppose you just happen to have a coin?" Sandy remarked.

"Of course. I always come prepared."

From her pocket, Kate removed her lucky coin, a silver half-dollar given to her by her father when she was ten years old. Tossing it high in the air, she caught it before it hit the sand. She plopped the coin in her open palm. "Call it."

"Heads I scale the damned fence, tails it's all yours."

Kate opened her palm, the coin tails side up. "Crap!"

Sandy laughed. "I'll be happy to offer you a boost."

Kate snarled quietly.

Without further ado, Kate and Sandy cautiously walked around to the area behind the structure. They'd decided beforehand it would be best to try and enter from the rear, just in case they were being spied on by Tyler or anyone else. Both had heard a boat motor minutes ago. Kate assumed Tyler was spying on them and didn't give it too much thought since she'd never considered him a danger or a risk. She knew she could and would kick his ass if necessary.

Both women remained alert, conscious of the fact that what they were about to do was breaking the law, because Jellard hadn't obtained any legal authorization for them to enter the premises. Remaining off the book had its advantages and disadvantages. On the slim chance they would need backup, they were basically out of luck.

In a harsh whisper, Sandy pushed Kate to make her move. "What the hell are you waiting for? You suddenly afraid of heights or something?"

Kate looked over her shoulder. "You want to do this, be my guest. I'm looking for wires; there is a security alarm, remember? I'll need to cut it, and I'm not absolutely sure which is which. Red, green, or yellow. One wrong slice, and I could activate whatever alarm this fortress has."

"Yeah, but remember—Mango Key doesn't have a police force. It'd have to be the Coast Guard, and something tells me they won't care one way or another if someone were to break into this place."

Kate acquiesced. "You're right. Give me a boost." Stepping into Sandy's cupped hands, she lifted one leg, then the other, easily mounting the brick wall. Standing on top of the wall, praying no one would decide to take a potshot at her, she removed her mini Maglite from her pocket and raked its beam across the top of the wall. Not more than three feet in front of her she spied a small black box. Lowering herself to her hands and knees, she crawled across the rough surface, scraping her knees on the stony texture and heaving a sigh of relief that there was no embedded glass. She removed the pair of miniature wire cutters she'd stuck in her pocket at the last minute. She pried the black box open with the tip of the tool. Inside were several strands of red, green, and yellow wires. Before she could stop herself, Kate snipped the red wire. When nothing happened, she snipped the yellow wire. Still nothing. *It's now or never*, she thought, preparing to snip the green wire. With shaking hands and her breath lodged in the back of her throat, Kate clipped the green wire. Waiting for the screech of a siren or some other god-awful noise to cause pandemonium, she remained on all fours. After several seconds passed without the wail of an alarm, Kate used the back of her hand to wipe the sweat off her forehead.

Not bothering to lower her voice, Kate said, "There's no alarm."

"How can that be? You'd think a place this size would be locked up as tight as Fort Knox."

"You would think. Maybe someone deactivated it over the years. I'm going to drop down. Go to those iron gates around the front. Meet me there. I'll see if there's a way inside."

Sandy gave her a thumbs-up.

Sandy raced to the front of what she now thought of as "the compound," where she found Kate waiting, a big smile on her face.

"You're just full of surprises, aren't you?" Sandy stated.

"No, I'm just handy with this." Kate revealed another tool of the trade, a small bolt cutter.

"Jelly?" Sandy asked.

"Yep."

"He must've suspected you wouldn't follow orders," Sandy said, a trace of humor in her voice.

"Something like that. Now listen up, here's the plan." Kate briefed her partner-in-crime, then both women entered the mysterious building inside the compound through a broken window.

Chapter 13

Pete trailed closely behind Tick as they waded toward the shore. When they reached the beach on the west side of that thing, Tick stopped and motioned for his brother to do the same. A few seconds later, as Tick prepared to remove his wet suit and gear, he whispered, "Take your suit off. We won't be able to move fast enough wearing wet suits. Let's hide them over there." He pointed to a large wooden hutlike structure that was probably used for storing beach gear for one of the island's elder's grandkids.

As they removed their suits, they both scanned the area to make sure no one was watching them. "What are you looking at?" Pete asked.

"I don't know. Ever get the feeling someone's staring at you, then when you look around and see no one there, you feel like an idiot but still you know there is someone watching you?"

"Well, sure. That happens to everyone," Pete said.

Still whispering, Tick said, "I feel that way right now."

Pete looked over his shoulder as Tick grabbed his arm.

"Don't look! They . . . someone *is* watching us."

"And you feel like an idiot?" Pete razzed.

"I'm serious, Pete! Take the gear over to that shack and

wait for me while I scope out *that thing*." He nodded at the mysterious building behind them.

Pete grabbed his and Tick's wet suits and the rest of their gear. "You want me to wait in the shack like some two-year-old? I don't think so. Remember, you asked me to come along. I'm not going to hide in some shack like a big wuss."

Anger sparked in Tick's eyes. "Look, dammit, I've already lost my family because of some sick bastard; I don't intend to lose you, too. Now do as I say, or I really will kick your ass."

"Then why in the hell did you ask me to tag along? So you could play big brother? I'm in this, too. If I get hurt, it's because I fucked up, Tick, okay? You don't have to baby-sit me."

Tick took a deep breath. Memories of those days after the murder of Sally and the kids flashed before his eyes. He'd been unable to protect them, unable to save them from the drug-crazed killer who took their lives so callously and care-lessly. He wasn't going to take a chance losing his twin. Though they hadn't seen much of each other in the past eight years, Tick was as protective as ever. He wished he'd never asked him to come along on this . . . *inane quest* . . . for what? To get themselves hurt? *Stupid, Tick, stupid, stupid, stupid!*

But life was all about taking chances, he knew that better than anyone. With a sudden change of heart, Tick said, "Follow me." If Pete was man enough to take an unknown risk, Tick had to be man enough to allow him to do so. But he'd cover his ass no matter what. Clearly, he hadn't been thinking straight when he'd decided to drag him along. He wasn't about to let his brother out of his sight, not even for a minute.

"Leave the gear. No one will bother it," he said over his shoulder. The gear could be replaced. Pete couldn't.

Pete dropped his goggles on the sand. "Whatever you say,

Patrick. You're the big man. Former Atlanta police officer. Famous author. You know what's best for everyone. Just do what good old Patrick Kelly says, and you'll never go wrong. No, sir."

Tick stopped, and Pete slammed into his back. Tick turned around to look his brother squarely in the face. "I'm an ass-hole, I know. It's just . . . I can't lose you now that you're back in my life. It just hit me back there. I don't know what I was thinking. I'm sorry, Pete. I didn't mean to belittle you or make you feel like a wuss. I'm the wuss. I'm . . . afraid to do anything anymore. I've been on this damned island so long, I forget things. Like common sense and good old-fashioned manners. This"—Tick held his arms out to either side— "midnight swim brought everything back. All those years as a cop kicked in, then left me as fast as it hit me. I'm not even sure I could protect you if something were to happen. Let's just walk back to the house, forget this ever happened."

Pete shook his head from side to side like a dog, his wet hair throwing water all over his brother. "No way. You're not taking the easy way out this time. You think something's going on at the place, so we're gonna find out exactly what it is. We look out for each other, Tick. No questions. Now let's go before this gets any mushier. Pull your dick out of the drawer, strap it on, and be the cop you've always been."

Tick couldn't help but laugh quietly, then he nodded and proceeded to walk toward *that thing.*

As he walked alongside his brother, Tick had a quickie heart-to-heart with himself. His blood pumped at the thought of getting involved with another investigation even though he thought he might've lost some of his nerve. Since he'd finished his last book and wasn't in any mad rush to start another, he figured he might as well see what he could find out about the place that had loomed in the background of his beach life for almost as long as he'd lived on Mango Key.

He thought about the two women, his neighbors, though they were only temporary. Kate, the quiet one. The one he had his eye on. Once he'd sobered up and started living again, if you could call what he'd been doing those first few years living, he'd met a woman in Miami who took care of his physical needs. Now, he wanted something more. A partner, a friend, and a lover. Could Kate be the one? He wasn't sure of anything just then. However, he'd made a mental decision, one he planned to stick to. Life was too short. From that second forward, he planned on living the rest of his life to the fullest. And deciding there was no time like the present, he walked a little faster, held his head a little higher, and flashed an ear-to-ear grin at no one.

Up ahead, he spied Bird waiting patiently on top of the iron gates at the front of the mansion. "Get the girls! Get the girls!" he squawked when he saw him and Pete.

"I think Bird is definitely male. He's always after you to 'get the girls,'" Pete said, as they made their way over to the gate.

"I think so, too," Tick added, before offering his arm to Bird. "When he says that, there's an urgency to it. Almost as though he's speaking about real people. You gettin' that?"

Pete laughed. "Yeah, there is an urgency to his words, but they all sound urgent, if you ask me. Maybe he's on a mission, and you just haven't figured out what it is."

"I don't know. I was planning to research parrots on the Internet but never got around to it. I just might do that someday soon. And I still want to brush up on my Spanish. He says a lot of words in his native language."

"You're sure of this?" Pete asked.

"No, I'm not sure of anything where that ball of feathers is concerned. Bird has mentioned Cuba, and that makes me think. It wouldn't surprise me in the least if Spanish wasn't the language he used to communicate with whoever owned him before he took up residence at my place. He started using it the other day when I asked him in Spanish if he understood what I was saying."

Amused, Pete offered, "A bilingual parrot."

"Yeah, I know it sounds nuts. Now, let's see if we can find a way inside this place and hope like hell no one sees us. Remember, stay behind me and do as I say."

"Or you'll kick my ass. I remember."

"Smart man," Tick said, grinning.

More than ready to finish what he'd started, Tick placed Bird on his shoulder and gave a slight push to the gate. When it offered no resistance, he was taken aback. Maybe this wasn't such a good idea after all. Someone must be inside for the gate to be open. At least he thought so, but reminded himself he'd never ventured this far, so the fact the gate was unlocked didn't really mean anything. After he glanced over his shoulder to make sure Pete was behind him, they quietly made their way past the gate.

Inside, in the center of the compound, was an Olympic-size swimming pool that looked as if it hadn't been used since it was built. Water covered the bottom. Algae skimmed the surface, the sides of the pool, and the steps leading down into it. Tick saw several frogs beneath its mucky surface and wondered how they managed to stay alive. Rainwater, no doubt.

Tick spotted an open door ahead. Touching the Glock he'd crammed in his shorts pocket at the last minute for reassurance, he walked slowly toward it. Using his foot, he pushed the door open, then out of habit jumped into a shooter's stance, with Bird still perched on his shoulder. Carefully, he went completely inside, looked from left to right, then behind the door. The room—he guessed it was meant to be used as a bedroom given its size—was empty except for several thin mattresses on the dirty tile floor. Tick motioned for Pete to step inside.

"What the hell is this? Summer camp for slumming?" Pete

nudged one of the mattresses with the tip of his bare foot. Dozens of cockroaches scurried out from beneath it, running every which way. "Oh, man, this is gross!"

Tick nodded but remained still.

"Let's see what else this mansion has to offer," Tick suggested.

Pete stayed close behind as they entered another room; though this room was much smaller than the other, there were more filthy thin mattresses scattered all over the floor. Two rooms across from them were identical. Dirty mattresses and bugs crawling everywhere.

"Get the girls! Get the girls!" Bird screeched.

"I thought something like this might be going on here, but I never took the time to check it out. Wasn't any of my business. Now I think I understand what Bird's been talking about."

Motioning to the mattresses, Pete asked, "What does this mean?"

Tick stiffened and put his index finger to his lips. Pete nodded. Cautiously, Tick tiptoed out of the fourth bedroom into the hallway. His heart hammered when he spied two figures silhouetted outside the window in the room across from the one he and Pete had just vacated.

Signaling to Pete to stay put, Tick removed his gun from the waistband of his shorts. With both hands directly in front of him, a firm grip on the gun, the pad of his index finger on the trigger, he clicked off the safety. Slowly, he crossed the hall, one step at a time, then he was in the room where he'd seen the two shadows looming outside seconds ago. Wary, he peered into the darkened corners, searching for someone or something. Nothing. He inched over to the window, eyes peering just above the windowsill so that he could see outside without being spotted by whomever he'd seen lurking in the yard. Again nothing. He moved away from the window and spied a small door on the north side of the room. Must be a closet. He inched his way across the room, his finger ready to pull the trigger at the first sign of movement. In his peripheral vision, he saw Pete step into the hall. Tick removed his left hand from the gun and motioned for Pete to stay put. Step after step brought him within inches of the closet door. Heart slamming in his chest, blood rushing in his ears, Tick saw a small crack in the door. Bird chose that moment to fly away while squawking, "I'm outta here!"

Using his foot to nudge the door all the way open, careful not to take his eyes off whatever lay beyond it, he gave the door a slight push with his foot. What he saw, cowering on the floor, almost knocked the breath out of him. He crammed the Glock in his waistband and stepped back.

"Pete, come in here."

Pete entered the room to stand beside his brother. He was as surprised as Tick was at what they were seeing.

"Damn, Tick! What—"

"Shhh, she's frightened."

A small girl, seemingly no more than ten or eleven, huddled on the floor inside the closet. Long dark hair tangled around her face, and clothes that were little more than rags barely covered her sticklike arms and legs. Though it was dark, Tick could see the fear in her eyes, thick tears streaming down her face. "I'm not going to hurt you," he said. When he saw the girl didn't seem to comprehend a word he said, he spoke softly, using words he thought she might understand.

"*No voy lastimas. No tenga miedo.*"

Big brown eyes stared up at him. Tick offered his hand to the girl, but she backed farther into the corner, her eyes downcast.

"*Mi nombre es* Patrick. *¿Cuál es su nombre?*"

"I thought you didn't speak Spanish," Pete said.

"I don't. Not much anyway."

Seeing the girl crouched on the floor reminded him of Emma, even though this girl appeared to be a few years older.

Images of Emma and Ricky overwhelmed him. Tears stung his eyes. He knuckled his eyes before the tears even had a chance to pool. He sniffed, then reached out to the child again, repeating what he'd just said. *"No voy lastimas. No tenga miedo."*

"Tick, what the hell are you saying to the kid? She looks like she's scared out of her mind."

"I'm telling her I'm not going to hurt her and not to be afraid."

"I don't think she understands." Pete knelt on the floor just outside the closet's small space. With her skittish behavior, the girl reminded him of the horses he used to ride in the rodeo. You had to earn their trust. Speaking in low, soft tones, Pete told the girl about his days with the ponies, and how he'd come to understand their every move. After several minutes, his soft words seemed to confirm to the child that he wouldn't cause her any harm. She held out her hand to Pete, and he gently pulled her upright and led her out of the closet.

Chapter 14

"I told you to stay down," Kate whispered to Sandy, who was standing outside the bedroom window peering inside, where all the activity was taking place.

"They're in there. And not only are they inside, they've found someone. I saw one of them carrying a body out of the room!" She gasped.

Squatting on her haunches, Kate managed to crab walk away from the window, dragging Sandy by her leg in order to keep her from peeping in the window. She didn't know who was inside and wasn't going to take any unnecessary chances.

Kate spoke sharply. "Shhh, be quiet. We don't know who's in there or what they're liable to do if they see us. Sit down! I need to think for a minute."

Sandy squatted next to her on the pebbled ground beneath the window. "I think I know who our visitors are. From what I could see, I swear it looked like our neighbors."

"It's pitch-black, Sandy! How could you tell?" Kate hissed.

"Unlike you, I pay attention to things. Like the shape of a man's ass, the width of his shoulders, the length of his hair. I'll lay odds our competition is our sexy hunkified neighbors. As a matter of fact, I'm so sure that's who's in there that I'm going inside to see what the hell they're up to." Without waiting for Kate to respond, Sandy jumped and ran around to the front of the mansion. Kate raced to catch up with her.

"What the hell do you think you're doing? You can't just walk in there like you want to borrow some sugar or something! This isn't like you. We're trained not to do this kind of thing without calling for backup. We're off the book, remember? I guess the heat is getting to you."

"For once, will you just trust me? Let me take the lead. If we weren't off the book, neither of us would be here," Sandy pleaded.

Not wanting to give in, but knowing Sandy wasn't dumb enough to do something totally stupid, she nodded. "If Jelly gives me any crap over this, it's your ass on the line, okay?"

"Yep. Now come on. I want to see what those two are up to." Sandy crawled in through the window they'd used earlier even though she knew there were doors that were unlocked. She never did anything the easy way. Without thinking, Kate followed her through the window. With Sandy in the lead, they sneaked down the long hallway where the four bedrooms were located without incident. *So far so good,* Kate thought. *We can do this,* she told herself over and over. Sandy was smart, plus Kate trusted her with her very life.

"Listen," Sandy said, coming to a stop outside one of the bedroom doors.

Kate strained, trying to hear the muffled voices coming from the bedroom. A few seconds passed, and she let out a sigh of relief. Sandy was right on the money. She heard the one who called himself Tick speaking in low tones. Both women jumped when their neighbor's parrot swooped through the doorway before them.

"I should've known that wacky bird had tagged along," Sandy hissed.

"I think it's a spy. Let's go inside, Sandy. You were right on the money. I want to know just what those two think they're doing, interfering in our investigation." Kate stepped inside the room, ready to chew out the brothers, when she stopped dead in her tracks. The redheaded brother, Pete, was holding a little girl. Kate thought she might be eight or nine—she wasn't sure of her age—but she was sure of one thing—the child was frightened, big-time. The parrot flew back into the room and sat on top of Tick's head. If this weren't a serious situation, Kate would've cracked up laughing at the sight.

"What are you guys doing here? This is private property," Kate said, all the while taking in the child, who looked as though she hadn't eaten a decent meal in forever and was scared out of her wits.

Tick took charge. "We could ask you two"—he motioned to Sandy standing in the doorway—"the same thing, but we know who you are and why you're here. Something tells me this isn't where we were supposed to meet for that late-night weenie roast."

"You would be correct. No fires being built tonight. For the record, we're here on official DEA business. Drug Enforcement Administration business," Kate snapped.

"Then I would say you're in the wrong place. There are no drugs here, or any to be found tonight," Tick shot back.

"That you know about," Kate shot back smartly.

She observed her temporary neighbor. Damn, he was a fine-looking specimen, she'd give him that. He was dressed in a ripped-up T-shirt and khaki shorts that had seen better days, and the dark hair matted to his head and a smoky five-o'clock shadow didn't distract from his good looks in the least. If anything, Kate thought the scruffy look made him appear sexier than ever. Add the parrot perched on top of his head, and he'd pass for a modern-day pirate. A slightly younger, sexier version of Johnny Depp. She did a quick mental run-through of her own dress, deciding it wasn't any worse than his. She smiled at her private thoughts.

"Nothing funny about it either," Tick offered in a low voice.

Kate looked at him as though he were one slice short of a loaf. "You're right, this isn't funny. Though I can't imagine why you'd think such a thing." Then she remembered her thoughts and how she'd smiled. Kate had the grace to blush, thankful no one could see, considering it was dark inside the abandoned mansion, the only light coming from the moon shining in through the window.

"I don't know about you three, but I think we need to get this child out of here before someone comes looking for her," Pete said.

"Of course," Sandy replied.

"Absolutely," Kate joined in. "I'll need to report this."

Sandy glanced at Pete, who was staring at Tick, who stared at Kate as though she were from another planet. One that hadn't been discovered. Yet.

"You can't report this now. We don't know who she is, where she came from, or why she's even here. For all you know, her parents could be out strolling the beach. What would they think if they returned, only to find their child had been carried off by . . . strangers?"

Kate thought he had a point, but the odds of that actually coming to pass were slim to none. "We all know that's highly unlikely. Why don't you ask her?"

"She's scared, and I don't know if she understands English. Tick tried speaking to her in his limited Spanish, and she didn't respond. As much as I hate to agree with the ol' bro, I think he's dead on the money this time." Pete shifted the weight of the small girl to his opposite shoulder.

"Let's get her out of here; then we can decide what to do. That fair enough?" Sandy suggested. In her native tongue, Sandy spoke in soft tones to the child, but the child didn't respond. Later, when they had a plan of sorts, she would try to talk to the frightened little girl. For the moment, it was enough that she was safe.

Agreeing this was best for now, they hurried out of the compound and back to the beach. Tick grabbed the wet suits, along with the rest of their gear. As it was almost impossible to carry all the equipment without dropping it, Kate took one of the wet suits from him and handed Sandy the snorkels and masks. "I don't even want to know why this stuff is here. I assume it belongs to you two?" Kate said, as they all walked away from the beach in front of the compound toward Tick's place.

Tick explained. "We were snorkeling after the storm. Pete and I have been wondering what's going on here. I've jogged in this area at night and heard . . . things. The Coast Guard does its nightly cruise-by regularly. They haven't reported their suspicions to me, not that they'd have a reason to. Since you're DEA, what's your take on it? I assume you were sent here to observe that place." Tick knew he sounded like a smart-ass whose turf had been invaded. Right now he didn't care. He just wanted to get the kid to safety and let the hot-bodied DEA agents do their thing.

"You assume correctly," Kate said, her voice firm and professional. "I'm not at liberty to discuss the details."

Mockingly, Tick supplied, "Of course you aren't."

"And if I did, I'd have to kill you," Kate said, as she rolled her eyes, glad for the darkness. When they finally arrived at the beach in front of the house on stilts, Pete shifted the girl to a more comfortable position before climbing the stairs. Looking over his shoulder, he called out, "Come inside, ladies. I think we're going to need your help. This little one smells like she hasn't had a good scrubbing in a while. I'm sure that you can make her bathing experience comfortable. If you're up to it, that is."

The last thing Kate wanted was another trip to her neighbor's house, but Pete had a point. None of them knew what the child had experienced. Being stripped down to her bare skin by two strange men was bound to cause the poor kid even more trauma.

Sandy acknowledged Kate's reluctance with a raised brow. Kate nodded. "We really don't have much choice."

"Well, I for one would bathe an alligator just to get close to the one named Pete. This has worked to our advantage for sure," Sandy whispered.

"Sandy, that's a terrible thought!" But Kate couldn't stop herself from smiling. Leave it to Sandy to see the bright side of any situation. One more reason they were such good friends.

Sandy leaned close, whispering in her ear, "It's true, and you know it. You shouldn't be so snippy with Tick either. I think he's interested in you. Don't screw things up before you even get a chance to know the guy. He is hot, don't you think?"

"Shhh," Kate whispered.

When he reached the top of the stairs, Tick opened the door and stood aside so Pete could carry the girl in. Kate and Sandy trailed behind him.

With a gentleness that surprised Kate, Pete placed the child on the sofa, tucking a throw blanket over her bare legs. She flinched when he tucked the cover beneath her chin. Kate's heart melted. Knowing that the child was beyond frightened and couldn't or wouldn't communicate with them, Kate sat next to her on the small sofa. Doelike eyes hesitantly gazed up at her. Kate smiled, wanting to reassure the child that she meant no harm.

"What's your name?" Kate asked.

The girl looked at Pete, then back at Kate.

"Rosita." She spoke clearly, though her voice was soft, quiet, as though she were used to whispering.

Tick, Pete, and Sandy looked at the child, then at Kate, all curious, wondering what it was about *her* that the girl trusted.

She'd been the one to linger in the background, allowing Pete and Tick the full responsibility for the girl since they'd found her. She had no experience with kids but knew that if she were in the same situation, in a house full of strangers, Kate would want to be treated in a normal way.

Smiling, Kate said, "Rosita. That's a beautiful name. It kinda rolls off your tongue."

A trace of a smile lifted the corner of Rosita's full lips. "Thank you." Again she spoke in a whisper.

Not knowing why the sudden change and unwilling to test the waters, Kate looked at Tick. "I bet Rosita would like something to eat and drink." She lifted her brow in question, giving him the opportunity to play host to his new houseguest.

"Of course. I . . . uh," Tick was at a loss for words.

"Bacon and eggs! Bacon and eggs!" Bird flew into the kitchen, landing on the back of a kitchen chair.

Rosita practically jumped onto Kate's lap, her big brown eyes full of fear.

"Can you get rid of him?" Kate asked without a trace of what she felt for the feathered creature. She didn't want Rosita to feel threatened by her voice any more than she wanted her to be frightened of Bird, who was obnoxious at the best of times.

Tick raked a hand through his plastered-down hair. "Sure. Bird, it's time to go to bed. Go."

Bird did as commanded, flying into the bathroom and settling on the shower-curtain rod.

"He's well behaved when he chooses," Tick offered.

"About that bacon and eggs. It sounds delicious. I bet Rosita wouldn't mind having an early breakfast." It was after two in the morning. Kate didn't know about the others, but she was starving and knew it had been a while since the child had eaten. Her eyes lit up like a Christmas tree when Kate mentioned bacon and eggs.

"Come on, Pete. You can help me cook, while our neighbors help Rosita with her shower," Tick said.

Kate nodded in agreement. "Great idea. A T-shirt and a pair of boxers would be great, that is if you have any. Clean ones."

"We have washing machines out here on this here island," Tick joked.

"Of course you do. I'm sorry, I didn't mean to imply that you didn't. I'm tired, and, frankly, I could use a hot meal myself. We have nothing but a microwave over at the shell. If I see another Lean Cuisine, I'll croak." She smiled, a genuine smile for the first time that night. When her host smiled back, her heart fluttered against her chest like Bird's wings. Damn, he was handsome. A little rough, but Kate liked that. A lover of pretty-boy types she was not. Which made her think of Tyler. The ass kisser.

"Did I say something wrong?" Tick asked.

"No, why?"

"You went from one hundred percent smile to frown in point-zero seconds."

"A bad taste in my mouth, that's all," Kate said, suddenly wanting to tell him all about Tyler. How she'd kicked his ass and what a waste of humanity he was, but the timing was off. They had Rosita to consider now.

"I'll get the clothes."

"Thanks."

Kate spoke to Rosita as though the incident with Bird had never happened. "Are you okay with a shower before we eat?" She wanted her to understand that no one would force her to do anything she wasn't comfortable with.

Rosita looked down at her clothes, which were nothing more than sun-bleached rags.

"Mr. . . . Tick has offered to lend you a T-shirt and boxers for the night, are you okay with that?" Not knowing what the child had been through and if the simple act of showering and changing into fresh clothes would have an effect on her, Kate made a mental list of things she and Sandy had that might be more suitable for the child, things that would make her feel more comfortable. Like a hairbrush and underwear that would be a bit big, but they'd surely fit better than Tick's.

"Yes, ma'am."

Whoa, Kate thought. This was the most polite kid she'd ever encountered. She caught Sandy's gaze. "Why don't you run over to the shell and get that little blue nightgown that's too small for me, and maybe some girly underthings for Rosita. And a hairbrush with one of those scrunchies for her hair. Bring the baby lotion, too."

Sandy caught on. "Great idea. By the time you're finished with your shower," she said to Rosita, "I'll be back."

Tick stepped into the small living area holding a tattered red shirt and silk boxers with fish on them. Kate raised her brow in question. "Nice. Uh . . . I mean, we're going to get her some girl things. If it's okay." Why did she say that? Of course it was okay.

"Good idea. Now"—he clapped his hands together—"if you'll follow me, I'll show you the bathroom. I've told Bird to go into the kitchen. There's a bit of . . . well, Bird sleeps on the shower rod. He uses the tub as a toilet sometimes. I cleaned it, but there might be a bit of . . . well, you get the picture."

Tick let Bird poop in the shower; yeah, Kate got it. "We'll watch our step," she said, as he closed the door.

With a caring touch, Kate brushed her hand through Rosita's snarled hair. "We'll get you cleaned up in no time, then we can have that bacon and eggs. Deal?"

Rosita nodded.

Inside the small bathroom, Kate helped her out of her raggedy clothes. She turned the shower on, adjusting the water to a comfortable temperature. She found a clean towel and washcloth and placed them on the back of the toilet tank, along with a fresh bar of Ivory soap and a trial-size bottle of dandruff shampoo. Probably a good idea, she thought, as she helped Rosita into the shower. She gave her the soap and shampoo and a thick pink washcloth, then pulled the shower curtain aside, allowing the child a bit of privacy even though she seemed completely comfortable undressing with Kate in the room. Kate swore she heard humming. *Poor thing, how long has it been since she showered and had a decent meal? In good time*, she told herself. *In good time.* If and when she found out who left this child out in the middle of nowhere, practically naked and starving, she promised herself she would kick ass and take names later.

Chapter 15

Tyler jolted awake at the sound of his cell phone buzzing on the night table next to him. Looking at the screen, he cringed when he saw UNKNOWN CALLER, UNKNOWN NUMBER. The blackmailer. He pushed the green button.

"What do you want? I told you I wasn't dealing! Are you . . . stupid or what?" Tyler spit into the phone, then wished he hadn't. Where this newfound set of balls came from he hadn't a clue. Must be the incognito thing.

The voice over the phone actually chuckled. "We're getting brave now, aren't we?"

Tyler felt his hands start to shake as he raced to the window to see if his blackmailer was watching him from afar. With only a partial view of the parking lot and one side of the beach, he couldn't be one hundred percent sure who was who. Locals, tourists, beach bums? Drunks and beach bums at this hour of the night . . . or morning.

"Look." Tyler turned away from the window, yanking the blinds shut. He started pacing, something he did when he was nervous. Right now he was past nervous. "I warned you not to call me again unless you have something to show me, something to let me know exactly what it is I'm buying, or rather, what I'm being blackmailed for. I know there's activity on Mango Key; what the hell do you think I'm here for? It sure as hell isn't the weather. I sincerely hope you've got something better than that, Mr. No Name Caller, because if not, I'm going to hang up, and you can shove whatever information you think you have straight up your ass! Where the hell are you? How is it you know every move I make?" Tyler demanded, again amazed by his sudden gutsiness.

More laughter. "Really, Agent Tyler, I'm happy to hear you and your cowardly ways have parted. In case you're curious, I don't like dealing with pansy asses. And to answer your question, it doesn't matter where I am. I know what you're doing and when you're doing it, but you've already figured that out. Smart boy, just like Daddy says."

If only he could place the voice! He *knew* he'd heard it before and was sure his blackmailer was male. He needed to arrange a meeting. Yes. That's exactly what he would do. A plan began to form.

Clearing his throat, Tyler spoke loudly and clearly into the phone. "First, leave my father out of this! He's unaware of my intentions." *Hell,* Tyler thought, *I'm unaware of my intentions.* He raked a hand through his ever-thinning hair. "Okay, let's say I've suddenly had a change of heart. I want to meet you in a place where we can exchange information. I'll call my bank and have the money wired to a bank in Key West. If the information you have is really worth a hundred grand, then all you have to do is follow me to the bank, where the money will be placed in your hands. Then we walk away, forget we ever met. Deal?"

Tyler felt proud of himself. He should have thought of this days ago. Plus, he really wanted this blackmail scheme behind him since he wanted to be the agent to bring down the house on Mango Key. If he could drag Jellard, Rush, and Martin down at the same time, then more power to him. Yes! He raised his fist high in the air. He could just see the smile on his father's face.

When the caller didn't respond, Tyler felt a moment of

panic. For all he knew, this blackmailer could have his head in his sights ready to blow him to hell and back. "Are you listening to me?" Tyler heard the fear in his voice. He felt tears well up and prayed he wasn't about to lose control of his bladder, something he'd done on more than one occasion.

"Actually, I think that's a good idea." The caller finally spoke, and Tyler's relief was palpable. He knew the bastard was toying with him. Why couldn't he have Rush's nerve or Jacobson's smarts?

"Someplace public. No meetings in the middle of nowhere. I won't go for that. And I want to know what this big secret is of mine you claim to have," Tyler said. He wasn't about to be more of a sitting duck than he already was.

"Of course not, I wouldn't expect you to. I'll tell you everything I know tonight at Sloppy Joe's. Eight o'clock."

"Wait! No, I can't—"

"Be there," the caller said, and disconnected.

Damn it to hell! He'd really screwed up now. Tonight was his big night. The night he was to meet Nancy Holliday at Sloppy Joe's. Positive that his blackmailer knew of his plans with the woman, the only question was how? Was Nancy Holliday his informant? Had their meeting in the traffic jam been prearranged? He didn't see how, but he couldn't pass it off as a complete coincidence either. His father always said there was no such thing as coincidence. He finally believed him.

Tyler glanced at the time. Four in the morning. The blackmailer must be an early riser or a late sleeper. He told himself none of this mattered, but it did. It was information like this that made a good agent. Maybe if he'd figured that out sooner rather than later, he wouldn't be about to be cashiered out of the DEA. Maybe if he hadn't bullied his fellow agents around and taken credit for their successes, he'd have a friend, someone who would help him dig his way out of the mess he'd gotten himself into.

Knowing he'd never get back to sleep and not caring because his usual six o'clock internal alarm would kick in the minute he drifted off, he opted to start the day. There was a lot to do before tonight's meeting.

First, he took a long, hot shower and started to think about getting a cup of coffee. The Southernmost Point Guest House didn't start serving until six, and he decided that he wasn't about to wait that long. He could go to the 7-Eleven up the street, but he really didn't relish the idea. So once he'd dressed in his Florida tourist garb, he decided that after forty years, it was high time he learned to make a pot of coffee.

His room had a minikitchen equipped with a coffeemaker, toaster oven, and microwave, plus a small refrigerator. Taking a bottle of Evian water from the fridge—there was no way he'd put Florida tap water in his body—he poured two entire bottles in the area indicated on the coffeemaker, then stacked the prefilled coffee filter in the basket, closed the back, and pushed the start button. How easy was that? Dad would be proud of him now. A month shy of his forty-first birthday, and he'd just made his very first pot of coffee. And without any help from the housemaid.

And isn't this just dandy? he thought. *No one gives a flying fluke if I made coffee or not.* He felt like calling his mother and asking her why she'd allowed his father to screw up his life, why she hadn't stood up to him. Maybe if she had, he wouldn't be such a milksop. Maybe . . . maybe nothing. It was what it was, and there was no getting around it. He was a chicken-shit coward, and everyone that mattered knew it. Except Nancy Holliday. Of course, if she showed up at Sloppy Joe's tonight and saw him, she would soon learn that he wasn't worth wasting her time on.

Tyler poured coffee into a cardboard cup, then added a packet of powdered creamer and two packs of sugar. He took a sip. Not bad. He contemplated his day as he sipped the hot brew.

First, he wanted to make an unannounced visit to the cop, see if he was on the up and up. If he knew anything about the goings-on at the compound at the tip of Mango Key, Tyler would demand that he turn over the information. If not, he'd pump him for info about his neighbors. Tyler knew the cop had to be aware that there were two good-looking women occupying that aluminum hut. He smiled.

The cop would also be told that he, Special Agent Lawrence Tyler, was in a position to stop them from doing whatever it was they were doing on Mango Key. (True, he knew that he couldn't fire them since they had never been rehired. His authority over Jellard might be more apparent than real, but there was no way that even Jellard could put them on the payroll without Tyler having been informed.) But the cop wouldn't care any more than his father did. The governor only liked to talk about his son in terms of where he was employed, not his actual duties. *Thank God for small favors*, he thought.

After he left the cop, Tyler would make a special visit to Rush and Martin to give them what for. He couldn't wait to see the looks on their faces when they answered the door.

Yes, today might be a good day after all.

Kate tucked the blanket securely beneath Rosita. *Poor kid*, she thought, as she turned off the light. The girl had eaten so much she'd fallen asleep within minutes of closing her eyes. Tick had been gracious enough to offer the child his bed for the night. Kate entered the kitchen, where a goggle-eyed Sandy sat staring at Pete while he told stories of his days in the rodeo. Tick, his back to the pair, stood at the sink, rinsing their dishes and placing them in the dishwasher.

Pete stopped talking when Kate sat down across from him.

"Unbelievable. She went to sleep almost immediately, hardly uttered another word. She seems so . . . mature. I did manage to ask her age before she drifted off. She said she was eighteen. It was all I could do to keep my jaw from dropping. I'm sure she was told if asked to say she was eighteen. I think she's around ten or eleven. Poor child, I can only imagine what she's had to endure. I wonder when she'll be missed and by whom. Something tells me it won't be a worried mom and dad."

Tick dried his hands on a kitchen towel, then sat next to Kate. "When I saw those mattresses scattered around, I knew something other than drug runners had occupied the place. A few weeks ago, when I was jogging, I thought I heard crying but didn't pay too much attention, told myself it was probably some wild animal. I've heard voices in the past and never given it too much thought. Now I know it might've been a young girl or girls. I don't think our Rosita has been there for weeks, at least I hope not. I can't believe I've been so stupid, so self-centered that I didn't see what was really happening at that place."

"Human trafficking isn't something your neighbors would advertise," Sandy pointed out kindly. "At this point, we're not even sure that's what's happening," she added. "And aren't you busy writing books and movie scripts?"

Tick blushed. "Yes, but you'd think as a former police detective, I would be aware of these things going on. I've been so immersed in my own little world the past eight years that I truly haven't paid attention to anything except my own needs."

Pete spoke up then. "Look, Tick, don't be so hard on yourself. We're not positive that's what's going on. I've been here, too, don't forget."

Kate chimed in. "That's why we're here. To investigate. As soon as the sun's up, I'm going to call Jelly. He's the guy who arranged for us to be here. If we can get Rosita to talk, she may help solve this. For now, I think it's best to let her sleep. Speaking of sleep, I think I'll head back to the shell for a bit of sleep and a shower."

She looked at the clock on the stove. After four. She'd be lucky to sleep for an hour. Years as an agent had taught her to grab a few minutes of sleep whenever the opportunity presented itself because one never knew when the chance to sleep might come around again.

Reluctantly, Sandy stood up, too. "Yeah, I guess I better try for a bit of shut-eye myself. I get these terrible bags beneath my eyes when I don't get enough sleep."

Tick and Pete followed them to the door. "We'll have coffee on by seven if you're interested," Pete called out to them when they reached the bottom of the steps.

Sandy waved. "I can't wait!"

Kate smacked her hand down. "Lord have mercy! Would you just stop for one minute. You're acting too eager, if you ask me. And remember, we're working, *Sandra. Working.* It'd be best to remember that."

"I don't see anything wrong with us coming over for coffee. Theirs was a sight better than that instant stuff we've been nuking in the microwave. Besides, I think you should be there when Rosita wakes up. She might be willing to talk to you after a good night's rest and a healthy breakfast."

"I'm sure you're right. Now, let's get inside and get some sleep. I, for one, can't run on adrenaline forever."

"Whatever, you're a party pooper," Sandy teased.

Fifteen minutes later, Kate and Sandy were lying on their cots with the air conditioner cranked as high as it would go and two oscillating fans blowing warm air across the room.

In a sleepy voice, Sandy said, "I think I'm going to move to Alaska when this gig's up."

"Then you'll be begging for heat. Good night, Sandra."

"Night," came the reply.

Two and a half hours later, Tick readied the coffee while Pete showered. He'd spent the past couple of hours on the small sofa and wanted to take a run on the beach to stretch his stiff muscles but decided it could wait until later. He had the little girl to think about, which made him think of Emma and Ricky. God how he missed those two. They had been the core of his existence, the reason he got up every day. Gone before they'd even had a chance at a taste of what life had to offer. Before he gave in to the memories and the depression that usually followed, he thought about the girl sleeping in his room.

Determined not to let something equally horrifying ruin Rosita's life, Tick considered asking Kate if he could join their investigation. Off the record, of course. It was time he got back into the loop of life. He allowed himself a mental picture of Sally cheering him on, giving him a high five. She wouldn't want him pining away the way he had been for the past eight years. Nor would Emma or Ricky.

Wearing nothing but a towel, Pete strode into the mini-kitchen and poured himself a cup of coffee before sitting down at the breakfast table. "Coffee smells good."

"I hope you plan on getting dressed. We have company, remember?"

"Yes, I remember. I just needed a caffeine fix, bro. Cut me some slack."

"You get any sleep?" Tick asked, pouring a cup for himself.

"Not much. I couldn't stop fantasizing about the neighbors," Pete said, smiling into his cup.

"Neighbors as in plural?" Tick felt a sharp pang of jealousy. Pete didn't have any business dreaming about *both* of their neighbors.

"Yep, bro, that's what I said. Though I think the serious one, Kate, has the hots for you. She kept staring at you when you weren't looking."

"Really? You saw her?"

"With my two very own eyes. For your info, I don't have any interest in her whatsoever, so if you want, she's all yours."

"Shit, Pete, you make her sound like leftovers!" Tick shook his head and got up to refill his cup. Something told him he was going to need all the energy he could muster even though the day was still young.

A tapping at the door sent Pete running for cover. Tick raked a hand through his hair, wishing he'd showered, but it would just have to wait.

Kate and Sandy stood on his minuscule porch, both looking as though they could use a java jump start. He opened the door and stepped aside.

"Good morning, ladies."

"It is, isn't it?" Sandy observed as she immediately headed for the kitchen, where she made herself at home by grabbing two cups and filling them with coffee. She handed a mug to Kate. "Our girl still sleeping?" she asked after she'd taken a sip.

"Sound as a rock; I checked on her when I got up. I swear she was smiling. I can't imagine why she'd smile under the circumstances, but it did my heart good." *Did I really say that? It did my heart good. I sound like a character in one of my novels.*

"Morning, Tick." Kate offered up a huge grin to her host. "Let's let her sleep a while longer. When she wakes up, I'd like to question her before I call Jelly."

Tick felt like jumping to the moon and back. Kate smiled at him like she meant it, like there was something more to come. Hot damn, if Pete wasn't right about this woman! Telling himself she wouldn't have smiled at him had she not been a wee bit interested, he quickly excused himself. "I'll leave you two alone while I take a quick rinse. There's more coffee. There are mangoes, bagels, and eggs in the fridge if you're hungry."

"I, for one, am starving. I'll start breakfast while you do your thing." Sandy made quick work out of slicing several mangoes, toasting bagels and placing them on two plates, then scrambling a dozen eggs. She scrounged around until she found paper plates, napkins, and plastic forks in the cupboard above the sink.

"If I didn't know better, I'd think you've been here before," Kate said, getting up to refill her cup. "You're comfortable here."

Sandy laughed. "I am, aren't I? Wonder what that means?"

"That you'll have dinner with me?" Pete declared as he stepped into the kitchen dressed in navy shorts and a yellow polo shirt with an alligator emblem on the top left of the shirt, his wet hair slicked back like a first-grader on picture day.

"I don't think so. I'm working, remember? I can't just up and take off to Key West or wherever for dinner just because . . . just because. Right, Kate?"

"No, actually you can go to dinner with Pete. I'm okay with watching the compound. I bet Tick would join me if I asked him to." Jelly would have her ass for this, but it would give Sandy a much-needed break. If she were completely truthful, it would also give her some time alone with Tick. That is, if he was game enough to join their team, on the QT, of course.

"Yeah, he would. He probably won't say anything, him being such a hermit all these years, but he really could use some female companionship. He didn't come right out and say it, but I'm his brother, I'll say it for him. I know these things."

Kate had the grace to blush. Sandy laughed until tears streaked her cheeks. "I do believe you've embarrassed Kate. She's never been very composed around men, just so you know. Not that experienced, either. You might want to mention that to your brother. I'd hate to see him take advantage of her, especially since he's in the need of some female companionship."

"I didn't mean that. I said he needs . . ."

"You'd better zip it up while you're ahead, little brother. I mean it." Tick had emerged from the shower smelling like Ivory soap and Old Spice.

"Would you all please stop?" Kate grinned.

"I second that. I don't need my little brother to . . . never mind." Tick gave Pete a scathing look that would surely kill if he stared a second longer. "I think I should check on my guest. It's about time she woke up," Tick said.

"I'll go to bed with you," Kate blurted. To cover her faux pas, she quickly followed Tick to his bedroom before Sandy or Pete had a chance to offer up another one of their unsolicited comments.

Rosita was wide awake and looking at the remote control in her hand like it was a foreign object. Kate guessed it was highly possible, given the appalling circumstances in which they'd found her, that she hadn't a clue what the contraption was or what it was used for.

Kate made her way across the room to the king-size bed. Being in such intimate surroundings with Tick made her heart race. She plastered a bright smile on her face, then sat on the edge of the bed next to the child. "Morning, Rosita. I hope you slept well."

She nodded, then carefully placed the remote on the nightstand. Kate observed her. Rosita appeared to be frightened. "I came to see if you're hungry." At the mention of food, the little girl's eyes sparkled like diamonds.

Tick remained in the doorway, shifting from one foot to the other. "Yeah, we've got breakfast."

Lame, Kate thought, then smiled. He acted almost as though he was embarrassed to be in his bedroom with her. She visualized him standing in the doorway, totally nude, and grinned again, only this time it caused butterflies in her stomach and her heart to race a bit faster than normal. Catching him staring at her, she quickly directed her attention to Rosita. "Sandy and I looked through our clothes, and we picked out a few things that might fit you until we can get you some new clothes. Want to come see?"

Brown eyes glowing, Rosita jumped to the floor, then expertly made up the bed as though she'd been doing this her entire life. *Sad,* Kate thought. If her suspicions were true, and there was human trafficking or *slavery* going down at that compound, it was likely that poor Rosita had been farmed out to work in a hotel or as a maid at a private residence. Exactly how the compound fit into the scheme of things she'd figure out soon enough. Her gut instinct clicked in, telling her she was right on the money, but she'd need more evidence than gut instinct.

If so, then who is behind it all? Who would take a child of no more than ten or eleven and treat her like a slave? Kate didn't know. But when she found out, she promised herself, she would personally see that they were prosecuted to the fullest extent of the law no matter how many favors she had to call in.

Chapter 16

They'd just finished their breakfast and were preparing to sit down to speak with Rosita, who was busily attacking her plate of eggs and bagels, when a loud knock on the door surprised them.

"You expecting more company?" Pete asked Tick.

Tick cast a wary glance at the door. "No. Either of you?" He glanced at Kate and Sandy.

"If we were, they wouldn't come here," Sandy offered.

More loud knocking, Pete went to the door and yanked it open. "What can I do for you?" he asked.

"You can tell those two . . . brownnosers that their superior wants to have a word with them. Now, as in pronto," Lawrence Tyler demanded.

When Kate heard the familiar voice, she catapulted to the door like her feet had springs mounted on them. She practically shoved Pete aside. "What the hell do you mean coming here? You're way out of line, *Lawrence*," Kate fumed. *How dare this self-righteous jerk question my whereabouts!*

"Apparently you've forgotten who's in charge, *Miss Rush*. If you and your colleague will step outside, I'll make this as painless as possible. I also want to speak to the cop when I'm finished with you two. Alone."

Kate doubled her hand in a fist as she prepared to knock

the smug look off her *former* superior's face. Sandy reached her just in time. "He's not worth it, Kate," she advised.

"Maybe not to you, but he sure as hell is to me. What's your business, *Larry?* Did big Daddy-o send you on a mission, or is this another of your fishing expeditions? By the way, next time you take that piece-of-crap boat out fishing, get some bait and a better book. Maybe one of Mr. Kelly's novels would be more entertaining."

Tick and Pete had told them about seeing a man in a boat spying on them. Kate had been right to send Sandy somersaulting on the beach. Blood rushed to her head as she stared at her *former* superior. She forced herself to step back and take a deep breath to gain control over the almost overpowering desire to strike out at him. Sandy was right. This idiot wasn't worth busting her knuckles over. But if he pushed again, next time she wouldn't stop to think before slugging him right upside his pretty-boy head.

"You're asking for complete and total dismissal, *Miss Rush.*"

Kate stepped outside onto the small front porch, not bothering to close the door behind her. Let them all hear what a coward her *former* superior was.

Shoving her finger in Tyler's face, she said, "Look, *Lawrence,* we both know you've got no business here. Sandy and I are no longer employees of the DEA, as you know full well. So what makes you think you have any business confronting us and claiming to be our superior in an organization to which we do not belong? If you want to ask us anything, I suggest you get a warrant that entitles you to ask questions. Perhaps you would like to explain to a judge why you think we are material witnesses to some crime you are investigating. Or would you prefer to get an arrest warrant for some crime we have presumably committed?

"And if you came here to rub the fact that we are no longer with the DEA in our faces, you shouldn't have wasted your time. We no longer have the slightest desire to associate with a bunch of . . . cowards and bullies. Which, judging from your high status in the DEA, it seems reasonable to guess members of that formerly elite organization have come to. If you're smart—whoops, scratch that—we all know that's not possible.

"So, before I decide to kick your ass a second time, *Mr. Special Agent Tyler,* I suggest you stick that pretty little head of yours between your legs and run for cover. You've done that for most of your career, so it should be very easy for you to do it now." Kate inched so close to Tyler's face, their noses almost touched. "You gettin' this, *Lawrence?*"

Tyler had the good sense to step back from Kate's intense glare and balled-up fists. In so doing, he lost his footing, which caused him to fall backward. Before he fell to the sandy area below, he managed to grab onto the porch railing. If Kate hadn't been so angry, she would've doubled over in a fit of laughter. From the sounds coming from the kitchen, neither Tick nor Pete felt any urge to restrain himself. Kate smiled.

Tyler brushed imaginary dirt from his shorts. "You're going to regret those words, *Miss Rush.* I need to speak to the cop. If he's smart, he'll give me the answers I'm looking for." Tyler stared back at Kate. For a split second, she thought he looked as though he was going to apologize. But if so, he had had a change of heart because he glared at her as though she were nothing more than dirt beneath his finger-nails. Normal behavior for the snobbish wimp.

Tick chose that moment to make an appearance. "I'm the cop you're looking for. Apparently, I'm smarter than some." Standing next to Kate, he placed a protective arm around her. "What do you want?" he asked Tyler, none too kindly.

Special Agent Tyler stood tall, shoulders back. He cleared his throat, then looked Tick directly in the eye. "This is none of your business."

In a tone so menacing it caused Kate to glance up at Tick just to make sure it was really his voice she heard as he spoke to his unwelcome visitor, he said, "If in addition to being exceedingly ill-mannered, you are also hard of hearing, let me repeat myself. I'm the cop to whom you referred. I heard you wanted to talk to me. Now state your business or get the fuck off my property.

"If you are very polite about it, and I'm of a mind to do so, I might give you some answers. If not, then you'll need to get one of those warrants Miss Rush spoke of. And if you decide to do that, something tells me you're not going to like my way of resolving this situation one bit," Tick proclaimed. "You see, I seriously doubt that you have any standing to get any warrants at all. In fact, your attitude tells me that you are desperate for some reason."

Now that his bluff had been called, Tyler was back in coward mode, and his gaze dropped to his feet, then back to Kate. "*Miss Rush,* this isn't going to bode well for you at all, trust me. When—"

"Stop!" Tick interjected in a firm voice, not allowing Tyler to continue. "Simply state what it is you came to say. You will *not* speak disrespectfully to Miss Rush in my presence. Are we clear on that, *Larry,* or do I need to clarify it for you?"

Kate's heart sang and did a one-handed cartwheel. She *really* liked Tick Kelly. A man's man for sure, standing up for her when he barely knew her. Sandy'd been right on the money again. He must like *something* about her. Why else would he come to her defense? For a split second, Kate almost felt sorry for Tyler. The big coward. Fortunately, the feeling passed as quickly as it came.

With an unusual air of bravado, Tyler taunted, "It's obvious you're sleeping with her, so there is really nothing to clarify."

Tick grabbed Tyler by his shirt collar and yanked him so

high he had to stand on his tippy toes. "Did you not understand a word I said? You really must be as stupid as you look." He observed Tyler's hot pink and orange shirt. "Now, tell *former* Agent Rush you're sorry, or I won't be responsible for my actions. Are you gettin' this, *Larry?*" Tick asked before relinquishing his grip.

Tyler's face turned a dozen shades of red. Before he had a chance to reply, Bird soared through the front door and planted himself on top of Tyler's head. The beast made quick work of pecking at the tender bald spot the hapless DEA agent had tried in vain to hide with a slicked-back combover. His hands flew in every direction as he swatted at Bird.

"Bullshit! Bullshit!" Bird screeched, buzzing around Tyler's head like a swarm of angry bees.

Kate gaped at the comical display, then, before she could stop herself, began to giggle uncontrollably. Tick caught on, and the two of them almost forgot their anger at their unwelcome intruder. Tears filled Kate's eyes as she watched Bird cut Mr. Special Agent Lawrence Tyler down to size. *In Bird talk, Tyler would be hummingbird size,* Kate thought, which caused her to laugh even harder.

Through his laughter, Tick finally managed to shout, "Stop it, Bird. Leave the man alone." On command, Bird's incessant pecking stopped, and he flew to his perch on Tick's shoulder. Then, apparently thinking better of it, he zoomed back, landing on top of Tyler's head, the agent's normally groomed hair now resembling a bird's nest. Roosting in the tangle of thinning black hair, Bird proceeded to leave a healthy dollop of bird droppings right on top of Tyler's head before resuming his position on Tick's shoulder.

Through her laughter, Kate managed to say, "You meant *bird*shit, right, Bird?"

Never in all the years she'd known Tyler had she ever seen him so . . . discomfited.

Using the hem of his brightly colored shirt, Tyler mopped

Bird's surprise gift off the top of his head. His face had turned so red, Kate feared he would suffer a stroke or a heart attack. *It'd serve him right*, she thought, then quickly admonished herself. While she didn't like the man one bit, she truly did not wish him dead. Not today, anyway, here on Tick's porch.

"I'm not going to allow you to leave until you've apologized to Ms. Rush," Tick stated firmly.

Tyler stared angrily at them. "I can't believe you two! Here I am, an officer of the law, your . . . animal uses my head as a toilet, and you expect me to apologize to a woman I detest? *I don't think so!*"

Tick took a step forward, Tyler a step backward. He grabbed the porch railing for support. "Kate Rush, you *are* a bitch, no matter what anyone else thinks. I bet you're PMS-ing again. I'm sorry, okay? Now there, are you happy?"

Tick stepped to the edge of the porch before grabbing hold of the arm Tyler had wrapped around the railing. He peeled his fingers back one at a time. "This is getting monotonous, Special Agent Tyler. She's not a bitch, and I for one don't accept your half-assed apology. Now, either come up with something more sincere, or I will personally call your superior myself. If that doesn't produce the desired results, which is a proper and *sincere* apology to Ms. Rush, then after I phone the governor and Florida's two senators, I will personally call the administrator of the DEA, whom I just happen to have known long before he took the position. Something tells me he wouldn't like your treating Miss Rush disrespectfully."

Hands on her hips, foot tapping at a mind-boggling rate of speed, Kate said impatiently, "It's okay, Tick. He doesn't need to apologize further. I won't accept it anyway. Lawrence, why don't you say what it is you really want, so the rest of us can get on with our day. You've wasted too much of my time already."

Deciding it was in his best interest to be compliant, at least for the moment, Tyler held both hands up in defense. "Okay, Rush. You win this time, but I won't forget. You owe me."

Kate rolled her eyes. "Get a grip, Tyler. I don't owe you squat." She thought about Bird and his actions. It was all she could do to control herself when she recalled the look on Tyler's face as Bird did his thing.

"I think we all can agree Bird took care of whatever any of us owed Special Agent Tyler," Tick said to Kate, a smirk on his face.

"Yeah, we can," Kate said, then turned her attention back to Tyler. "Explain why you're still here?"

As he had no other choice, Tyler decided to spill his guts. He'd already been humiliated to the nth degree. What would a little more suffering matter? All he wanted was to state his business and get the hell out of here. "All those months ago, when you were assigned to that stakeout, I . . . something was going down at that abandoned mansion at the tip of Mango Key. My informant's information wasn't on the money."

"No kidding," Kate said. "I'm listening."

"This is off the record, and if anyone finds out I'm telling you this—" He stopped, realizing it wouldn't matter who found out. His days were numbered anyway. "Forget I said that. Whatever's going down there is big. As in promote-to-the-top big. Don't ask how I know this because I won't tell you. I know you and Sandra are off the radar, so to speak. And don't ask me how I know that either. I do. You and Martin and the rest of the old Phoenix crew know I'm about to be kicked to the curb."

Tyler looked away, so she wouldn't see the tears in his eyes. "I'd like to have something substantial on my list of career achievements before they toss me out on my ass. You," he said directly to Tick, "have been here on the island for a long time. Have you witnessed anything unusual? Night visitors? Boats coming close to shore?"

Tick looked at Kate. She winked at him. "As I'm sure you must know, I didn't come to Mango Key to make friends with my neighbors. I work on my books and scripts. When I'm not working, I'm out on my boat. So to answer your question, no, I haven't seen anything that would arouse my suspicions. Of course, I haven't been looking, either, and it's hard to see if you don't look."

Tyler seemed to ponder Tick's words. "So, what you're saying is in all the years you've spent on this secluded . . . *island,* you haven't seen or heard anything remotely suspicious going on at *that place?*" He pointed to the stretch of beach behind him.

Tick shook his head. "You're asking me if I heard anything? Okay, well . . . yes, I've heard voices, seen the Coast Guard there a few times. If you're asking me if I've heard or seen anything *significant, unusual,* my answer is still the same."

Tyler leaned against the railing. "I'm not sure I believe you. You were a homicide detective. Aren't detectives supposed to have some sort of sixth sense or something?"

Kate took a step toward Tyler, then Tick gently grabbed her by the elbow, pulling her beside him. "I told you he isn't worth it." Tick directed his steely gaze in the annoying man's direction. "I think you have your answer. I want you to leave, and I'm only asking once. You gettin' it, *Special Agent Lawrence Tyler?*"

Tyler stuffed his hands into his shorts pockets, then used his foot to propel himself forward from the post he'd been leaning against so casually. "Yes, I do believe I've got it." Turning his back on Tick and Kate, Tyler started down the steep steps, then stopped and looked over his shoulder.

"We're not finished, Miss Rush, I promise you, we are not finished."

Tick hiked a foot high in the air, aimed it at Tyler's back, preparing to kick him down the flight of steps, then slowly lowered his leg. "I'll take my own advice; you're not worth it."

"We'll see about that," Tyler tossed back as he practically skipped down the remaining stairs. "We will see about that," he repeated in a whisper meant for his ears only.

Chapter 17

Kate wanted to chase Tyler down the stairs and kick his butt all the way to Cuba, but now wasn't the time. She had a young girl who required her immediate attention. Tyler was like an old shoe; he'd likely be stuck in a corner desk somewhere in some dank little office for years. Kate would find him when and if.

Tick opened the screen door for Kate. "If I'd had to work with that bastard for more than a day, I would've killed him."

Kate stepped inside. "Trust me, I've had to use all the restraint I could muster. My saving grace, rather *his* saving grace, was that both of us moved around a lot. Otherwise, I think I would've killed him a year ago, when he assigned me to do surveillance here on Mango Key after making me wait hours and hours before he showed up at the meeting place.

"That's when I finally realized I'd had enough and turned in my resignation. Something he said made me so mad that I snapped and pummeled him real good, letting him know it was for what he had done to good agents over the years. So much for my restraint."

Pete called out as they entered the kitchen, scratching any chance Tick had of responding.

"Hey, you two, breakfast is getting cold." Rosita was still seated at the table, a plate of scrambled eggs and a bagel in front of her. Pete nodded toward the child. "This is her second helping."

A slow burn crept up the back of Kate's spine and came to a halt at the base of her skull. The son of a bitch who did this to this helpless girl had better say his or her prayers, because when and if, no, *when* she got her hands on the slimy worthless piece of humanity, she was not going to restrain herself. She forced a smile as she sat down beside the little girl.

"Hi, Rosita."

Rosita dipped her head, but her gaze found Kate's. She offered a slow smile, then lifted her head so that she was looking directly into Kate's eyes. "Who was that man?"

Taken aback, Kate took a few seconds to gather herself. "I used to work with him, honey. He's nothing to worry about. Is there some reason you're afraid of him?" Kate wanted to pull the words back, but it was too late. "He's nothing to concern yourself with. He can't hurt you if that's what you're afraid of."

"Kate," Sandy interjected, then sat beside Rosita. "Can you eat another bagel? I don't think I can finish mine. All those mangoes filled me right up." Sandy shot Kate the all-knowing look, which Kate knew was meant to tell her to stop her questions, give the child a moment to recover from her questions about Tyler.

Kate nodded. "I think I could eat another bagel, too. Pete, would it be too much trouble to ask you and Tick to toast two more?" She gave a slight nod in Rosita's direction.

Pete grabbed the sack of bagels from the refrigerator. "I could eat the entire bag myself, so I'll just toast them all. You hungry, Tick?" Pete asked.

Tick lingered in the kitchen doorway. "You bet. I'll have one, too."

Rosita lifted the edge of her mouth in a small smile, as

though she knew what they were trying to do in order to make her more comfortable. "I would like another as well, please."

Kate's eyes widened. She'd never been around kids that much, but she was sure of one thing: The few she had been around weren't nearly as polite as Rosita. Before anyone had a chance to reply, Pete placed two bagel slices slathered with cream cheese on Rosita's plate.

"Thank you, Mr. . . . Pete."

Smart, too, Kate observed. She hadn't been told how she should address them, yet she had enough manners to know what was proper and what wasn't. Kate was sure she was nowhere near eighteen just by the looks of her. Last night, rather early this morning, she'd thought she was possibly ten or maybe eleven. Now, in the bright light of day she thought possibly Rosita was thirteen, fourteen at most. However, her mannerisms were those of a refined adult. Someone had spent a lot of time with this child. Could it be that her parents were a wealthy Cuban family, and she'd lived a privileged life in Cuba? If you could call living in Cuba privileged. But Sandy had lived there as a child, and now look at her. She had a doctorate.

When Rosita was out of earshot, she would ask the others their thoughts on the subject. Maybe Rosita had been kidnapped, and her family was looking for her this very moment. There was no time to waste, Kate figured, and with that in mind, decided to ask Rosita a few more questions. But she would make sure they were worded just so. Pete dropped a bagel on the plate in front of her.

"Thanks," she said.

"Sure." Pete placed a plateful of bagels in the center of the table with a large container of cream cheese and a jar of jelly beside them. Kate guessed the twins liked bagels. She smiled. Maybe they didn't know how to cook. Hell, it wasn't a crime not to be on *The Next Food Network Star*, a show she'd become addicted to before Jelly brought her back on board.

Pete took a seat next to Sandy, and Tick leaned against the counter. Kate took a hefty bite of her bagel before speaking. "Rosita, I know this isn't easy for you, but it's important that you tell us how you came to be at that . . . house." Kate looked at Sandy. She gave her a slight nod, indicating she was heading in the right direction.

Rosita wiped her mouth, then placed her napkin to the side of her paper plate. "I was told not to speak of that, Miss Kate. I'm sorry." She looked as though she were about to cry.

Kate tried another tactic. "Sweetie, whoever told you not to talk about this isn't a very nice person. We know you're afraid to tell, but I promise you that you have absolutely nothing to be afraid of. I'm going to see to it that whoever took you there never does this to anyone else. Do you understand what I'm saying?"

Rosita nodded. "Yes, but they said they would . . ." Her dark eyes drifted toward the screen door and beyond. "They said they would drop me in the middle of the water where it's real deep. I cannot swim." Rosita paused, not for impact but to wipe the tears from her face. "They told me one large cement block was all it would take, and I would be shark bait or food for the bottom feeders, whichever came first." She cried freely, her small shoulders trembling as she sobbed.

A raging inferno coursed through Kate's veins. She eyed the others. She could see that the child's words had affected them just as deeply. She would strangle the person who'd said that to Rosita, then she'd dangle the bastard . . . Oh, what the hell, before Kate finished with them, whoever did this would remember Kate Rush for a long time. In order to continue her questioning of Rosita, Kate took a deep, calming breath. And another.

"That's a very mean thing to say to someone. Was this person someone you know or a stranger?" Kate knew she came off as though she were talking to a three-year-old, but this was just her way of calming herself. What she really wanted to do was find the SOBs and choke the life out of them and feed them to the sharks, though Kate thought surely the sharks would spit them out, and the bottom feeders would gag at the first bite.

Rosita finished her milk and wiped her mouth before taking her paper plate to the garbage. When she finished, she sat back down. "It was both."

Kate could hardly contain herself. Sandy saw this and took over the questioning until Kate was calm enough. This was her baby, and Sandy knew she'd want to finish what she'd started.

Sandy leaned across the table and took Rosita's hand in hers. She spoke to her in Spanish first but stopped when Rosita shook her head. "I speak better English. In Cuba, I spoke a little Spanish, but not much. I was trained at an early age to speak English. They said I would have a good future if I learned and followed the training. I practiced every day until I could think in English."

Kate couldn't hold back. "My God, how old were you when you were told this?"

Rosita shook her head. "I was maybe five or six. I cannot remember."

"Can you tell me how old you are now? Your real age. Not the age they told you to say."

Rosita seemed to consider Kate's question with such intensity that she almost wished she hadn't asked.

"I will be fourteen my next birthday."

So she was only thirteen!

Kate observed Tick as he balled his hands into fists. She could feel his inner rage across the small room. She glanced at him, saw pain slashed across his face, and knew that having Rosita here in his home brought back all his painful memories of the past. She knew about his family but certainly didn't know him well enough to go there. Maybe, in time, he would share that part of his life with her, but for now, they had to find the son of a bitch who had treated this child as though she were nothing more than a thing to be toyed with. Animals were treated better.

"Exactly what were you being 'trained' to do?" Kate asked even though she had a strong suspicion she already knew.

"I cleaned the houses for the rich people in Cuba. They told me I would make a lot of money in Miami, and I could have my own room, plus I would be with my family."

Tick stepped over to the table. "Rosita, where are your parents?"

The million-dollar question Kate was dying to ask, but she wanted to glide into those waters without upsetting the child any more than she had already. She watched the child carefully. She didn't appear to be upset in the least. As a matter of fact, Rosita was smiling like she'd been given the pot of gold at the end of the rainbow.

"I was told they would be in Miami waiting for me. I have not seen them since I was a very small child. Around three, I think. I so wanted to get to Miami so I could find them. Mateo . . . uh, I was promised if I worked very, very hard, they would help me locate them."

"Who is Mateo?" Tick asked. Kate knew this was the cop talking, not the father who'd lost his family. He wasn't wasting words.

She shook her head again. "I am not sure. He . . . he said he was my cousin."

Pete slid out of his chair, and Tick sat down across from Rosita. Kate observed this, thinking, *Okay, we're back in father mode.*

"Why don't you just tell me your story. The way you remember. Think you can do that for me? I swear on my life I will not allow anyone to hurt you. Do you trust me, Rosie?"

Rosie?

Kate watched in amazement as Tick continued. He must've been one hell of a cop. The DEA, FBI, or DOJ would snap him up in a New York minute if he put himself on the market.

Rosita stood up, removing all the paper plates, napkins, and plastic utensils from the table. She seemed comfortable doing this, so no one asked her to stop. She found a damp kitchen sponge and proceeded to wipe the crumbs from the counter, then the table. When she was finished, she wiped out the sink, then neatly folded a kitchen towel, placing it next to the sink. She looked around. When she saw there was nothing else that she could clean, she sat back down.

"I don't usually . . . well, what I mean is, I have been around some very bad men. I don't always trust them." She looked at Tick as though she wanted to burn his face into her memory. "You have good eyes. I . . . Yes, I will trust you. Where do you want me to begin?"

The small kitchen was so silent you could've heard the proverbial pin drop. Even Bird managed to keep his trap shut.

"The beginning, Rosita, that's always the best place to start."

Chapter 18

Rosita chewed on her bottom lip for a few seconds before continuing her story. She placed both hands in her lap, one atop the other, as though she were posing for a formal photograph. With her dark hair free of the tangles and grime, it reminded Kate of a rich warm cup of coffee. Her eyes pooled with unshed tears, leaving a silvery glaze over her deep brown eyes. Rosita cleared her throat as an adult would do. "There are some things that I do not remember clearly, so I cannot be totally sure of everything. I don't want you to think I am telling a lie." She looked at Kate directly in the face as she said this, as though if Kate even thought she was telling anything but the whole truth, she would break down.

Kate reached for her hand. "Just tell us what you remember. I expect it would be impossible to remember every single detail, right, Sandy?" Kate kicked her friend's leg under the table, and Pete jumped. Kate almost laughed. Damn Sandy. She already had poor Pete wrapped around her leg. Later, she would comment on how fast she worked.

Sandy chimed in, "We don't expect you to remember every last detail, sweetie. Just tell us what you can."

Rosita nodded. "I think I was around three or four when my parents were taken to Miami, though I am not sure. I remember crying when they left me with Aunt Constance. I think she is my father's sister, but I'm not sure of that either. She taught me how to speak in English. She said someday it would pay off. I never knew what she meant." She brushed a strand of hair away from her face. "I still don't understand. But then Mateo came along, and Aunt Constance said that I must work very hard so she could send me to Florida to live with my family again.

"I think I was about seven or eight by this time. I remember crying because I could not remember my parents' faces anymore. There were no pictures. They were just like a shadow in the back of my mind." Rosita paused. "You understand this, Miss Kate?"

Amazed at the child's keen perception, Kate wanted to tell her she totally understood where she was coming from since she'd felt the same way about her grandfather after he'd died. She had pictures, but it wasn't the same as actually *seeing* him. She'd remembered the smell of cigars, his spicy scented aftershave for years after he died. Then the memories became cloudy and vague. So yes, she knew exactly what Rosita referred to. "Of course I understand."

Rosita took a deep breath. "I did everything Aunt Constance asked of me. I spent three hours every day studying English. Aunt Constance said I should not listen when she and Mateo spoke Spanish as it would ruin me for the future. So I forgot much of my native language because Aunt Constance insisted speaking English would pay off. She used those words a lot. I still don't know why.

"After English studies, I would polish silver for the rich and undeserving, that's what Aunt Constance always called them. Mateo brought all kinds of beautiful silver to the house almost every day. I loved to see it shine, so I worked very hard to make sure I did not miss even a tiny speck of tarnish. If I did, I would have to do each piece all over again.

Mateo would bring gold and jewels, too. I was not allowed to touch them, but sometimes I was allowed to look. But I never touched. Aunt Constance said I was her best girl ever, and she would make sure once I went to live with my parents that I would get my very own bedroom, so I always tried to follow her rules."

"Did you ever attend school?" Sandy asked before Rosita continued her story. Being born in Cuba had its downside, but Sandy had been very well educated while living there.

"No, ma'am. I was taught at home. Aunt Constance is very smart. She had all sorts of books. After I finished with the silver, I studied the lessons Aunt Constance prepared. She was . . . is very, very smart. She knew her numbers better than Mateo. When they thought I was asleep, sometimes I would hear them arguing about numbers, though I think it was money numbers."

Tick cleared his throat, raked a hand through his uncombed hair. "What do you mean by money numbers?"

"I never understood what they really meant. But Aunt Constance always said her payoff was less than it should have been. She said she did all the training, the hard work. I don't remember ever having a hard time with my numbers, but I think she told Mateo this so he would be nice to her."

Kate's hair rose on the back of her neck. "What do you mean, Rosita?"

"When the numbers were high, Mateo was always nice to her and to me. Though he wasn't always so nice to the others."

"Others?" Kate interjected. "There were other girls there with you and Aunt Constance?"

Rosita smiled. "Oh yes, there were a lot of girls. Aunt Constance told me they were my cousins though I never remember my mother or father telling me I had so many cousins. I am sure that I was just too young to remember them."

Kate shot a look at Tick. He gave a slight nod. Now they were getting somewhere. Bird chose that moment to swoop into the kitchen, his wings flapping so fast they created a slight breeze as he hovered above the table. "Get the girls! Get the girls!"

Rosita's mouth hung open. "That's what Mateo used to say to Aunt Constance. All the time he would tell her to 'get the girls, get the girls.' I wonder why your bird says this?" Rosita looked at Tick.

"Uh, well . . . I'm not really sure why he says that. He's not really my bird. He just flew by one day and stayed."

Kate's eyes rounded like saucers. She bit the sides of her jaws to keep from laughing. They were onto something critical here, and the last thing she wanted to do was laugh. Poor Rosita would think she was making fun of her.

Rosita nodded as though this were the most normal thing in the world. Birds that talked and came for a visit and never left. Bird had yet to reveal his bilingual capabilities.

Not wanting to get sidetracked by talking about Tick's foul-mouthed bird, Kate quickly took over the conversation. "So, tell me about the other girls. Did they have families in Miami, too?"

Rosita directed her gaze away from Bird and back to Kate. "I suppose. They usually left after a few weeks. Some stayed a long time but none as long as me. Aunt Constance always said I was special, and I had to be in perfect condition before I was allowed to leave. She told me Mother and Father would not want me if I wasn't perfect. I . . . I don't know that I believe that anymore. I have done everything that has been asked of me, and I still have not heard from my family."

Subdued after hearing the child's story, Kate spoke to her in a gentle tone. "Rosita, do you know why you were brought here to Mango Key?"

"There were twelve of us."

Tick, Kate, Sandy, and Pete stared at one another. As was becoming customary, Kate took the lead. "Were these twelve girls your cousins?"

Rosita dropped her head to her chest. Small sobs caused her thin shoulders to shake. She cried for a few seconds, then lifted her head. "I am sorry. I get so very sad sometimes."

"It's okay to be sad. No one here is going to hurt you or say anything hurtful to you. You have our word. Right?" Kate looked at Sandy, Pete, and, lastly, Tick. They all promised they would protect Rosita.

"Thank you. I know you mean no harm. I know when people are good, as I have seen so much evil." She dropped her chin to her small chest again as though she were ashamed at what she'd just said.

Kate waited until Rosita looked up again. This seemed to be her way of avoidance when she felt sad or ashamed. Damn, she was thirteen and acted like an old woman. Whoever was responsible for this had better give his or her soul to God, because Kate planned to kick the living hell out of them. Big-time and legally, of course. But then again, maybe not. Perhaps among the four of them, they could just toss the low-life scum into the ocean for shark bait. Right now she would like nothing better.

"What are your parents' names? I have a friend who will help me locate them. I'll make arrangements for you to be with them immediately." Kate mouthed, "Call Jelly," to Sandy. Sandy gave her a thumbs-up.

Rosita's eyes sparkled. "You can really do that, Miss Kate? Really?"

Kate didn't want to disappoint the young girl any more than she'd been already, so she simply stated, "I promise to do everything within my power to find them for you."

"My mother is Raquel Vasquez and my father is Felipe Vasquez."

Sandy jumped out of her seat, searching for something to write with. Pete raced into the bedroom, returning in seconds with a pencil and paper.

"Can you spell those names for me?" Kate asked while Sandy prepared to take notes.

Rosita spelled their names out loud and clearly. Knowing what Kate was going to ask of her, Sandy spoke up before Kate had a chance to. "I'm calling Jelly now."

Kate nodded and continued to question Rosita.

"Do you know who brought you and your cousins to the island? Do you have any idea how long you've been here?"

The young girl shook her head, "I do not know except it was a friend of Mateo's. He is an American man. He kept telling us that we were very lucky to have him guide us into US waters because he was a very important man in the United States. He said some of the girls wouldn't be so lucky. We did not know what he meant, so none of us really talked to him. The boat was fast, but it was very small. We were all cramped together, and there was not much water to drink. We were very hot. We asked the American if we could go inside, where it was cooler, because some of the girls became very ill from the rocky boat ride and the sun. He just hit the girl who asked." Again, Rosita's eyes filled with tears. This time, however, she did not bother to lower her head. "One of the girls"—she looked around the room as though she were afraid—"died. The boat man just pushed her into the water. I remember him saying he hoped the sharks were hungry for Cuban food."

For the second time, those gathered around the small dinette table were silent. Such words coming from a thirteen-year-old were unheard of in their own world; but sadly in their line of work, they were accustomed to such stories. Kate stiffened nonetheless. She wasn't so hardened that she did not feel for the young girl. Treatment of this caliber would most likely scar Rosita for life and maybe ruin whatever small chance she might have for a normal life. Taking a deep breath, Kate continued, trying to be as direct as one could in such a delicate situation without losing sight of her ultimate goal. Get as much information as she could on these bastards without hurting Rosita or, even worse, losing her trust. "Do you know what her name was?"

Rosita knuckled her eyes. "She was called Maria. That's all. A lot of the girls were Maria."

Figures, Kate thought.

"Could you take a guess at how old she was? Her true age?"

"Maybe fifteen?" Rosita said.

"Rosita, were the girls in the boat with you . . ." Kate paused, as she wasn't quite sure how to word her next question. "Did any of the girls in the boat stay with your aunt Constance?"

"Oh yes. All twelve of them. Aunt Constance said they always saved the best for last. She told me I had completed all my training and that I would make my parents very proud. When I left with the others, though, I thought something was wrong. On the night we left, we were brought to the old church in Havana. Aunt Constance said we were going to be blessed by Father Domingo, but he never came. Several of Mateo's men arrived, then Aunt Constance hurried us out of the church and drove us to the place where the boat was. When we arrived at the boat landing, I heard Mateo curse a lot. Once I think I even heard him punching one of the men, but I cannot be sure of this. We were told to be quiet or else."

Kate could only imagine what the *or else* meant.

"What happened to the girls? Where did Mateo take the other girls who came with you? We searched the house and didn't find anyone else." *Unless they hid themselves extremely well,* Kate thought. But that was highly unlikely, she realized, given how thoroughly they'd searched the place.

Rosita dropped her chin once again. Several minutes passed before she looked up at them. "That man, the American, came to the house. He said he was there to pick up his—" Rosita stopped as though she were afraid to continue.

"It's okay, Rosie. All you have to do is tell what you remember," Tick finally said. Kate could tell he was in full cop mode. Totally law and order, no bullshit. She was glad because she had a feeling she was going to need an extra hand.

The child nodded, taking Tick at his word. "The American man said he was there 'to pick up his . . . *whores.*'" The last word was barely a whisper.

Kate caught Tick's gaze, saw the dark vein in his neck beating wildly. This was worse than she'd even imagined. Prostitution.

Pete looked shocked. Sandy was still on the phone with Jelly.

"And that was when you decided to hide?" Kate questioned.

Rosita nodded. "The girls were very frightened of the American man. He called them bad names. He touched them in places where he shouldn't, too. I did not want to go anywhere with that mean man. I knew I had to save myself, and that is when I decided to hide. I thought since I was on US soil, later I could locate my parents myself. I just kept waiting for the right time to leave. Then some people came and I thought it was the American coming back to get me, so I didn't dare go outside. I saw boats and then you . . . and then I was saved. I owe you my life. All of you."

Kate was shocked, as she'd never heard such passionate words from one so young.

Sandy stepped back into the kitchen. "I told Jelly everything. He's sending Josh and Roy to Cuba ASAP. On the QT, of course. He said he would be here this afternoon."

Kate had one more important question. "Rosita, if you saw the American man, the one you say is mean, could you identify him?"

She nodded. "I will never forget his face, Miss Kate. Never."

Chapter 19

Lawrence Tyler paced the length of his room at the Southernmost Point Guest House. He kept reliving the scene with that bitch Kate Rush back at Mango Key. He planned to make her suffer if it was the last thing he ever did. She had humiliated him beyond anything he'd ever experienced. And that goddamn bird. He'd kill that mangy ball of fluff and make a dream catcher out of its feathers.

Nothing was going as planned. He was back at square one, which wasn't really square one since he'd never had a plan to begin with. He'd hightailed it to Mango Key in hopes of orchestrating a big bust at that compound. Then nothing. He'd been made fun of, picked on, walked on, and crapped on. No wonder his father didn't want anything to do with him beyond boasting that his son was a big-shot DEA agent. Other than his professional status, he'd been a disappointment to his parents as far back as he could remember.

He'd spent most of his early years at one boarding school or another when really all he ever longed to do was stay at home and go to a regular school like real kids did. He'd watched dozens of movies and television shows where kids got up in the morning and their moms always had smiles on their faces and big healthy breakfasts prepared. Their fathers were always there to listen and advise.

But no, his parents had always had their sights set on the White House. His father's greatest aspiration was to be the man in charge, president of the United States. Top dog, number one, as in the buck stops here. It wasn't that he had strong political views or any vision for the country. No, his father just wanted the office, and his mother, to be the power behind the throne, not to say the First Lady.

Tyler had been nothing more than an inconvenience to his parents. Once, when he was twelve, he'd been home for spring break and overheard his parents talking when they thought he was in bed sound asleep. His father had stated quite clearly that he would've gotten rid of the little bastard had it not been too late and illegal. And his mother had agreed. It hadn't been real complicated to put two and two together and come up with four. Pure and simple. He had been an accident. And his parents had to live with it, or rather, him. No wonder he was such a gutless wonder and a lowly coward.

He would never, *ever* let Kate Rush get away with humiliating him again. He'd hunt her down like a rabid dog, and when he found her, well, he'd do what they did to rabid dogs. He'd put the bitch down. D-O-W-N, as in dead. He smiled at the image but knew in his heart of hearts that he was not capable of killing her. He was simply too much of a coward, though it made for one hell of a fantasy.

He smiled as he visualized Kate running through a heavily wooded area with him right on her heels. Rivulets of blood would be streaming down her pretty face as branches scraped across it, then . . . well, hell, he was even a coward in his fantasies because he wasn't sure what he'd do with her when he caught her. He didn't see himself simply shooting her and putting her out of her misery. Besides, Rush would fight back. He knew all too well what she was capable of. A coward she was not. Deep down he had a warped sense of respect for her. She'd never backed down from him in all the years they'd worked together, even when he was her immediate superior and she knew she was risking her job. Kate Rush had the guts and courage he'd spent his entire life searching for.

He still hated the bitch.

Deciding that another trip to Mango Key was out of the question, and with the rest of the afternoon looming in front of him, Tyler decided he might as well go sightseeing just like all the other tourists in town. Maybe, if he was lucky, he would bump into Nancy Holliday, and they could have drinks together. First things first. He would take a refreshing icy-cold shower, then dress in his tourist garb to wander the streets of Key West. Maybe he'd go to the Hemingway house and catch a six-toed cat. He grimaced at the thought. Tyler hated cats.

Tyler grabbed his travel kit and was heading to the bathroom when his phone buzzed. He wasn't sure if he wanted to answer or not. His day had sucked enough already, but then he decided it couldn't get any worse. He grabbed the phone off the desk, glancing at the caller ID before answering. It read UNKNOWN CALLER, PRIVATE NUMBER.

"Tyler here," he said, with as much authority as one could muster after being crapped on by a bird.

"I see you came hightailing back to the safety and comfort of your room."

The blackmailer.

"What the fuck do you want?" he asked with as much bravado as he'd ever had.

"Well, well now. Aren't we getting a little big for our britches." The caller laughed. "Speaking of britches, those shorts you bought at that tacky tourist trap, the ones in the second drawer next to those loud T-shirts you bought, have a rip on the left pocket, which happens to be the pocket where you keep your wallet. You might want to make use of the sewing kit the guesthouse supplied. It's on the bathroom shelf; if memory serves me correctly, it's on the top shelf next to those little bars of gardenia-scented soap."

Tyler was totally speechless for a minute. Gathering his thoughts, he realized that the son of a bitch had been in his room. "How dare you break into my room and go through my things! I'll have your ass arrested!"

The blackmailer laughed. "Oh, stop with the threats, *Larry* my boy. I've been in your condo, I've touched your silk boxers. What's a little search of your room? Nothing. Trust me. And did you know that I've always thought of you as *Larry*. Lawrence never suited you."

"We're supposed to meet tonight at Sloppy Joe's. What more could you possibly want?"

He heard the caller laugh. He wanted to reach through the phone and wring his neck, choke the life right out of him.

"You really don't have a clue, do you, *Larry?*"

Such anguish. Goddammit, he *knew* the voice from somewhere, he'd heard it before. He couldn't place exactly where and when, but when it came to him, the bastard was going to be sorry.

"Stop calling me Larry. No one calls me that. What the fuck do you want? I thought we'd made our plans?"

A wicked laugh caused him to hold the cell phone away from his ear. He could not wait for this to be over and done with. With his days numbered as a DEA agent, he just wanted to get on with his life. Maybe he'd move to the Bahamas when all was said and done. He wasn't known there, at least as far as he knew. It might be the perfect place to start over. Maybe he could convince Nancy Holliday to come for a visit. What the hell was wrong with him? Suddenly he was having all these fantasies, now it was Nancy Holliday, and he didn't even know the woman.

"I think you're getting very brave, Agent Tyler. Actually, I'm calling because I want to help you."

Tyler shook his head. He wasn't that gullible. He said

nothing and waited for the blackmailer to resume his emasculation for the day.

"You've been watching that compound on Mango Key for over a year now, haven't you?" the blackmailer asked.

"That has nothing to do with you," Tyler said. He removed the phone from his ear and was about to press the END button when he heard the blackmailer raise his voice.

"Don't hang up."

Now Tyler was sure the bastard had a camera on him, as there was no other explanation. He sure as hell wasn't psychic. "Where is it?" Tyler asked. "I know you've been in my room, so I can only assume you weren't in here just to touch my things. Though maybe you were. You tell me." Tyler smiled. Two points for him.

"You can wipe that shit-eating grin off your pretty mug, sonny boy. Of course I've been in your room, and of course I've planted a camera, along with an audio device, and your phone is bugged, as you surely must know by now. You can toss everything and start anew, but it will be a waste of time. In a matter of minutes, maybe an hour or two at most, I will have the new items bugged just as easily as I did the first time. Now that we have that matter cleared, I want you to listen to what I have to say. We both know you're about to become DEA refuse. Let's just say I have recently been made aware of a certain event that not only will allow you to keep your job, but to rise to the top, as I've told you in previous phone conversations."

Damn! Who in the hell is this? I know the voice, know it's disguised, but I can't pin it down. Think, dammit, where have I heard this voice before?

"Don't waste your time trying to figure out who I am. You'll never guess. Now, I am running out of patience with you, *Larry.* As they say, time is money, and I have wasted too much time already. Do you want to hear what I have to say or not? It's your call."

Did he? Tyler wasn't sure, but if the blackmailer had a plan to dig his ass out from under the mile of crud he'd wedged himself under, he figured it wouldn't hurt to listen to what he had to say. "I'll give you one minute, then I'm hanging up. And I will not meet you tonight if this info turns out to be another line of your bullshit. You got that?" Tyler puffed his chest out. See? He *could* call the shots when he needed to. If only his father could hear him, he'd think twice before making fun of him again.

The blackmailer gave him the details of what he would need to do and when and where to do it in order for him to come out smelling like a rose with the big promotion to boot. If what his blackmailer said proved to be the real thing, then maybe, just maybe, he might have a snail's chance of proving to his father, his former colleagues, and the world that he wasn't simply the low-life, backstabbing coward they thought him to be. More important, that damned task force would disappear as soon as it became evident that he was headed for bigger and better things in the DEA. And he would be one up on that ball-busting Kate Rush.

"And you're sure of this?" Tyler demanded one last time.

"One hundred percent. I'll see you at eight o'clock sharp. By the way, since I have just saved your neck, I'll want more than the original hundred grand we agreed on before. I think this is worth at least . . . let's say half a million bucks."

Tyler almost wet his pants. Half a million dollars! "I say no fucking way! I can't get my hands on that kind of money, and if you're so good at what you do, you should know that by now." Tyler wanted to scream, kick the walls, and pound his fists on the bastard who continued to torment him with his unreasonable demands, but he couldn't. If there was a way for him to save face, he would do whatever was necessary.

"Lawrence, *Larry,* I know *you* don't have that kind of

money, but I know you know someone who does. Figure it out."

Without allowing him a chance to reply, the blackmailer ended the phone call. Tyler wanted to kill the son of a bitch. You didn't have to be a rocket scientist to figure this out. The blackmailer must know that his father had a boatload of money, and if he knew that, then he also knew his father was the governor of the good old Sunshine State.

What the blackmailer didn't know: It would be a cold, icy, downright frigid day in hell before he asked his father to lend him half a million dollars. He'd find it elsewhere.

Chapter 20

Jelly assured Kate that Josh and Roy were on the right track. "They're smart, Kate. We've got hundreds of contacts in Cuba; in fact, one of them just so happens to be an old college friend of Roy's. They're pros, remember? And don't forget, they once covered your ass, kept you alive."

Kate nodded. "I know, but *Cuba*? You should have sent Sandy. She was raised in Cuba, knows the lay of the land, so to speak."

"Trust me, they know what they're doing."

"I know, I know. I just hate it that you had to send them *there*."

Jelly had arrived just hours after Sandy called him to tell him what they'd learned from Rosita. He'd immediately sent Josh and Roy to Cuba in search of Rosita's aunt Constance and the man who called himself Mateo. The agents were sure that the two hadn't used their real names in front of the girls, but then again, stupid is as stupid does, Jelly reminded them. Once Rosita had a chance to get to know Jelly, she would have him ask her if he could question her about her life in Cuba. She'd submitted to his questions, but Kate knew the poor girl was getting tired. Hell, *she* was tired. Sandy and Pete had just left for their dinner date in Key West. Jelly had whispered something in Sandy's ear before she left. Kate saw the glum expression settle on her dearest friend's face and knew her "dinner date" was going to be anything but. More like a stakeout, and not the kind of stakeout one equated with dinner.

She made the umpteenth pot of coffee, and Tick made ham sandwiches for the four of them. As was becoming the norm, Rosita's eyes lit up like shooting stars when she was offered food. Kate wondered how often dear Aunt Constance had fed the child or if she'd used food as a means to control her and the "cousins."

After they'd consumed the stack of sandwiches and drained the pot of coffee, Kate told Rosita she should rest for a while and led her into Tick's room without bothering to ask if he cared. Somehow she knew Tick was as taken with Rosita as she was. The child was wise beyond her years, but Kate saw a side of her that possibly only a mother could see. The need to be loved and cared for. When Rosita spoke of her mother and father, Kate's heart broke. She doubted that, after all these years, they were even alive, let alone waiting for their daughter to arrive to provide her with a room of her own. Kate had wanted to ask Rosita just how many girls shared a room in Cuba, but she'd seen the scattered mattresses over at the compound. A room of one's own would be a luxury unlike any other.

After Kate settled Rosita in for a late-afternoon nap, she, Jelly, and Tick migrated to the porch, where they could talk without fear of being overheard. Rosita had seen enough. It was time to allow her to be taken care of until they knew exactly where things stood.

Out on the porch, they settled themselves in the lounge chairs. The late-afternoon air was balmy, with the temperature still hovering around the ninety-degree mark. Bird chose that moment to swoop out the front door and settle on Tick's shoulder. "Get the girls! Get the girls!"

Jelly almost fell out of his chair. "What did that bird just say?"

Tick laughed. Jelly hadn't been introduced to Bird's extensive vocabulary yet. Wait until he heard the bird when he got up a head of steam.

"He's been with me almost since I found this place. He sort of adopted me at some point after I moved here. I suspect he might have belonged to someone over at the compound. He's got quite a vocabulary. He even speaks Spanish."

Jelly rolled his eyes. "I'd have to hear that to believe it."

Tick rolled off a few words in Spanish. When Bird replied in Spanish, Jelly just shook his head in bewilderment. "Never say never. I sure would like to know what the old Bird has seen over there. Or maybe not. It doesn't look good on finding the girl's parents alive."

"Are you telling us you know something, or are you just assuming?" Kate asked.

"Actually, a bit of both. Southwest Florida being such a breeding ground for immigrants wanting to touch US soil, I know you're both aware of this, but hear me out. They're coming by the boatloads now. Someone is providing them with fancy speedboats, cigarette boats, and enough fuel to take them to safety in Miami. Once they touch our sandy beaches, we have no choice but to take care of them. It's truly a pitiful sight seeing the hundreds of men, women, and children who manage to make it here safely. They actually kiss the ground or your feet. Now that Castro's brother Raúl has taken the reins, it appears to some that those ninety miles to freedom are worth the risk. We've seen more immigrants in the past year than ever before. Then come the smugglers, who are looking to make big bucks. It's a food chain in a sense. There's the HMFIC, and I know you both know what that means, so don't ask me to repeat it because I won't. Plus there are tender ears just inside. From what I can see, that poor kid has heard and seen enough to last a lifetime."

"Get to the point, Jelly." Kate turned to Tick, who was seated next to her. "He can really go on and on if you don't put a stop to it."

"I don't know what HMFIC means," Tick offered out of the blue.

Kate whispered, "It's *head mother F in charge.*"

Tick simply shook his head and smiled a smile so broad it sent a sparkle to his eyes and butterflies directly to the pit of Kate's stomach.

Jelly laughed at Kate, then continued where he left off. "Someone with big bucks is financing these immigrants. Even worse, someone is promising them a pot of gold when they arrive. They're told they must pay for the risky trip to the US, and, of course, they're agreeable, anything to set foot in the good old US of A. This is where they're exploited by the big boys. Once they're here, more often than not, families are torn apart. The men are sent to work in the citrus camps, the women, depending on their age and looks, are either sent to work as sex slaves, prostitutes, maids, or strippers. They do this willingly because they're so damned grateful to be here. The jerks who do this know it and use it to their advantage. They threaten the immigrants with being sent back to Cuba, so they continue to work in the lowliest professions. The children are used in ways that I don't even want to put a voice to, but they're farmed out to perverts and pedophiles; some of them hit the streets at eight or nine to prostitute themselves for these scum suckers. I think that"—Jelly nodded in the direction of what they all referred to now as the compound—"is what's going on over there. We're still digging for the current owner of the house. Can't find a damned thing either. Someone with either deep pockets or political connections has hidden the current owner's information so deep it may never be found. The person who built the compound, Benito Cruz, has been locked up for the past five or six years. I doubt it's anyone connected to him. He's watched like a hawk. I made a few phone calls to the warden up at Starke, told him to keep an eye out for any new visitors Cruz might have, anything out of the ordinary. The warden assured me nothing had changed, but I'm not naive. They're behind bars because they're criminals. Get a thousand or so together, and you're bound to stir the pot, so I'm not positive Cruz is out of the picture, but I doubt his pockets are deep enough that he's the big boy behind this operation. I called Tom Dolan, told him what's going down, so he's in for the long haul if we need him." Again, Jelly motioned to the compound at the end of the island.

"What's your gut telling you now, Kate? I know how you pride yourself on listening to your instincts."

Kate felt Tick's stare but didn't bother to acknowledge it. She needed to keep her mind focused on what was real, and right now, her thoughts on Tick Kelly were anything but real. Lustful, yes; real, no way.

Kate cleared her throat a little too loudly. "I'm glad Homeland Security is covering our butts. That's always a plus. My instinct is telling me this isn't just your average run-of-the-mill human-smuggling operation." She held her hand out, palm up. "Before you disagree, I don't mean to imply that human smuggling of any kind is acceptable. This place here"—she mimicked Jelly's move, nodding toward the compound—"is big stuff. My gut tells me we might find our ringleader safely ensconced right here in the United States. And something else that's been bothering me since I spied that jerk Tyler out on the boat pretending to be a fisherman. Why is he here? Even if he's supposed to be supervising the Miami operation, he's been relocated to LA, so what brings him all the way across the country to Florida, and in particular, here to Mango Key?"

Jelly laughed. "Let's just say this. When he shows up in Miami, which is not very often—hell, as you said, he operates out of LA and spends more time in Phoenix than he does in Miami—no one, and I mean absolutely no one, speaks to him. Not even the secretaries or the custodial staff. He's the black plague. Of course, there is the ongoing investigation. He's going to be out of a job soon. I don't think his father will be able to pull strings this time around since he's pulled all there are to pull. Tyler isn't suited for this business, never has been. I kinda feel sorry for the guy." Jelly took another sip of his now-cold coffee.

"Well I, for one, can't wait to see the glory hound kicked to the curb. He's been nothing but a pain in my butt since day one. Right now we have more important matters to deal with. Gut instinct aside, what are we going to do with Rosita if we can't find her parents?" Kate knew the answer, but she did not want to hear it for fear her heart would simply crack and never heal.

"We'll have to go the usual route, and while I know it's not what either of you want to hear, it is what it is. She'll have to go into foster care until a suitable family can be found to adopt her."

Tick leaned forward, elbows on knees. "I don't want to see Rosie go to a foster home. They're not always up to par. I've taken kids away from foster parents who were worse than some of the lowlifes I put behind bars. Isn't there something else we can do?"

Kate watched Tick and knew he was feeling the same way she felt. But Kate knew Jelly was right on the money.

"Unless we find a relative, odds are good that Rosita will have to go into foster care. I don't see a way around that," Jelly explained.

Tick stood up, stretched, then sat back down. "Why can't she simply stay here until a relative is located?" He looked at Jelly, then at Kate. "I know how to take care of a kid. Remember I . . . let's just say I've had a bit of experience."

Kate's heart shattered into a million tiny pieces. Tick had had children in another life, as she knew. Did he really believe he could take care of Rosita? He was a recovering alcoholic and a loner who lived on an almost secluded island, plus he talked to that Bird. Kate didn't think his chances were good if he were to appear in court to apply for temporary custody. She wanted to tell him that, save him from the possible disappointment and heartache, but she didn't have the heart to break his any more than it had been broken already.

Jelly rubbed his hand back and forth over the stubble on his chin. The sound reminded Kate of sandpaper. "Actually, Tick, that might not be a bad idea. The girl has been through enough as it is. I'll place a few phone calls. I might be able to get a temporary custody order without all the hassle of going to court."

Kate looked at Jelly as if he'd taken temporary leave of his senses. "Do you think that's a good idea? I mean . . . it's just that, Tick is a man, and—"

"Men can't take care of children? Or were you going to say alcoholics can't take care of children?" Tick's facial expression grew serious. His eyes hardened as he stared at her.

Kate wiped her damp hands on her shorts. She took a deep breath. "I'm not sure what I was going to say, though I'm sure you're quite capable of caring for Rosita. I've seen it with my very own eyes. It's just, I don't know if staying here on Mango Key is such a good idea after what she's suffered over there, at that . . . that hellhole."

Jelly nodded in agreement. "Kate has a point."

"Then I'll rent a house in Key West. With the economy and everything, it shouldn't be hard to find a place suitable for a child," Tick said.

"Okay, okay. I'll keep that thought in mind. She's fine where she is, at least for now. Kate, you and Sandy can help Tick out. That is, if you . . . can you even take care of a kid?" Jelly gave a short laugh. "Forget I said that. You're Kate Rush, and Kate Rush can do anything she sets her mind to."

"You're right, Jelly, I can. And I *can* take care of a child. I've always wanted a kid . . . well, you know how it is. I'm not getting any younger. I wouldn't mind caring for Rosita for a while." She cast a glance at Tick. "Until a proper family can be found."

"Then I'll make those phone calls now." Jelly stood, stretched, then excused himself and walked down the steep flight of steps leading to the beach.

"So you're saying you'll come to Key West with me?" Tick asked.

Damn, damn, and double damn. She'd set herself up big-time. "I'll do whatever is necessary to care for Rosita, even if it means moving in with you and that damned Bird."

Tick smiled, and this time it definitely reached his eyes.

To quote Bird, Kate was in deep shit!

Chapter 21

Thurman Lawrence Tyler slammed the phone down so hard the handset shattered. Bits of plastic littered the top of his custom-made mahogany desk. His carefully constructed life was about to fall apart, but he refused to let that happen. He'd been in the weeds before and managed to salvage his political career. He could do it again.

"Elizabeth, can you come in here?" He knew his wife was eavesdropping outside the door.

Seconds later, the oak doors parted. "What's happening, Thurman? I overheard you on the phone."

Elizabeth Tyler, wife of the esteemed governor of the state of Florida, was dressed impeccably as usual. She wore a white Oleg Cassini shift dress that probably cost more than most people spent on a college education. Diamond studs glittered in her ears. Not a hair out of place could be found on her professionally dyed blond head. Polished, socially perfect was his wife. He expected nothing less of her, and she knew this. Had known this since the day she gave birth to Lawrence, their pitiful son. A day he regretted with every ounce of his being. They'd made a pact. He'd kept his end of the deal thus far and knew Elizabeth had as well. Now it appeared as though the choice to keep the pact between them was being taken away.

"Thurman, dear, why did you destroy your phone?"

The governor paced in front of his large desk several times before answering. "I believe there is a wiretap, a bug, whatever they call it on my phone." He examined the bits of broken pieces on his desk. In the plastic rubble he discovered a small, round, nickel-plated device the size of a dime. "This is why I destroyed my phone." He held out the small object for her to examine.

Elizabeth surveyed it with interest. "I see." She walked over to the bank of windows that overlooked the gardens. It was time. She knew this day would come but honestly had not expected it to arrive quite so soon. She turned to face her husband of more than forty-five years. "What will you do?"

Thurman shook his head. "I'm not sure. I have to come up with something. This is not the way I've envisioned this stage of my life. I am about to announce my intention to seek the nomination of the Republican party for president! This is the worst possible time for this to surface. The race is wide open. This is my year, goddammit! I've worked too long and too hard to allow someone to ruin it for me!" Thurman slammed his fists against the top of his desk, sending debris flying in every direction.

Elizabeth briefly thought of all the money and the endorsements they'd privately accepted. If word of this . . . *incident* got out, it would all have to be returned. They would be ruined politically.

"Thurman, first you need to calm down. Nothing is ever resolved with anger. Let's go into our private quarters." She waited for him to reply. When he didn't, she said, "We will have complete privacy there."

The governor swiped the rest of the broken phone from his desk. "Call Robert and have him clean this up immediately. I'm going to need another phone. Ask Jacob to meet us in our private quarters. It won't look good if anyone comes in here and sees the office of the governor looking like a pigsty."

Elizabeth smiled. "Of course. I'll see you in our quarters in ten minutes." She hurriedly left Thurman's office in search of Jacob, the lieutenant governor. He was completely devoted to the governor, and Elizabeth decided that was a good thing. She found him in the main lobby with a group of college students.

"Excuse me, Jacob?" she said politely. "May I have a word with you?"

The students oohed and ahhed when they spied Florida's first lady. She smiled at them, asked about their studies, and even made a few suggestions on next year's curriculum. After their telling her how much they admired the governor, Elizabeth thanked them again, then practically yanked Jacob away. "The governor needs to see you in our private quarters."

"Of course, as soon as I finish with these students." He turned his attention back to the group clustered in the lobby.

"Tell them there is an emergency. The governor specifically asked that you come immediately."

Jacob took a deep breath, then gathered the students in a semicircle. "I'm afraid I'm going to have to cut our tour short. There has been an emergency, and the governor has asked that I come to his office right away." The group made their disappointment clear, but Florida's lieutenant governor was not lacking in political skill. "This is one of the lessons you will all learn if you choose a career in government. The well-being of the public must always come first. Now, if you will excuse me. Have your professor arrange for another tour. I'm sure we will be able to accommodate you all in the future."

After the students thanked him, Jacob followed the governor's wife to the private living area.

"Is the governor ill?" he asked as he trailed in her wake.

"Yes, but not in the physical sense," Elizabeth answered swiftly.

Outside the door to their private quarters, Elizabeth paused before entering. "Jacob, this is one of those times that your absolute discretion is a must. I do hope you understand?"

Jacob, barely six foot, with a slender build, a receding hairline, and wire-rimmed glasses, looked like any ordinary man. Elizabeth knew better. Not only was he brilliant, he was kind and had a quick wit about him that she and the governor admired and had come to rely upon. "Of course, Elizabeth."

Elizabeth touched Jacob's arm. "This particular matter is very . . . delicate. I wouldn't be too far off the mark were I to say this *delicate* matter could cost Thurman his bid for the presidential nomination."

Jacob hurried ahead of her. "Then let's not waste another moment." He pushed the double doors open and entered.

Thurman stood next to the fireplace. He'd since removed his suit jacket. His hands were jammed in his pockets, his tie lay discarded on a settee beside him. When he heard them enter, Elizabeth saw him stand a bit taller. That was her Thurman. He was tough as shoe leather, always prepared for one crisis or another. One of the reasons she'd married him in the first place.

Thurman turned away from the fireplace. "Let's have a drink." He went to the bar opposite the fireplace and did the honors. Scotch on the rocks for himself, a white wine for her, and Jacob's usual vodka martini.

Drinks in hands, they gathered around a small table in the kitchen, Thurman's personal choice. Said it made him feel more at home.

"There isn't time to mince words, so I will get straight to the point. Elizabeth, it has never been nor will it ever be my intention to hurt you or Lawrence. However, as is sometimes the case when one is in a powerful political office, one must do certain things."

"You're scaring me, Thurman," Elizabeth said, her voice quivering. "What? What is it that's got you so riled up?"

He took a sip of his drink, then placed it on the table. "I've had to stoop to a very low level. For the past eighteen months, I've had every office that Lawrence has worked out of monitored. Telephones, cell phones, video surveillance. Everything."

Elizabeth just sat there, her mouth agape. "I don't understand."

Thurman reached across the expanse and took her hand in his. "It came to my attention a while back that Lawrence wasn't the most popular or accomplished agent in the DEA. Rumors surfaced that he was backstabbing his colleagues, not following proper procedures. Recently, I learned the DEA has formed a special task force, and they're planning to give the poor boy the heave-ho."

Elizabeth placed her hand over her mouth. "But why? He's an excellent agent. He's been promoted repeatedly, to the point that, with the manpower shortages, he's supervising three offices across the country, including the one in Miami. I discussed this with him just a few days ago. He said everything was fine and that he couldn't be happier."

"Then he was trying to protect his mother," Jacob said.

"Were you aware of this?" Elizabeth asked Jacob.

"Yes, I was," he said, without bothering to elaborate.

Thurman glanced at Jacob before continuing. "Time and again, I have called in favors, yanked on every string I've been able to tug for Lawrence. I'm afraid there isn't anything more that I can say or do to help him this time around."

"He'll be devastated. I . . . Is this why you're having him watched? Or is it something more?" Elizabeth took a very unladylike gulp of her wine.

"I'm afraid there is more. Apparently, Lawrence has gone in 'deep,' as the DEA agents call it. He's in Key West now, but he's been seen in Mango Key, that small island in the lower Keys. There is a large compound there that the Coast Guard has had its eye on for a long time. A drug lord used to own the place before he was busted and sent to prison. About a year or so ago, Lawrence received some intel that turned out to be useless. Now it seems this source has contacted him again with information, and he's down there trying to make one last effort to salvage his career. I can't say that I blame him. It's the manly thing to do. A few of his former colleagues are also there on the island observing what, if anything, is taking place at that former drug lord's place. On top of his failing career, it seems he's also being blackmailed."

Elizabeth placed her hand on her heart. "Blackmail? Why? Who would do this?"

Thurman took a deep breath. "Take a guess, Elizabeth."

Elizabeth racked her brain for anyone who would want to blackmail her son and why. Other than street people and drug addicts that she knew he sometimes used as sources, she couldn't think of anyone who would want to blackmail Lawrence. "I haven't a clue. Why don't you enlighten me?"

"Carlton Staggers."

Elizabeth turned a pasty white. "Oh my God! He was sworn to silence. We've paid him handsomely for his . . . services! Why now? What does he hope to gain? He'll destroy us and himself in the process."

"That, my dear, is the reason I am breaking phones."

Elizabeth took a few minutes to recover from her shock. "Let me get this straight. You're having Lawrence electronically monitored and someone is having *you* electronically monitored as well?"

"That's a good way of saying that while I've been spying on Lawrence, someone has been spying on me. I know this sounds like something out of a bad movie, but as governor of the state of Florida, I have to cover myself, and of course I was protecting Lawrence in the process, and now it's become one huge convoluted cluster fuck, and I'm not asking you to excuse my language here."

Elizabeth drained the rest of her wine. "Are you sure the *blackmailer* is Carlton?" She pursed her lips as though she had a bad taste in her mouth.

"Positive."

"Does he know he's being *monitored?*" Elizabeth asked.

"I'm not sure. I would like to think not, which will give me some time to find out exactly what's going on."

"Thurman, this could ruin us, completely ruin us and any hope we have to secure you the nomination, much less win the election."

"Those were my thoughts exactly." The governor turned to his right-hand man.

"Jacob, you've been my right hand for eight years. I doubt there is anything about me or Elizabeth that you haven't been privy to." Thurman looked at Elizabeth, saw the nervous twitch in her right eye. She was upset and had every right to be.

Jacob took a sip of his cocktail. "What's going on, Thurman? Who is this Carlton fellow? If this affects your career, it's liable to affect mine as well," Jacob said without a trace of anger. Anyone else would lose his cool, but not Jacob. He would make an excellent governor when Thurman left office.

Thurman looked at Elizabeth, seeking her permission to tell Jacob just exactly who Carlton was and the role he'd played in their lives.

"It's all water under the bridge, dear, go ahead. You have my permission to tell Jacob. Like you, I trust him to keep this under wraps for as long as we're able to."

"This doesn't sound good, Thurman," Jacob said in his usual professional, smooth way. "But, whatever it is, we'll deal with it. We've had issues before."

"Yes, we have, haven't we? Well, before I get off the topic

at hand, let me tell you the story. When I finish, you might
want to advise me what course to take."

They settled themselves around the table. Thurman reached
for Elizabeth's hand. "You're sure about this?"

"Yes. It's time, Thurman. And who knows, it just might
garner a sympathy vote with female voters."

He patted her hand. "That's my dear Elizabeth. Always
looking at the bright side."

*Elizabeth Jane Waldie felt out of place among her college
classmates, felt as though she would never really belong as
she dished up trays of lime green Jell-O with a dollop of
whipped cream on top. After she finished with that, she had
to work the cash register in the student lounge for two hours.
Then she would hightail it back to her dorm, where she
would spend the rest of the night studying to keep her grades
up. She had a partial scholarship to Florida State University,
and maintaining her grade point average was a requirement.
To obtain the extra funds she needed to attend school, she
worked three part-time jobs. Thank God she only had one
on campus. Most of the students who attended were wealthy,
their families taking care of their every need. How she wished
she had a family to support her, not just in a monetary sense,
but to have someone she could lean on when she was down,
someone to tell her it would be okay. But she didn't, and
Elizabeth was not one to wallow in self-pity. Hated it, actually. So there she was, earning money by serving those who
ate their lunch on campus. The job wasn't so bad, but there
were times when the girls from Alpha Chi Omega would
tease her, make fun of the fact that she had to "work to eat."
Elizabeth ignored them, but it still hurt and embarrassed her.
She reasoned they were all adults now, so she could not understand what their point was, but she dealt with it and managed to get through her days.*

Although tomorrow was the first day of spring break, she

still had to work at her other jobs. The Pony Keg, where she served pizzas and beer three nights a week, and The Book Exchange, which was her favorite job of the three. She had a great love of reading. Her major was library science, so it was her hope to someday work in a grand library, maybe the esteemed New York Public Library. This was her senior year, and she was looking forward to beginning her life in the real world. She'd spent her entire life in Florida, in the small town of Crest, where the most exciting things that happened were weddings and funerals. She never knew her parents as her mother had died in childbirth and, immediately after, her father had committed suicide. She had spent her entire life with her father's spinster sister. Hardly a day passed that Aunt Evelyn failed to remind her of the sacrifices she'd made in order to raise her. Personally, Elizabeth had never figured out just exactly what those sacrifices were, especially as so much of what they lived on came from her social security survivor's benefits.

She was motivated to make something of her life, and she knew that the first step was getting an education. She'd studied hard in high school, earned a partial scholarship to Florida State University in Tallahassee, and never looked back. Out of respect, she wrote Aunt Evelyn twice a month, and if her work schedule permitted, she returned to Crest for the holidays.

Her only real friend, Marlene Janus, who was basically in the same boat as she—no family money and no relatives to speak of—had invited her to a party that night given by Chi Phi, the oldest and currently the most popular fraternity on campus. Elizabeth didn't ask how she'd managed to get an invitation, but she knew Marlene wouldn't go if she didn't agree to go with her, so she'd said yes and was now looking forward to an evening out, an evening away from studying and her day-to-day responsibilities.

When her shift in the student lounge was over, Elizabeth hurried back to her dorm room, where she dressed in the only decent dress she owned. A simple sleeveless black dress with a small leather belt. She'd found the dress stored in the back of Aunt Evelyn's closet on one of her visits home. Later, she learned it was the dress Aunt Evelyn had worn to both Elizabeth's mother's and father's funerals. Her aunt told her she'd thought about throwing it out but decided not to, as it was quite expensive. Though certainly not an expert where clothes were concerned, Elizabeth had an eye for quality and knew this dress was very well made and wouldn't go out of style anytime soon. She'd asked her aunt if she could borrow the dress, and of course Aunt Evelyn had gone on and on about how much it cost, it was the only memory she had left of her brother's funeral, and made Elizabeth promise to have the dress dry-cleaned before returning it. Apparently, Aunt Evelyn had forgotten about the dress. Now Elizabeth considered it her one and only decent article of clothing.

She'd arranged to meet Marlene at The Pony Keg for pizza. From there they would take a taxi to the party on campus. Both had agreed that if the party turned out to be a bust, they would go to the movies to see Elvis Presley's Blue Hawaii. Elizabeth would have preferred simply to have pizza and go to the movies, but Marlene was adamant about meeting her future husband before they graduated in three months, and did anything and everything humanly possible to ensure she increased the odds, hence tonight's party.

Elizabeth walked the six blocks to The Pony Keg, her feet killing her in the three-dollar pumps she wore, but unfortunately, Aunt Evelyn hadn't had any decent shoes to go with the dress. She found Marlene seated at their favorite booth by the plate-glass window. She'd taken the liberty of ordering them each a cherry lime Coke and their favorite pepperoni and mushroom pizza. Elizabeth sat down in the seat across *from Marlene and kicked off her pumps beneath the table, where no one was likely to see her bare feet.*

She took a sip of her Coke. "So, want to tell me what's so special about tonight's party?" Elizabeth asked.

Marlene was Elizabeth's complete opposite. Elizabeth was quite elegant in the looks department. Long blond hair, a figure that would put Sophia Loren's to shame, and clear blue eyes that always seemed to sparkle no matter what. Marlene, on the other hand, was short, a tad on the plump side, and had thick, black wiry hair, which she ironed once a week in order to straighten.

"Oh my God, Liz, don't tell me you haven't heard!"

Elizabeth smiled. Marlene was the typical Italian girl. Loud.

"I haven't, but I know you're about to fill me in."

"This could very well be my last chance to snag a husband, you know? There are men from Princeton and Yale attending. Do you know what this means? I could meet and marry a scholar, maybe even a doctor or a lawyer! I think tonight is going to change my life forever."

Elizabeth smiled at her dearest friend's enthusiasm. "Then I wish you the best. Now, I for one am starving, so let's eat."

They spent the next hour eating and talking, anything to kill time. The party started at eight o'clock. Marlene said they would look juvenile and desperate if they got there early. When the appropriate time arrived, they hailed a taxi and headed to the Chi Phi fraternity house.

Thurman continued, "That was where Elizabeth and I met. She was the most beautiful woman at the party. I was taken with her the moment I laid eyes on her."

Jacob asked, "What does this have to do with anything?"

"Just listen," Elizabeth said.

The room was overflowing with well-dressed men and women. Elizabeth looked at her secondhand dress and de-

cided it could rival anyone else's. While she knew this was trivial, it mattered to her. She wasn't just the girl at the lunch counter or the waitress who served pizza and beer; nor was she just a book bender. Elizabeth was quite sophisticated in her own way. She'd never been taught any of the practiced social graces; for her, it seemed to come naturally. She decided her dress was perfect, and she planned to enjoy the evening.

Marlene got lost in the crowd in her constant search for husband material, so Elizabeth wandered throughout the downstairs, stopping when she came to a room that was filled with wall-to-wall books. She skimmed the titles, saw several of her favorite authors. She was about to remove Hemingway's For Whom the Bell Tolls, *one of her all-time favorites, when a hand stopped her. She yanked her hand back, then looked up into the bluest eyes she'd ever seen.*

"No touching the books," the man said to her, smiling, "without introducing yourself first."

Elizabeth laughed. "And here I was thinking I was about to make a terrible faux pas. I'm Elizabeth Waldie." She held out her hand. When he clasped it in his strong, lean hand, she was instantly smitten, knowing she'd just met a true gentleman.

"I'm Thurman Tyler."

Elizabeth looked at their hands, still clasped together. "It's very nice to meet you, Mr. Tyler."

"You're a Hemingway fan, I see?"

He'd noticed the book she'd been about to remove from the shelf.

"I am."

"This is one of his best," Thurman said.

"Yes, it is, but there are those who think—"

"Thurman, Thurman, Thurman, you sly son of a bitch! It's not like you to have a piece of tail lined up so early in the evening! You plan on sharing?"

Elizabeth was mortified, and it must have shown on her face because Thurman turned to the short stocky guy who'd been so crass and punched him squarely in the nose.

Elizabeth was sure her night was ruined. After bloodying the man's nose, Thurman removed a monogrammed hand-kerchief from his pocket and gave it to him.

"Carlton Staggers, if I ever hear you speak this way again in front of Miss Waldie, you will live to regret it."

The man, Carlton, mopped his bloody nose with Thurman's handkerchief, then walked away without even bothering to apologize.

"I can't tell you how sorry I am for Carlton's behavior. He's obviously had too much to drink."

Incredulous, Elizabeth asked, "You know that man?" He didn't look like the type a man like Thurman Tyler would befriend.

"He's been my roommate for the past two years."

"Carlton never forgave me for busting his nose that night. Said I'd ruined his chances of meeting a decent girl. For the most part, we remained friendly, but Carlton had a chip on his shoulder. He had transferred from Harvard to Florida State after his freshman year and joined the fraternity second semester sophomore year. After graduation, he stayed on to attend law school. For the rest of our senior year, he harassed Elizabeth whenever the opportunity arose, but it wasn't anything she couldn't handle. After college, Elizabeth went to work in New York City, and Carlton Staggers was forgotten about. Elizabeth and I married three years later and returned to Florida, where we'd decided to make our home. When I ran for Congress in 1966, he appeared out of the blue. He asked to work on my campaign. At first I told him no, as I'd never forgiven or forgotten what he'd said about Elizabeth the first night we met. He convinced me that was nothing more than booze, and I relented. He was good at what he did, so I hired him as my campaign manager.

"I won and no longer needed him, at least not until the next election came along, but he just couldn't let it go. He wanted to work for me, he said, telling me I was his only friend. Well, sucker that I am, I hired him in numerous positions throughout the years. He always performed, I'll give him that much." Thurman stopped when he saw tears streaming down his wife's face. "If you want me to stop, I will."

She simply shook her head. "No, just finish what you started. Jacob needs to know this."

"When we married, I discovered I couldn't father a child. It was tough at first, but we both decided we could always adopt, and we were so busy trying to build my career that a child would have been in the way.

"After I won my second term in Congress, we were all high on the win. Elizabeth had arranged for a huge celebration. It was the best; life couldn't have been better for us. Later that night, Elizabeth and Carlton had words. He'd had too much to drink, as was becoming the norm for him. She asked him to leave, even going as far as to escort him to his car. She was as brash then as she is now." Again, Thurman smiled at his wife.

"Just say it, Thurman, this has gone on too long. Get it over with," Elizabeth insisted.

He took a deep breath and downed the last of his scotch. "Carlton attacked Elizabeth that night. And that was the night Lawrence was conceived."

Chapter 22

In spite of all the negative factors currently at play, Tyler couldn't stop himself from being just a little bit excited. He was going to Sloppy Joe's tonight to meet up with Nancy Holliday. He wasn't going to allow the son of a bitch who was blackmailing him to ruin his evening either. He knew the chances were good that his secret caller would be watching him, and Tyler hoped to hell he would recognize the son of a bitch since they'd arranged to meet there. But as far as Tyler was concerned, the entire deal was off.

It no longer mattered to him if he was fired and chased out of town with his ass between his knees. Well, to be completely honest, it mattered, but not as much as it once had. He was tired of fighting the endless battles and never winning the war. And he wasn't going to ask his father for one red cent. He had plenty of money of his own, but half a million bucks wasn't in his budget, and even if it were, he would not pay the jerk who had made his last few days miserable.

However, he wasn't finished with Kate Rush and Sandra Martin. He would ruin that pair if it was the last thing he ever did. He'd virtually begged the Rush bitch to listen to him when he'd showed up at the cop's place. He even tried to appeal to her sense of duty, or he thought he had, but she still refused to relent and listen to what he had to say. When all was said and done, he would take care of Kate Rush. And that was it.

For the rest of the evening, Lawrence Tyler was going to be Lawrence Tyler, whoever the hell that was. Right now, he was content to be the guy Nancy Holliday had met on her way to Key West.

He dressed in the soft worn denim jeans he'd purchased at the secondhand store and a white dress shirt. He left the two top buttons undone and rolled up the sleeves for a casual look. Eyeing the dirty sneakers he'd tossed in the closet, he had a change of heart. He wanted to look casual, snappy, like everyone else in Key West, so he opted for a pair of the leather flip-flops he'd purchased at that tacky tourist gift shop. He slipped the newly purchased Ray-Bans around his neck, grabbed his wallet, along with the keys to the rental car and his room key. As he was about to lock the door behind him, he remembered his cell phone. He ran back inside and grabbed it off the small dressing table. He'd keep it on vibrate. The last thing he wanted was a call from the black-mailer while he was getting to know Nancy Holliday.

Tyler jogged downstairs and outside onto the front porch of the bed-and-breakfast. The warm evening air was a pleasant surprise. It had been so hot and humid the past two days that Tyler wondered why he'd ever considered living in Florida again. He'd hated it when he had to spend time here as a kid, especially when he was trotted out for his father's political campaigns, and when Jellard had assigned him to the Miami office before he turned the tables and ended up switching places with Jellard, Tyler had hated it even more.

Inside the Mustang, he poked a few knobs to lower the rag top. He cranked up the engine, found an oldies station playing The McGuire Sisters singing "Teach Me Tonight." He smiled, thinking about how fitting that song was. He cranked up the volume and drove the short distance to the other end of Duval Street. Lady Luck was with him, and he found a parking spot on the corner of Greene Street, mere feet from the famous Hemingway hangout. He didn't bother closing up the rental. He'd taken out insurance. If anyone wanted to screw with it, so be it.

He walked the short distance to Sloppy Joe's, where the music was so loud it could be heard several blocks away. He frowned, thinking the environment sure as hell wasn't conducive to getting to know Nancy Holliday unless they used sign language. If she showed, maybe he could convince her to take a stroll on the beach. Later, of course. He didn't want her to think he didn't like the loud music and party atmosphere. He couldn't have cared less about the racket, but he truly did want to get to know the woman better. For some reason, he hadn't been able to get her out of his head. Normally, he was with a different woman every other night. He was lucky if he remembered their names. But not this time. He checked the time on the watch he'd purchased at the drugstore—7:50.

He stood outside on the sidewalk in front of Sloppy Joe's, hoping to spot Nancy or someone whom he would recognize as his blackmailer. He stood there for twenty-five minutes, his mood turning more sour by the second. *Fuck it,* he said to himself as he went inside. It was eight fifteen. Nancy wasn't going to show, and it looked as though his blackmailer wasn't going to either. He found a beat-up wooden bar stool at the bar. The bartender, a young guy with a pierced lip and tongue and a Mohawk, wiped the bar off in front of him, slapped down a wet cardboard coaster, and said, "What ya havin'?"

Tyler rolled his eyes. "I'll have a glass of white wine."

The bartender smiled. "Ahhh, one of those types." He turned his back to Tyler, reached for a wineglass on the rack above him, then stooped so low Tyler lost sight of him for a few seconds. When he popped back up, he had a bottle of white wine in one hand. He set the glass on the coaster, filled the glass. "You wanna run a tab?"

"What did you mean when you said I was 'one of those types'?"

The bartender shook his head. "Aww nothin', man. Most of the dudes that come in here don't drink wine. They're beer drinkers. You look classy, ya know?"

Tyler smiled. He'd thought the bartender might've thought he was gay. It wouldn't be the first time. "Thanks, man, I guess you could say that."

"Cool. You just raise your hand when you're ready for a refill."

Tyler nodded. He positioned himself so he could watch the open area that led outside. Throngs of people walked the streets. Some wore bathing suits, others wore the usual attire: shorts, flowered shirts, and flip-flops. He heard a horn honk, someone hollered, "Fuck off," and a loud group of underage girls giggled as they passed by the open door. Key West had something for everyone, he thought as he stared out at the busy street. Except him. There was nothing here for him. Hell, the goddamn blackmailer hadn't even bothered to show up. He turned around, raised his hand in the air so the bartender could see. The bartender waved, held up his index finger indicating to him he'd be right there.

No longer interested in the nightlife in Key West, Tyler turned his back on the open door. He'd have one more glass of wine, then head back to the guesthouse. He removed his phone from his shirt pocket, checking to make sure he hadn't missed a call. Nothing.

A group of rowdy drunks, who'd been taking up most of the seats at the bar, apparently decided to move on to the next watering hole, leaving Tyler as the place's only patron other than those who were seated at the few tables scattered about. There were thousands upon thousands of business cards stapled all across the walls, the ceiling; everywhere one looked, there was a business card. Wanting to leave his mark, Tyler opened his wallet in search of his official Miami District Chief Officer of the Drug Enforcement Administration card. When he located one, he deliberately left it on the bar for a few minutes, hoping the bartender would see it. He tossed the card out there, waiting for his refill; then maybe he'd have someone to converse with while he finished his drink.

The bartender mopped up the spills at the end of the bar, then tossed his towel on a counter behind him. He bent down and grabbed the bottle of white wine. "Sorry, dude, those people were drinkers. This one is on the house."

Tyler watched him pour the vanilla-colored liquid in his glass. Frankly, he thought each drink deserved a fresh glass, but this was Key West. Normal social graces and manners probably weren't much in evidence in places like Sloppy Joe's. He was about to take a sip of his wine when a loud female voice caused him to wince.

"I can't believe this shit!" Sandra Martin said, as she and Pete Kelly pulled up to the bar.

Damn! Sandra Martin and Pete Kelly.

Wanting to keep his cool, Tyler looked over to where they were sitting. "I should have known. You've always had a big mouth."

"Well, you just kiss my . . . my . . . you know what, Lawrence Tyler. Aren't you supposed to be capturing drug runners and bullying female DEA agents?" Sandy slid onto the bar stool with Pete's assistance.

"Buzz off, Martin. I came here to relax," Tyler said as casually as he could. Inside, he was shaking like a leaf. If Sandra Martin was here, chances were good that bitch Kate Rush wasn't far away. If, and it was a really big if, Nancy Holliday walked through the open entryway, the last person he wanted to be seen with was Kate. No doubt she'd tell the entire bar how she'd kicked his ass.

"Good, because we did, too. Right, Pete?" she asked Pete, who was standing behind her.

"We're here to have a beer, that's it. Nothing more," Pete said pleasantly.

"Good. Enjoy yourselves," Tyler said in the usual prissy tight-ass tone he reserved for people he didn't like—lately just about everyone.

Pete nodded.

"I don't think I can stay here, Pete. Let's go to the newer Sloppy Joe's. Wanna?"

"Whatever you like, Sandy," Pete said.

"Hey, Lawrence, we're going to the other Sloppy Joe's. Have a nice night." Sandy hopped off the bar stool and left without another word.

Another Sloppy Joe's? What the hell! I thought there was only one Sloppy Joe's in Key West!

He tossed a twenty-dollar bill on the bar and left in such a hurry he forgot to staple his card up along with the others. *Screw it,* he said to himself.

Once outside, he had to ask a group of young twentysomethings where the other Sloppy Joe's was located. "It's not really Sloppy Joe's; it's where the original owner started his bar, but the locals call it the other Sloppy Joe's," said a young guy who seemed to be the only sober one in the bunch.

"Do tourists usually know about this?" he asked before he walked away.

"Hell yeah," one of the drunks in the group called out. "It's right around the corner."

Tyler didn't bother thanking them. He ran around the corner, where he saw a small sign that read ORIGINAL SLOPPY JOE'S.

He hurried inside but was surprised when he saw that the

place was empty. Shit! His luck couldn't get any worse. He was about to make his exit when a woman of an undeterminable age poked her head out of what must have been a small office. "Hey, don't leave, we're just opening up for the night."

Tyler stopped. "Sure. What time do you usually open?"

"Nine o'clock sharp."

Not sure if he should stay or if he should hightail it around the corner to the known Sloppy Joe's, Tyler figured what the hell. "Okay, just let me have a Coke. I have to drive a boat later tonight." A lie, but it was a good one.

"Sure thing," the woman said, reaching inside a large cooler for a small bottle of Coke. "You want a glass and ice?"

"Nope, this is good," he said, and meant it. He hadn't had a small Coke in the little pale green glass bottles in ages. He tipped the bottle up to his mouth, downing the entire bottle in one long gulp. He took another twenty from his wallet and gave it to the woman. "Here you go. That hit the spot."

She took the money and went to an old-fashioned cash register at the end of the bar. "Keep the change, really. I wonder if you could do me a favor?" He watched her and saw the look on her face. "It's nothing weird, trust me."

She smiled and walked over to the small table he stood by. "Look, buddy, I've heard every line in the book. What some think isn't weird is, so what is it you want?"

Tyler removed his last DEA agent card from his wallet and gave it to her. "I was supposed to meet a friend at Sloppy Joe's at eight o'clock. I'm not sure if she'll show up here, but if she does, tell her to call me."

"So does this gal have a name, a description?" She picked up the card but didn't look at it.

"Yes, sorry. Homespun type of girl, nice brown hair, tanned. Her name is Nancy Holliday."

The woman looked at the card. "Hot damn, you're DEA?"

That's more like it, Tyler thought. "Yes, I'm undercover so . . . well, tonight I was taking a bit of a break. Was supposed to meet Nancy, but I think we may have gotten our wires crossed. If you see someone who resembles her, ask her if she's Nancy Holliday and just give her my card."

"Absolutely; I don't want to piss off no DEA agent . . . Mr. Tyler. I'll keep my eyes open."

He knew that was how he should be treated all the time. Too damn bad Rush hadn't been around to witness what respect looked like. The bitch.

"I would appreciate it," Tyler said. "Nice talking to you." He left without giving her a chance to reply.

Tyler took his time walking back to his car. The street was noisy, people shouting at one another, laughter bubbling out from the various bars and restaurants. It was after nine, and the gift shops and ice-cream stands were closing their doors for the night, allowing artists, psychics, magicians, and the like a chance to make an extra buck or two at Trafalgar Square, the area made famous for its stunning sunsets.

Tyler wished he could close off the mess that was his life as easily, but he couldn't. As his father always told him, "You made your bed, son, now you have to lie in it." Until recently, he'd never really given much thought to what that actually meant. But here he was again, on the verge of ruining a fifteen-year career just because he wanted the glory, the respect that came with the job. He'd had anything but. He didn't want to work the shit jobs that the other agents were assigned to, he wanted the fame and glory that occasioned national news coverage and invitations to the White House.

After this last escapade, meaning his racing down here to, as it turned out, beat Rush and Martin to the pot of gold, he'd acted foolish and stupid. But they were foolish and stupid, too; otherwise, why were they here working off the book? They wanted the fame and glory as much as he did. And Tyler knew *something* was going down at that mansion on Mango Key. He'd raced down, hoping to discover exactly what it was, only to find Rush and Martin had beat him to the prize as they usually did. He wanted, *needed* one last big bust under his belt before they kicked his ass straight to the curb.

He saw that his rental was no worse for the wear; no one had keyed the paint job, and the tires were all inflated. He took the keys out of his pocket, slid in behind the wheel, put the key in the ignition. Just as he was about to crank the key to the start position, a hand reached in and touched him on the shoulder.

"What the hell?" he said, then looked over his left shoulder. Surprise didn't describe what he felt. "Oh my God, I'm sorry! I thought someone was about to yank me out of the car!"

Nancy Holliday in the flesh.

"Oh, I didn't mean to frighten you. Sorry." She stood on the edge of the street beside his car. "I saw the car and thought it might be yours."

Tyler wasn't sure what to say. For starters, she hadn't bothered to show up at Sloppy Joe's as they'd planned, and now here she was acting like . . . well . . . *Shit, Tyler, if she was looking for your car, there must be some reason she wanted to see you,* he thought to himself. He wanted to smack his head and say *Duh.*

He stepped out of the car. He saw a Ben & Jerry's right across the street. He'd bet anything Nancy Holliday would rather have an ice cream than a beer. "Want to get an ice cream?" He nodded to the small yellow structure across the street.

Nancy was dressed in white knee-length shorts with a cherry red tank top. She wore red sandals, and Tyler noticed that her toenails were also painted a bright cherry red. Her hair was pulled back in a low ponytail secured with a white ribbon. To Tyler, she looked like an angel. A candy-apple red angel.

"That's the best offer I've had all day," she said.

Tyler reached for Nancy's hand as they made their way across the street. "And you've had lots of offers today?" he asked, once they made it safely across the street. They joined a long line that snaked around the shop. He figured this would give him a little bit more time to find out as much as he could about her.

Nancy laughed. To Tyler it sounded like choir bells. And wasn't he getting snookered? *Rush would love this side of me,* he thought.

"No, I'm afraid not. I went to Sloppy Joe's, and you weren't there," she said. "I was running late because the spa where I'd scheduled a massage for the evening had over-booked and, of course, instead of relaxing and letting myself enjoy the luxury, this being my first massage and all, I just couldn't because I knew I would be late meeting you. And what's even worse, you never told me your name, or if you did, I can't remember. All I remember is that you said you lived in LA."

"I remember you teach tenth grade at J. P. Stevens High School in Edison, New Jersey, but I don't recall telling you my name. What an idiot I am! Well, let me introduce myself. I'm Lawrence Tyler."

Nancy had a sense of humor, and normally he didn't like women with a sense of humor, thought they were goofy air-heads. But if she didn't have a sense of humor, he figured she'd never have taken the time to meet him at Sloppy Joe's. So now, he decided, he liked women who had a sense of humor.

The line was slowly moving forward. They had at least ten people in front of them. Enough time to pick her brain.

"So, you said you've been here before. What brought you back?" Nancy asked.

Should he tell her the truth, or at least a version of the truth? Or should he make up a fantastic story to impress her.

Normally, the women he dated were impressed simply by his profession. Somehow, he didn't think his title would impress her. He would tell her the truth. The whole truth and nothing but the truth. A pumped-up version of the truth.

"Actually, I'm not here on vacation. I'm the chief of the Miami district of the Drug Enforcement Administration, the DEA, though strangely enough, I am usually located in LA. I'm here . . . well, let's just say I'm here on official DEA business."

Nancy looked as though she'd been hit by a truck.

"Wow, a real live officer of the law. I must say that's the last . . . well, I thought you looked like the accountant type, or maybe an attorney. I just . . . well, I feel very safe standing here with you." She shot him a toothy grin as wide as the sunset.

For the first time in his almost forty-one years, Lawrence Tyler knew what *smitten* truly meant. "Thank you, I think."

They both laughed. The line continued to move. Tyler wished it would slow down. He was liking every minute standing here with a woman who really seemed to be what she was. Good, clean, and wholesome.

"Lawrence, would it be too brazen of me to ask if you're related to Governor Tyler?"

His night was ruined. No, he wasn't going to let the mere mention of his father ruin the rest of the evening. "Actually, he's my father, but don't tell anyone you heard it from me."

"Wow, you're really something. I can't wait to tell my students I met the son of Florida's governor. And he's a bona fide DEA agent. I'm sure this will be the talk of the cafeteria once the cat is out of the bag. I'm a little bit impressed, I must say."

Tyler didn't notice the short, stocky, seventy-year-old man who had come up behind him until he felt the pressure of cold metal jammed into his back.

"Lawrence Tyler, I can't believe it's you! What in the world are you doing out this late? I thought little boys were supposed to be at home in bed."

Carlton Staggers! What the fuck?

Tyler swiveled his head around. "I think I should ask you what you're doing here? I'm here on official business."

Staggers wedged the barrel of the gun deeper into Tyler's lower back. "So am I. I'm here to take you home, Lawrence. Your father's been taken to the hospital. You'll need to come with me right away."

Tyler's heart was pounding so hard he thought his chest would explode. He no more believed his father was in the hospital than he himself was. If that were the case, it would be plastered all over the news. And there were plenty of television sets hanging around in the bars in Key West.

"What do you want?" he asked his godfather between gritted teeth. He hated this man more than anything or anyone in the world.

Staggers had the decency to whisper in his ear. "Aren't you supposed to meet that blackmailer tonight?"

It was then that Tyler finally remembered where he'd heard the blackmailer's voice.

He'd been hearing it his entire life.

Carlton Staggers, godfather and lifelong friend of the family.

"I think you'd better come with me."

So as not to create a scene, as much as he hated to desert her, he knew he must. And it was important that he not give her any indication of who he was walking away with. "Nancy, I'm sorry, but my father is ill. Here." He reached into his wallet and pulled out a twenty. "Get yourself an ice cream. I'll be in touch."

Nancy looked stunned. She just nodded.

Staggers dug the gun deeper into the tender spot at the

base of Tyler's spine. "I'll call you," he shouted to Nancy, as Staggers forced him out of the line and toward the street and the spot where he'd parked the Mustang.

And the fun just keeps on coming, he thought as he raced across the street with the muzzle of a gun jammed in his back.

Chapter 23

"I've never been on a real high-speed police chase before," Pete said, as he and Sandy jumped into the unmarked sedan parked in front of Ben & Jerry's.

"And you aren't going on one now either. This is going to be nice and slow. I don't want to attract attention. But just in case, make sure your seat belt is fastened," Sandy said as she pulled out onto Duval Street. "I'm just going to follow him for now, just like Jelly said."

"Tell me again why I had to sacrifice our dinner plans? What's so important about this guy we're following?" Pete asked, as they cruised a safe distance behind Lawrence Tyler's rented Mustang.

Sandy checked her rearview mirror. "Long story. Here's the short version. Jelly's friend, Tom Dolan from Homeland Security, seems to think the governor's son is in danger. As usual, he needs someone to babysit his useless ass. Hence what you and I are currently doing."

Pete laughed. "I think there's more to it than that. Remember, my brother was a cop. I know you have to keep this under your hat, so I'm not offended that you're not telling me the truth."

Sandy rolled her eyes and cast a quick glance at her passenger. "You know, if I weren't driving, I just might smack you upside the head for that comment. I am telling you the truth. Tyler is a total asshole. He's been a thorn in both my side and Kate's for all the years we've been with the DEA. We're always pulling his ass out of a jam. Pure and simple. Tonight's just more of the same. Almost makes me want to return to teaching."

Sandy perked up when she saw the Mustang pull into the parking lot of TIB Bank of the Keys, a Florida-based chain of banks. "I wonder what he's up to now?" She pulled into the Darling Dolls Day Care parking lot across the street from the bank.

"Why are we parking?" Pete asked.

Frustrated with his nonstop questions, Sandy turned to Pete. "We're here to make out." Sandy couldn't help but smile. "Look, if you want, get out and hitch a ride back to Mango Key. I'm supposed to tail this piece of human crap. You knew that when we left Tick's place. So if you can't take the heat, get out of the kitchen. My mom used to say that all the time. Took me years to understand what it truly meant."

"Okay, I get it, but you still haven't told me why we're in this empty parking lot."

"Someday, we're going to make out in a parking lot. Consider this foreplay, practice, whatever. Did anyone ever tell you that you talk too much?" Sandy asked, keeping her eye on the Mustang.

"I could ask you the same thing," Pete said. "This isn't my kind of foreplay, just so you know," he added.

"I'll keep that in mind. And I would tell you to kiss off. I like to talk, and if you don't like that, well, you know what you can do."

Pete burst out laughing. "You're really funny, but you already know that, don't you?"

"Be quiet, and yes, I've been told I'm funny. And no, I don't have any plans to take my act on the road, before you ask."

Sandy saw the Mustang's passenger door open. "Shit, and I've got on my new white jeans. I swear if I get one drop of blood on these pants, the good old state of Florida is gonna buy me a new pair." Sandy opened her door, checked her shoulder harness to make sure her gun was within easy reach. "I just might shoot the son of a bitch. Put the governor and the first lady out of their misery."

Pete knew the situation was more serious than Sandy was letting on, so he decided to keep quiet until he knew exactly what was going down. In a loud whisper, he said, "I thought Tyler is a DEA agent."

Sandy nodded, then proceeded to open her door all the way. Once she had the door opened as far as it would go, she crouched behind it. She whispered, "Hand me my purse."

"What?" Pete questioned.

Sandy spoke between gritted teeth. "I said give me my purse. Now!"

Pete thought it was a helluva time for her to ask for her purse, but he did as she asked.

With her left hand, she reached for her gun. Using her right hand, she dumped the contents of her purse on the seat. She saw her cell phone, flipped it open, and held down one number.

"I've got him in my sights," Sandy whispered into the phone. "They were sitting in his Mustang in the parking lot, then the passenger door opened. But I haven't seen anyone come out yet. I'll get back to you as soon as something happens."

For what seemed like hours, but surely was just a few long, drawn-out minutes, Sandy watched the Mustang, waiting for something more to happen, waiting for Lawrence to jump out of the driver's seat, wailing like a hungry baby. But nothing.

"Pete," she whispered, "how long have we been here?" As usual, she hadn't remembered to wear her watch. She didn't want to risk opening the phone again to check the time. That little green screen put out more light than one thought.

"Fifteen minutes," came his reply.

Sandy nodded. "I want you to stay here. If I'm not back in fifteen minutes, hit the number one on my phone and tell Jelly I need backup."

Without waiting for his reply, Sandy kicked off her three-inch heels and sprinted across the street to the bank parking lot. Approaching from the side, only a row of shrubbery at least eight feet high was between her and the Mustang. She kicked herself for wearing her white jeans, knowing she'd be a moving target for whoever had forced Lawrence into the car.

While she couldn't stand the sight of him, he was an agent, and she'd taken an oath to protect her fellow agents no matter what the case. Leave it to Lawrence Tyler to screw up a date with the first decent guy she'd met in like forever. If she got his ass out of this alive, no *when* she got his ass out of this, whatever the hell *this* was, she would personally kick his ass all the way to the governor's mansion. *If he thinks Kate's an ass kicker, wait till I let loose with my Cuban temper.* The image caused her to smile.

Sandy took a few steps closer to the tall shrubbery, hoping to get a better view of what, if anything, was taking place inside the Mustang. It was dark, and the streetlights were too far away for her to make out anything other than shadows. She'd have to get closer. With that thought in mind, Sandy squeezed through the bushes. She was cussing beneath her breath like an out-of-work sailor. She felt something crawl along the back of her neck and wanted to scream. Taking a deep breath and trying not to think about tarantulas, and God forbid those icky brown recluse spiders that were so deadly, she shivered in the warm night air. She was getting pissed just thinking about the thought of a spider when she heard a muffled cry coming from inside the car. Spiders aside, Sandy cleared the small hedge in front of the shrubs in one giant leap. She stepped on several tiny pebbles but remained quiet until she knew what the situation was.

Holding her breath, gun aimed directly in front of her, Sandy crab walked around the back of the Mustang. She inched her way over to the driver's side, where the door still remained closed. Stopping again, she again heard muffled cries from inside the car. She slithered on her belly like a snake underneath the Mustang. Tyler had better be dead; if he wasn't, she planned to kill him on first sight. Not only were her jeans ruined, but she could feel the asphalt as it dug into her belly.

With her entire body under the car, Sandy positioned her head so that she could view the inside of the vehicle. What she saw almost made her pee her pants. She pulled herself out from under the car and slid into the passenger's seat.

"What the hell have you got yourself into this time?" Sandy asked, as Tyler tried to talk with layer upon layer of duct tape across his mouth. She stuffed her gun back inside her shoulder holster. "I should leave you here just like this. Maybe I'll even take a picture." Sandy laughed loudly. "Would make a hell of a screen saver for my computer, but, Mr. Tyler, today is your lucky day because I don't have my phone on me. Rather I do, it's just not in a convenient location. So—"

". . . et eh," Tyler mumbled.

"Oh, all right. Let me see if I have a knife in the car." Sandy raced out of the Mustang to her unmarked car across the street.

Pete looked scared.

"I was starting to get worried. It's been almost fifteen minutes. Everything okay?"

"Peachy," Sandy said as she rummaged through the glove compartment. She found a pocketknife. "I'll be right back."

Without giving Pete an explanation, Sandy raced across the street. Her feet were raw from the damned pebbles, her stomach had a scrape the size of a melon, plus she had to pee.

Seeing Lawrence Tyler's mouth taped was priceless. Seeing Lawrence Tyler's upper body duct taped to the steering wheel was even better. Sandy couldn't help herself. She laughed so hard tears pooled down her face. Before she cut him loose, she wanted to see the bastard squirm just a few minutes longer. After a couple of minutes of watching him writhe and twist, she whipped the pocketknife out and sliced the heavy-duty duct tape away from his mouth.

As soon as the tape fell away from his mouth, Tyler yelled at her, "You idiot. There's a bomb under the seat set to go off at midnight. Cut me free and let's get the hell out of here."

"Oh my God," Sandy said as she began hacking away at the tape pinning him to the steering wheel. "Are you sure about the timing?"

"How the hell would I know any more about the timing than what my loving godfather said?" he replied.

"Your loving godfather? What the hell are you talking about, Tyler?" she asked as she frantically continued with her efforts to cut him loose.

"It's a long story."

Before either of them could say anything else, the last of the tape came loose, and they ran from the Mustang as fast as they could. And it was a good thing, too, because no sooner had they crossed the street to get to the car Pete was still sitting in than the bomb in the Mustang went off and flames shot ten feet into the sky. Pieces of the car shot out in all directions, and only the tall shrubbery kept them from being hit by flying debris.

Pete jumped from the car and ran over to where Sandy had instinctively pulled Tyler to the ground. "Are you all right?" he asked. "What the hell just happened? Did that car over there explode?"

"Pete, help us to the car and let's get out of here. Give me the cell phone so I can call Jelly. As for you, Tyler, just get in the car and shut up. As soon as we're away from here, you and I are going to have a serious chat."

For once, Tyler was quiet.

Up till now, Sandy had joked and made light of the entire evening, but now it was time to get down to business. "Lawrence, it seems your father has had your ass covered again. Jellard got word that you're being blackmailed. Want to tell me about it?"

Tyler looked at her as though he'd like nothing better than to chew her up and spit her out, but didn't. "No, but I guess I don't have much choice, do I?"

"Not really."

Without arguing, without calling her every name in the book, Lawrence Tyler told Sandra Martin his story about the blackmailing informant, who had turned out to be his god-father.

"I thought they knew what was going on at that . . . damn compound, so I took off hoping to make a bust before my ass got kicked to the curb. Now I find out this was personal. I don't get it. I still don't know what I was being blackmailed about. That miserable bastard never said before he forced me to let him tape me to the steering wheel and told me that now that I knew who he was, he was going to have to eliminate the evidence against him, namely me. That's when he planted that bomb he said would go off at midnight."

Sandy almost felt sorry for Tyler. Almost.

"I don't know why you were being blackmailed either, but here's what I think." Sandy held her hand up. "I know you don't want to hear this, but you need to hear me out."

Tyler just nodded as though he knew he was defeated.

"This blackmailer, your godfather, knew you would do whatever it took to make a grand-finale career move. He knew you were about to get the boot. He knew Kate and I were sent to Mango Key to watch that damned place. What better time to blackmail you? You were sent there so you'd be distracted, Tyler. This blackmailer, who, by the way is still running around out there somewhere, knew you were at the bottom of your career path and simply took advantage of you. Admit it, Tyler, you are just as vulnerable as the rest of us."

"How do you know this?" he asked.

"Apparently the governor was keeping an eye on you. He had your phones tapped."

Tyler was defeated and dropped his head against the steering wheel. "You knew who the blackmailer was when you found me, didn't you, Sandra?"

Sandy looked at Tyler, who looked as though his world had just turned completely upside down. "No. I wasn't given that information when Jellard sent me to babysit your ass tonight."

Tyler grimaced. "Well, now you know. It's my frigging godfather, can you believe that? Of all people. I've always hated the son of a bitch, and now I know why."

Jelly hadn't given her details. "What's his name, this godfather of yours?"

Tyler gave a shaky laugh. "Carlton Staggers. I think he lives in Miami."

"Then I'll send a car to find the bastard. Your father has pulled out all the stops for the DEA, said anything we needed to do was sanctioned by the governor himself. If we find him first, do you want me to kick his ass?" Sandy asked.

Tyler just shook his head. "You'd do that for me after all the bullshit I've given you over the years?"

Now it was Sandy's turn to laugh. "You're damn right I would. Remember, that bomb almost killed me, too. So it's personal with me."

Tyler thought there was a very, very *slim* chance that someday he just might actually come to like Sandra Martin.

Someday.

Chapter 24

"I'll contact the governor's office and meet you in Miami as soon as I can," Jellard said.

He closed his cell phone, and shook his head.

"What? *What?*" Kate asked impatiently. "Are they okay?"

"You know you're starting to sound more like a mother hen rather than a DEA agent. And yes, they're okay. Josh Levinson and Roy Jacobson are two of the best agents I have."

"Gee, thanks," Kate offered up.

"Along with you and Martin, I was about to add, but you keep interrupting me. Now, do you want to hear what went down or not?" Jelly asked.

"That can wait. First, you need to follow through on making arrangements for me to meet Aunt Constance. I have something very important to impart to her."

After Sandy had called to tell them about rescuing Tyler from the bomb Carlton Staggers had planted in the Mustang, they'd been up all night, waiting to hear from her again. After she'd filed her report with the locals, she and Pete had been taken by a private plane to Miami, where Tyler was placed in protective custody until Carlton Staggers could be found and arrested. Tyler's location was known only to Jelly and the governor.

On the second front, Josh and Roy had been able to nab "Aunt Constance" and "Mateo" just hours after they'd arrived in Cuba. It would be a long time before either viewed sunlight other than from behind bars.

As soon as Kate had learned Josh and Roy were back from Cuba, she begged Jelly to take her to their location. Aunt Constance and Mateo were being held in a secret location until the DEA and Key West authorities received further notice from Tom Dolan. But Homeland Security wasn't going to get a chance at these low-life child abusers before Kate did.

"Kate, you know I can't sanction this, especially since you're not officially DEA. But I might be able to arrange a visit. I know a gal there, she's in charge of security for things like this. I would bet when she gets the full story, she might allow a visit. We're going to forget this conversation as soon as I make a few calls. You got that, Rush? I know this has pissed you to the bare bone; hell, I wouldn't mind a couple of minutes in a jail cell with these scum feeders myself, but that's what distinguishes us from the bad guys. We catch them, Kate, the rest is up to the justice system."

"I get your meaning, Jelly. You do whatever you can, I'll take it from there, and this conversation never happened. Make that phone call. I'm going to see what Tick and Rosita are up to."

Kate left the stilt house, allowing Jelly a few minutes to find out Jacobson and Levinson's location now that they were back on US soil. And as she vowed, the sorry excuses for humanity were going to be on the receiving end of her temper. And that wasn't always a nice thing.

Three hours later, after a hasty boat ride to Key West via Tick's cigarette boat, Kate docked at the marina, found Tobias waiting just as Tick said he would be. From there, a local private investigator, another friend of Jelly's, drove her to a small concrete-block office building located on the military naval station next to Key West International Airport, where they picked up Roy and Josh.

Jacobson didn't waste time once he saw Kate. "You're going to get thirty seconds and not one second more. I mean it, Rush. If anyone finds out what we're doing, they'll have all our asses. You think you can do this and stick to these rules?"

Kate nodded. "Let's stop wasting time, I want to get back to Tick's before Rosita gets wind that I'm doing something I shouldn't be. She's had enough to deal with in her short life."

"Follow me," Jacobson said.

Kate followed her former colleague down a narrow hall to a small room at the end. A military guard jostled a set of keys, found the one to unlock the door. He pushed the door aside, revealing what looked like a concrete-block cell of no more than eight by ten. A woman, maybe in her late thirties, with long black hair that almost touched the back of her knees, sat huddled on a metal-frame bed, minus the luxury of the two-inch-thick standard prison mattress.

Kate knew there was no time for words. Without further ado, she glared at the woman, who returned an equally hateful stare, then turned away as though Kate were nothing more than scum.

Kate took three steps across the small cell and stopped in front of the woman who called herself Aunt Constance. Before she could stop herself, Kate grabbed the woman's hair and twisted it until the woman couldn't move and had no choice other than to stare up at her.

With her free hand, Kate smashed her fist into Constance's nose. She heard the cartilage pop, then blood spewed from her nose. The woman's face twisted into a mask of rage, hands thrashing about wildly as she tried to return Kate's punch, but Kate had the advantage and smacked her across the face. Heart racing, she was so pissed at this . . . bitch, she wanted to do so much more but knew this was way more than Jacobson had promised. She dropped her hand by her side, wiped the blood on her jeans, then turned to leave, but before she could stop herself, Kate couldn't resist adding, "That was for Rosita and all the other girls whose lives you ruined. May you rot in hell." Trembling, she opened the steel door, where Jacobson waited. Kate saw the look on his face when he saw her.

"I'm going to forget I ever saw that," he commented when he saw the blood on her hand.

But good old Jacobson. He was smiling as he spoke.

While Sandy and Pete, who had returned from Miami while Kate was in Key West, were getting some needed rest, Jelly picked up the explanation he had been giving Kate before she went out for her "discussion" with Aunt Constance.

"Apparently this Mateo's brother, Jorge, was the master-mind behind the human-trafficking scheme. About a year ago, the brother drowned as he was bringing another group of immigrants to Miami. This shut the operation down for a while. Remember that stakeout Tyler wanted to send you on during the hurricane?" Jelly asked.

"How could I forget?"

"Mateo says that's when his brother drowned. And that was when all the intel we were getting ceased. Somehow, according to Mateo, Jorge obtained ownership of the house until the original owner served his time. In return, when Jorge died, ownership went to Mateo. And upon Mateo's death, or as is the case now, his future imprisonment, the ownership reverts to the original owner, who's currently serving a life sentence at Starke."

"Confusing, but it makes sense," Kate said. "So you really believe Lawrence's snitch was on the money when he told him something was going to happen at that damned compound?"

"I know it's the last thing you want to hear, but yes. Lawrence was on to something. His snitch got scared off when Jorge and his passengers drowned. Jump forward almost a year. Lawrence started getting phone calls. Knowing he was about to lose his job, Lawrence just assumed the calls were connected to the happenings on Mango Key. He hightails it from LA to Mango Key without a plan, without telling anyone in the DEA what he was going to do. Basically, he went AWOL. Carlton Staggers, his godfather, knew what was going on because he had the father's phone bugged as well as the son's. We still haven't figured out how long the governor's office was being bugged, but Carlton did have access to the governor's mansion."

"Why? That's the part that makes no sense to me. Why would Governor Tyler have anything to do with such a low-life scum bucket? And why, for the sake of all that's holy, would this Staggers character be Lawrence's godfather? I just don't get it." Kate peeked over the porch railing to make sure Tick and Rosita were safe. "They're still romping in the water." Tick had taken Rosita and Bird to the beach, so that she and Jelly could talk in private.

Jelly nodded and grinned. "I like this Tick. Maybe I'll ask him if he wants to come to work for me."

"Bullshit. As soon as this is cleared up, you're going to take early retirement. I know you too well, Jelly."

He stretched and yawned. "It's possible. I'm too old for these all-nighters anyway. If I don't retire soon, I'll be too old to enjoy myself, so you're right on the money. I think I'll travel for a bit before I call it a life. Always wanted to go on an African safari."

Surprised at Jelly's announcement, Kate replied, "Really? I never knew."

"Yeah? I expect there are a lot of things we don't know about each other, Kate. It's not like these past twelve years have been one great big social gathering."

Kate nodded. "True, now finish up before Tick returns."

"Governor Tyler went to college with Staggers, they were fraternity brothers and roommates for a couple of years. Apparently Carlton has a law degree. He's worked for several firms across the country. Personal injury."

Kate took their empty coffee cups and refilled them. "Figures, all those ambulance chasers. Never cared for the type."

Jelly took a drink of his coffee and grimaced. "When I retire, I plan to give this crap up. I don't know how I've managed to avoid an ulcer all these years."

"Stop changing the subject and tell me what you're dying to tell me. I know you, Jelly. It's a bombshell, too. Am I right?"

"You're very perceptive, Kate. That's what's made you such a damned good agent all these years. So to answer your question, yes. What I am about to reveal to you could possibly make headlines across the country, if not the world. The governor is going to do everything in his power to keep this out of the media, but you know as well as I do, that's easier said than done."

Impatient, Kate asked, "And what would that be?"

"In the governor's early days, when he first ran for Congress, he hired Staggers to act as his campaign manager. Back in the day, after Thurman and Elizabeth were married, it seemed Staggers had a sick fascination with Elizabeth. He'd met her the same night the governor did. Apparently Staggers made some crude comments about Florida's future first lady. Elizabeth detested him, but he continued to pop up in their life. They would pity him and take him under their wing. On one such occasion, I believe the governor said he'd just won his second term as congressman, there was a big celebration, lots of hoopla, lots of booze. You know how those parties are."

Kate nodded. "I've been to a few myself."

"Keep this between you and me, Kate. I wouldn't even mention this to the cop. He's been through enough, he doesn't need to hear any more bullshit. Staggers attacked Elizabeth that night at the party." Jelly paused, suddenly unsure if he should spill the governor's secrets. But he trusted Kate with his life. He could trust her to keep this quiet. "There really isn't any other way to say this, so I'll just say it. Staggers raped Elizabeth, and Lawrence was conceived that night."

The room was stone silent. It took Kate several minutes before she was able to reply. "And Lawrence doesn't know about this?"

"Nope, and that's why Staggers was trying to blackmail him. He wanted Lawrence to go to his father to get the big money. The original demands were just the opening act. Not only did Staggers want the money, but apparently he wanted the whole family to suffer. He must have set up the meeting he did to soften Lawrence up some more and get him to agree to go to his father. But for some reason, Lawrence had reached the point where he just didn't give a damn anymore, and he told Staggers to go to hell.

"That left Staggers in an awkward position. Lawrence knew who the blackmailer was but had no intention of covering up whatever it was the blackmailer had on him and his family. Staggers, of course, had no idea that the governor knew about the blackmail and who the blackmailer was. So Staggers figured that if he got rid of Lawrence, *his own son,* he was home free. Anticipating the possibility, he had a bomb prepared and ready to be set in place. Why he lied about when it was supposed to go off, I do not know. I suppose it could have been sheer incompetence on his part that it went off almost two hours earlier than it was supposed to. Maybe we'll find out once he's in custody."

"I never thought I would say this, but poor Lawrence. What a shock this will be."

"The governor and Elizabeth want to be the ones to tell him. The governor knew after he and Elizabeth married that he wouldn't be able to father a child, so he raised Lawrence as his own. When the time is right, they'll tell him or not. We all know Lawrence has self-esteem issues. This would kill what little he has left. He's always been told that Staggers is his godfather. The governor needed an excuse for his popping up all the time."

"Wow." For once, Kate was at a loss for words where Tyler was concerned.

"So you understand why we can't let the media get hold of this. Nancy Grace would eat Lawrence and the entire family for breakfast. So would Larry King and Bill O'Reilly. He'd be the topic of every news story in the world. Then they'd jump on the protecting-your-rapist story. We'd have every do-gooder out there pounding down the governor's door. I think it's up to the Tylers to reveal this information. When the time is right or not. The governor was quite clear about that to me on the phone. I feel sorry for him. He said he was going to retire. He'd planned to announce that he was going to seek the nomination of the Republican party for president in 2012, but after this disaster, he wants out of the limelight, and so does the first lady. With Staggers about to be locked away for a very long time, effectively the rest of his life, once he's apprehended and prosecuted, at least they won't have to worry about him. They've been paying him to keep silent for years. He knew Lawrence was his son because he had somehow learned that the governor wasn't able to father a child. They've been his meal ticket too long."

"Wow. Poor Lawrence. I hate to change the subject, but

what about finding Rosita's parents? Did Roy and Josh learn anything about their whereabouts? I didn't think to ask Roy when I was with him."

Jelly took a deep breath before he spoke. Kate knew this wasn't going to be good news either. "Mateo was a cousin, though how many times removed I don't know. When Roy called me after you had left to come back here, he told me Mateo told him that Rosita's parents never made it to the States. The boat they were on was rickety at best. They, along with eighteen others, drowned in the Gulf of Mexico."

Kate's eyes filled with tears. "Oh, Jelly, tell me this isn't true? She can't stop talking about her parents. She thinks Tick and I can find them for her. This will devastate her. She's been through so many nightmares already."

"I don't know what to say to the poor kid. But I did manage to pull a few strings. For now, Tick's been given temporary custody of her until a proper foster home can be found."

All of a sudden Kate broke down and cried like a baby. She cried for the child she would probably never have. She cried for the family that Tick had lost. She even cried for the misery that Lawrence was bound to go through at some point in the future. And then she just cried because it felt good, almost like an emotional cleansing.

"I'll be back." Kate went to Tick's small bathroom, where Bird made his home. She stripped off all her clothes and stood under the hot water, allowing it to cleanse her soul. Right now, it felt in need of a good purging, a baptism of sorts. A light knock on the door told her she'd been in here long enough. She hurriedly toweled off and dressed.

She opened the door. Tick.

"There is something I've been meaning to ask you."

Kate followed him back to the kitchen, where Sandy and Pete, somewhat rested, and Rosita were gathered. Jelly had already left for Miami.

Tick was the first to speak. "Remember when you girls invited us to the beach for a weenie roast?"

Kate and Sandy nodded.

Tick continued to speak. "Well, I think tonight's the night to roast weenies since the weather's looking good."

Kate and Sandy nodded again.

"Then let's get busy. I know how to make the best guacamole in the world," Rosita said, her eyes sparkling.

The adults gave each other that special look. They all knew now wasn't the time to tell Rosita her family had never made it to US soil. Now was the time to celebrate just being alive.

Epilogue

Ten Months Later

Kate checked her beach house one last time, just to make sure she wasn't leaving anything she needed behind. Nothing caught her eye, so there was nothing to keep her here any longer. A single tear dripped from her eye when she entered the bedroom she and Sandy had recently decorated. Soft yellows and creams and splashes of bright green here and there. A new Mac computer sat on top of a brand-new oak desk. Opposite that was a giant plasma television set, Pete's contribution to the makeover. There were books and videos, CDs, posters of the latest pop stars. The closet was so stuffed with clothes, Kate had to remove some and put them in her closet. She scanned the room one last time before she left. More than anything in the world, she wanted this room to be as perfect as possible. She decided it was as good as it would get until Rosita moved in and made the room her own. When she and Tick had told Rosita about her parents, she'd been so sad. But since she had learned that she was being adopted by Tick and Kate, the child hadn't stopped smiling.

First, there was a wedding to attend.

Gathered out on the beach were all the people who were near and dear to her. Each and every one of them had made a mark on her life. She was honored that they'd taken the time out of their busy lives to share in the celebration. She closed the door and walked down the steps that led to the beach.

She stopped and turned for one last look.

"You know it'll never be the same again," Tick Kelly said.

Kate placed a hand over her heart. "You scared me, and I know it won't be the same. I don't want it to be the same, Mr. Kelly."

Tick pulled Kate close to him, then kissed her long and slow. When they broke apart, both were breathing a little heavier than normal.

"Tick, are you okay with this? I mean . . . you've been here before. I just want to make sure that Rosita and I aren't, well . . . you know."

"Substitutes for the family I lost? Is that what you want to say?"

Kate nodded. Tears, like tiny silver rivers, dripped down her face.

"These last months with you and Rosita have been the best time of my life. Truly. When I went to Atlanta and stood by Sally, Emma, and Ricky's graves, I felt as though another person had lived that life. In a sense that's true because I'm not the man, not the father that I was then. I will always love them, but you're my life now. You and Rosita. I've gained a few of life's bruises and bumps since they died. Some of them have been for the good, and some not so good. You"—he gazed into her eyes, which shimmered with tears of happiness—"are the best of everything good. Rosita, she's a blessing. The two of you are the angels who gave me a second chance at life. And you ask me if I'm okay. If I were more 'okay,' I'd have to be in heaven because, Kate Rush, in my opinion, it ain't gonna get any better than it is right now. So, what do you say? Shall we go down to the beach, where our friends are waiting?"

Kate hooked her arm between his. "Let's go."

The warm May breeze from the Atlantic greeted them as they made their way to the beach, which Kate's grandmother had always said would be a "killer spot for a wedding." And today those words were coming to fruition. Not only were Kate and Tick getting married, but Pete and Sandra were as well.

Never in a zillion years had Kate thought she and Sandy would do something so corny as a double wedding, but somehow it didn't seem corny at all. It seemed perfect for all.

"Do you think the minister will mind when we tell him there are two extra couples who want to get married today?" Kate asked, as they slowly made their way over to the canopied area where their reception would follow.

"I think it will be just fine, now stop worrying and let's get this show on the road. I have two beautiful ladies to escort down the aisle."

While it had taken months to plan, the ceremony would be over in minutes, and Kate wanted this day to last as long as possible.

The minister, a friend of Jelly's, would be performing the service. As Kate and Tick, Pete and Sandy, and now Lawrence and Nancy formed a semicircle in front of the minister, they each said their vows, and when they all said their final "I do!" the party began.

"Hey, Rush, get your ass over here. I need to ask you something," Lawrence called out, as she was on her way over to the reception.

"What is it now?" she asked when she raced back over to where he and Nancy were still standing.

"I want to apologize to you. For all the shitty things I've put you through. The PMSing, calling you a bitch, and ordering you to go on a stakeout in the middle of that hurricane. Do you think you can forgive an old chum?" Lawrence was so sincere, Kate almost started to cry.

"I'll think about it," she said, then hurried back toward the tents where they were holding the reception.

"Wait! Kate, I need an answer now," he shouted. "Please?"

With that, not only did Kate return to the beach, but Sandy followed her. And Bird. And Tick. And Pete.

"Gather around you guys and listen up, 'cause I'm only going to say this once. Lawrence Tyler, I forgive you for every low-life, mean-spirited, uncaring, thoughtless act you've ever committed against me."

"Well, since Kate's in such a forgiving mood, I guess I can forgive you, too. But you do owe me a new pair of white jeans for making me crawl like a snake under that Mustang to save your worthless hide. Then you puked on me on the plane ride to Miami; that's a bit hard to forgive, but since I'm in a forgiving mood, okay, you're forgiven," Sandy said, grinning from ear to ear.

Kate wore a plain white dress, Sandy wore a cream-colored dress, and Rosita was dressed in the palest yellow. Nancy wore a white silk dress that had belonged to her mother. The three men trailing behind them wore cutoff jeans, flowered shirts, and flip-flops.

Today three marriages had been made in heaven.

Pete looked at his older brother. "You okay, bro?"

"This has got to be the very best moment of my entire life. I'm just tryin' to drink it all in." Somewhere from above, Tick knew, Sally, Emma, and Ricky were giving him a big high five.

The three men gave one another high fives and were running toward the canopy when the music began to play.

Connect with Us

Visit us online at
KensingtonBooks.com
to read more from your favorite authors, see books
by series, view reading group guides, and more.

Join us on social media

for sneak peeks, chances to win books and prize packs,
and to share your thoughts with other readers.

facebook.com/kensingtonpublishing
twitter.com/kensingtonbooks

Tell us what you think!

To share your thoughts, submit a review,
or sign up for our eNewsletters, please visit:
KensingtonBooks.com/TellUs.

36042198R00159